Tiara Borealis

Four Crowns
Book Two

Erin Lark Maples

Lodestar Literary

Copyright © 2024 by Erin Lark Maples

All rights reserved.

This book is a work of fiction. Names, characters, places, and incidents either are products of the author's imagination or are used fictitiously. Any resemblance to actual events, locales, or persons, living or dead, is entirely coincidental. No portion of this book may be reproduced, distributed, or transformed in any form, or by any means, including photocopying, recording, or other electronic or mechanical methods, without written permission from the author. The only exception is by a reviewer who may quote short excerpts in a review and certain other non-commercial uses permitted by copyright law. Please obtain only authorized electronic editions and do not participate in, or encourage, the electronic piracy of copyrighted materials. Your support of the author's rights is appreciated.

Cover designed by MiblArt.

*To Heather,
for faith and the bookplate*

Prologue

The first who came to our realm, the fae, an old word that means *from,* made peace with their fate. Removed from Elysium in a failed mutiny on their queen, they assimilated here. Cast out among the normal, those like you and me—well, not really me so much as you—they built a new life among the humans, content with easy access to the Otherworld, a second parallel realm that provided a vacation from the trappings of Earthbound life. Known as the Gentry, they traded the life of the untouchable for one of safety.

For hundreds of years, this was enough.

Many reveled in this new world where the centuries enabled them to amass riches and treat our world as a playground. The Gentry bought fancy houses and cars, then countries and governments. They controlled what they wanted, ignored what they didn't. Some chose to remain in the old ways as inhabitants of the wildest places, and still others established themselves somewhere in-between. So long as they had the weirs for travel and a collective understanding of how they could coexist with humans, all was good.

Forgoing what few whispers of hope any had for a reunification with Elysium, the first of the fae considered how to secure their future. Attempts were made to procreate. Creatures were born or made. Humans became an obvious plaything. A little regulation from the Netherworld, though, and things settled—albeit with some resentment—for a few more centuries.

But then their former queen's cherished lover was slaughtered one night under the cover of darkness and drink. Enraged, she set off on a rampage through Elysium, striking against those who failed to protect her treasure. The courts fought among each other in failed attempts to prove their innocence and rule dissolved into chaos. Each court blamed the other. The queen, heartbroken and furious, sealed off the weirs, one-by-one, in a wrathful search for the traitors, leaving what few remained heavily guarded. She ejected the courtiers who'd failed her, casting them out with little hope of survival.

They became the Fallen.

What does this have to do with a middle-aged plant nursery owner on Whiskey Row?

Not a godsdamn thing—unless you're me.

One

"The plumber made eyes at me."

I eyed my best friend. "And you swept him off his feet?"

Christopher sighed. "Sadly, no. I scoped out that tight butt from behind, like a proper maiden."

I snorted. "Alas, we don't live in a Golden Age movie." I shifted a lipstick plant from under the sink faucet. I hung it from a rack to drip dry, it's bright red flowers lining the vines. "Gone are the days in which you can seduce a man with well-cut linen pants."

Christopher, the epitome of fashionable, poured us each a cup of coffee from my decades-old machine and replaced the carafe. That day he'd paired a woven short-sleeved shirt that played to his shoulders with a pair of jeans, cuffed over too-clean sneakers. "Which is an utter tragedy," he said, bringing the *I Wet My Plants* mug to his lips. "You would be my Hepburn, darling. Hair swept up, that ridiculous red pout on your lips. Pearls, perfect pumps. A little dog named Boots. I would wear a suit—"

"You hate suits."

Christopher was the master of wearing everything but a jacket and tie. In our decade working together for a high-profile wedding planner in Chicago, he'd worn nothing but suits to work. Our dress code was muted professional, nothing wild that would steal the spotlight from the hosts. After the cake was cut, the bouquet tossed, and the last drunken bridesmaid packed off in a rideshare, Christopher would strip in the bride's dressing room, paint on some two-hundred dollar jeans and a Prada sweater, wrap a scarf around his neck, and drag me off to the bars in Boys Town where he chatted up anyone who bought him a drink while I questioned how far I could push the babysitter with her curfew. Of course, this story makes us sound like wild twenty-somethings when I assure you this was our thirties and we always took the train home. This was another city, another time, and what feels like, most days, another life altogether.

"But I look damn good in them," Christopher said, pursing his lips at me. "Anyway, that would have been some action, something I'm sorely lacking. This place is a high desert in more ways than one."

With an overdramatic roll of my eyes, I gave the plant a little shake, then unhooked the plastic handle from the bar and handed it off to my best friend. Christopher added it to the rack he'd affixed to the wall near the tropical plants that crowded the front window. "You've been here all of two months. It takes time to find your scene," I said. This is what I told myself, too, when I lamented the narrow scope of my existence.

To be frank, I was scared shitless, even two months in. The first week after I moved to Whiskey Row, I found out this place is crawling with the extranormal, a term Christopher created to describe everyone who wasn't what they should be —a boring, average human being. Prescott, for a host of reasons I'd only begun to explore, drew the extranormal like moths to a flame. Unlike the soft-winged insects, however, many of those who combed these streets at night were dangerous—and they weren't leaving.

A typical boutique plant shop in a tourist town would see a balance of locals wanting something for their office and visitors in search of a gift for someone back home. In the Apothecary, where I was in charge of a weir to the Otherworld on top of a selection of houseplants and a growing menu of teas and cocktails, I had to usher through members of the Gentry and deny entry to any of the Fallen. The former paid me for this service, and the latter tried to kill me for its enforcement. Two jobs in one. Joaquin said the average person would have freaked out, packed up, and left town.

But I'm not average, no matter what society says about women my age. None of us are. We've become cured beings, true individuals who are tough and learned, weathered and strong. And it's long past time we own that.

At our height of business, Christopher and I co-ran one of the premiere event planning businesses in the greater Chicagoland area. You wanted a Palmer House wedding, a seance-themed funeral, or a baby shower for two hundred? You called us. We'd handled everything from lost grooms to a congressional representative caught smoking with the serving staff to reality show-style baby daddy reveals mid-cake cut.

That doesn't mean we didn't go home and scream into a pillow. If you're going to throw parties, you're going to hate people from time to time. You'll have to swallow all of your pride and then some when all you really want to do is tell the mother-in-law exactly how far she's pushed your buttons, let the head chef know his pâté sucks, or inform the gathered employees that you overheard massive layoffs are in store fresh off the Christmas season. It just means that in the moment, we were nothing short of consummate professionals, treating every disaster like an exciting challenge yet to be solved.

Prescott, this new life, had yet to be fun.

"Did he say anything about the inspection?"

"Don't think so. He said he hooked up your misters, though. Even rigged one up at the back door, which is pretty convenient as I'm guessing that atrium bakes in the summer."

"Huh." I studied the copper pipes that bent along the walls and up above our heads. Zip-tied at even intervals, a set of misters lined two walls of the front room near the ceiling. One of the black tubes snaked toward the back of my shop. "How did he manage that?"

The shop was all industry: cement floors, brick walls, and racks for my burgeoning plant collection. As safe a place for amping up the humidity as I could get. I'd section off the plants who preferred things on the drier side, like my succulents and the five-foot Peruvian apple cactus, while the orchids, bromeliads, and begonias would have a veritable rainforest. The wiring for the grow lights was safe, wrapped and angled away from the wetness, and there was a damp-free zone erected near my makeshift bar and sales counter.

What might seem like overkill to the average plant owner was anything but for me. Plants and I have always had a tumultuous relationship, and I was only just beginning to learn why. I wanted every advantage I could swing in this new adventure.

"Said it wasn't a problem—once he had everything sorted. There's a control over there." Christopher pointed to a little box hanging from the closest piping. "In another month or two, you'll be glad you paid this man."

The Apothecary maintained a steady, natural heat. What had been comforting in the chillier months was likely to become miserable in the summer. Prescott was far milder than the booming metropolis of Phoenix several hours south, but still, summer in Arizona was nothing to be underestimated.

Beyond my comfort, I had to think in terms of the plants.

Balancing the water needs of the variety I wanted to carry was tricky enough without the upcoming shift in the weather. I'd asked other business owners on Whiskey Row if their shops were as hot, but it seemed I was the lucky one. Not that extra heat was a good thing to a woman my age. But I suppose it was free.

The historic building had pipes to match. Their advanced age caused failures which had flooded my shop more than once. If this guy had been worth his fee, those days were behind me.

I twisted the dial, and a fine mist shot out of the pinholes and drifted over the plants beneath. I blinked in the afternoon light as the sunbeams filled the shop with prismatic rainbows.

"Beautiful." As much stress and heartache as the shop had caused me in our short acquaintance with each other, I found myself falling for both the space and the potential I could taste in its future.

"Lotte swears Prescott will get hot come summer. She has to move her displays back from the windows. The water guy agreed." Christopher dropped his smooth radio DJ voice and affected a burly baritone. "Hope you like it hot and sweaty, baby."

"Is this the part of the story where you cocked an eyebrow and said, 'Well actually, Mister, I sure do'?"

Christopher laughed. "He only flirted with me to get the details on you."

"As in, when will she pay me or what happened to the old owner? The one who knew what he was doing?"

My best friend shook his head and stooped to pick up a few dropped leaves from a spotted croton. "More like, when will she be back, how is she settling in, does she like the place, and what is my relationship to you...Awkward—maybe. Hunting for your dating status? Definitely."

"I hardly doubt that a glorified plumber I've never met

was trying to get my number, and if he is, that smacks of some kind of bizarre desperation."

Christopher spent the bulk of the last two months since his arrival on three things: rearranging the aesthetics of my shop, adventuring with Lotte and Prescott Hiking Club, and getting on my case about my continued lack of company between the sheets. I pointed out that I'd relinquished the only bedroom with official sheets to Christopher, but he said a dedicated woman wouldn't let details stop her.

He may be right.

"You just wait. I wouldn't be surprised if he comes back. Seemed willing to fix anything else you needed. Even asked if I wanted him to check out any of the other rooms for old pipes," Christopher said.

I puffed out my cheeks and exhaled. "Sounds expensive. I could use a few weeks and a dozen sales before I consider anything extra." I rubbed at my forehead, considering which bills I could postpone, if any, should this so-called expert find more to fix. "Anyone else come by?"

"Not while he was here, no."

"Good, except..." I opened my Uncle Hollis's ledger, where he tracked the tithes offered to him in payment, and noted what happened to each traveler. When he died and I inherited the shop, this duty came as part of the package—serving as an ersatz ticket master. The fae show up, pay me a little something for their access and my protection, and I let them through. These items range from a feather from an exotic bird I couldn't find in any guidebook to a wrap made of fluttery silk so fine I doubted its likeness could be equaled. Occasionally, I was offered a jeweled pin, an elaborate hair comb, or a ring. These items I kept in a locked box. I opened it when bills stacked up, considering the heft of the pieces, the dent they would make on my debt, and the distance between the Apothecary and the nearest pawn shop. But I'd yet to part with any of the items. Not that I was above selling them—at least, most of them—it was how to explain their origin, the intricate carved designs, the otherworldly materials. Gaven, my practical sometimes-assistant who was technically a member of the Gentry himself, offered to melt them down for me in one of his college classes, but I'd yet to give in.

"You're glad you didn't have to explain supernatural beings disappearing into your glass closet except you're hoping one of those very beings will come through and hand you a fat stack of cash that solves all your problems?"

"That would be ideal," I mused aloud. "But there's also the practical solution—drumming up more customers."

Moving to Prescott to run my own business meant more than growing plants. It was like becoming a mother. You think that if you read all the books, buy the latest products, and join the right groups on social media, you'll be the best at parenting. Then the baby arrives, fresh and wiggling and needy, and you find out how hard life has become, and no amount of squeaky giraffes or amber teething necklaces will save you. Raising my son Patrick has been the hardest thing I've ever done, however much I wouldn't trade a minute. I'm so proud of the man he's grown to be, the work he's put into his life. Yet only a mother knows the blood, sweat, and tears that got me through those early days. Running a business came in second, but there were more than a few similarities.

While a business could be locked up for the night, revamped, or even closed should fate require it, it was still your baby. You poured so much of yourself into its success, and determination was an essential ingredient in the outcome. I showed up to this place with nothing to hold me to the past and found every reason to dig deep into it. I would succeed, come hell, high water, or in my case, the Fallen.

"We'll get there," Christopher said. He stepped over to the Birds of Arizona calendar I'd pinned to the wall. The edges curled back, casualties of the amped-up humidity in the room. "Lotte said she clears the bulk of her business in the holidays. The town goes all out with lights, caroling, and some poor schmuck dressed in a Santa outfit. Street fairs and roasting chestnuts everywhere. It sounds glorious, and we need to be ready for the onslaught."

The thought of the busy season pressed at my chest. I had so much to do before the crowds got anywhere close, let alone settled in for a season. There was maintaining any kind of inventory, figuring out what tourists would buy and stuffing the shop with that, then making sure I had a clue (and some practice) as to how to keep those plants alive. *In-one-two-three, out-one-two-three...* Whenever the overwhelm threatens to drag me under, I breathe. It doesn't fix anything, but it gives me the space to start over, to think, and to otherwise regain a smidgen of control over the situation.

When I'd steadied my nerves, I flipped back through Hollis's book, his faded handwriting scrawling across the pages. "This is Christmas City, according to every tourist site. Apparently it's some kind of concession for having lost the Capitol—twice." The owner of the year-round ornaments shop sang her praises of the holiday season. She'd already placed an order for three dozen Christmas cactuses as part of her shop decor. But I couldn't make it to Christmas on one future sale. "I've got to make it through the next six months—at least—before I've got a shot at the holiday crowd."

"Sorry I didn't bring a dowry, sis."

"You make up for it with your sunny disposition. I'm going to need it to last that long."

Christopher and I both lost our jobs when the owner of the business went tits up into debt and released the both of us. I'd moved west after the call from Hollis's lawyer. Christopher tried to make it as the display designer for a downtown department store. One month of dressing mannequins in cheap synthetics and the catty coworker politics and he'd arrived up on my doorstep, suitcase in hand. "If only money really did grow on trees...tried that with that hand of yours?"

I looked down at my hand, turning it to take in the tattoos that decorated my skin. "If only I could magic my way into money. I can sprout weeds through the sidewalk—that's new. But not useful." June, my mentor, was a begrudging teacher of my abilities. A divination witch who ran a bicycle shop, she agreed to give me lessons on how to find and wield what power I'd inherited. Thus far, her exercises had been lacking in anything with purpose. "I'll let you know when I can charm people into forking over cash."

Christopher smirked. "So, the training with old Junie is going well."

No one would dare call my trainer anything other than June to her face. Yet Christopher loved his pet name for the wiry, silver-haired woman with a gaping chasm where a sense of humor existed in the average person. I sighed. "It's...going. Feels like I keep breaking every unknown rule in the witch book, though. Don't expect more than the moment requires. Ask for permission. Keep my movements small. She says I need to learn control first."

"But is it helping?"

I flexed the fingers of my right hand, then curled them into a fist. The leafy tattoos vined outward from my wrist. The surprise inking over which I'd had no control shimmered. "I think so." I unfolded my fingers in a slow release. In the palm of my hand sat a tiny striped seed. As we watched, it sprouted one leaf, a tiny stem, and then a second leaf. As it stretched upward, a bud appeared, flowered into a tiny primrose, dropped its petals, then withered and died. I brushed the dust into the nearest potted peperomia. "Fertilizer."

"Whoa," Christopher said. "How long until you can crank

enough out for a banquet hall? Think of the margin of profit if you could pull that off."

I sighed. "A while yet. June says I need to learn the destructive side of my power alongside the creative aspects. There's so much more to hedgeriding than I'd imagined."

Hedgerider. This was my new identity on top of figuring out how to turn a profit at the Apothecary. If I believed June—and I tended to, given that she was the local coven leader—an unchecked witch of any kind was dangerous. As a hedge witch, a *hedgerider*, someone who could connect with the dead—or the nearly dead—this went double for me. There's no hedge without dualities, and no hedgerider without a balance act between life and death.

"You'll get there."

"Will I?"

"Of course," Christopher said. "Why wouldn't you?"

I thought of the sessions with June. She'd started with small work, sprouting seeds, identifying plants, and basic defense. The minute she'd presented an old mannequin, eyes painted red, and directed me to attempt an offensive move of some kind, any kind, my resolve fell apart. I'd seen plenty of Fallen. Some had attacked my shop, killed my friend, and threatened everything I held dear. That night, I hadn't had to stop to think. I was all reaction, pure impulse. But now, accepting the Fallen as an enemy to be eradicated wasn't clicking. I'd seen so many others who hadn't attacked me. Stumbling around the square at night, huddling for warmth. Dancing in a night club, strung out, yes, but also just feeling the music, finding a moment of goodness in what had to be a disorienting, dangerous life. I'd watched what happened as those ousted from their utopia by a dysfunctional high court and a mad queen battled an inevitable addiction to fae elixir, a drug that made the moment verge on euphoria instead of their constant state of desperation. That they medicated with a taste of home while they waited for a chance to leave the human realm was a tragedy, and I was conflicted as to what to do about the situation.

Joaquin and I differed on this. As a mercenary, he's accustomed to fulfilling a contract and asking questions later. His preferred, callous end for those unable to control themselves would never sit right with me, no matter what he—or his bully of a boss—said was necessary.

My instinct was to help people get what they wanted—not murder them. I'd built a career out of finding a middle ground where the bride gets her afternoon tea and the groom gets his hunting party. Soon-to-be-mother-in-law insists on chocolate but you want vanilla? We'll have a miniature cake. Uncle Ralph can't be trusted with an open bar? We'll do drink tickets. At the first sign of conflict, I dialed into the middle ground. Killing would never be my first option. The idea of asking Joaquin—and by proxy, Ansel—what other options were available crossed my mind, but I quickly squashed it. After all, some of the Fallen had tried to kill me, too.

I puffed out all the air in my lungs. "Got some mental blocks to work through. If I could turn my party tricks into a business, I would. Pretty sure half the witching community would be after me for exposing all of us, though."

Over a stupidly expensive bottle of wine, I'd spilled the details of my new life to Christopher the first week after his arrival. He'd professed needing a pair of aspirin and a long night's sleep to sort it out in his head but woke up the next morning in full acceptance mode. We had yet to tell anyone else he knew, but that day was coming. There were only so many secrets I could keep from my next-door neighbors, and this was unlikely to remain one of them.

I'd introduced Joaquin to Christopher after my friend's arrival. The shifter gave my bestie a once over and a quick sniff before stepping outside to use his phone—no doubt to alert Ansel.

Anything Ansel set me on an edge from which I feared I would topple any day now. The man alternated between accosting me for damning him to seven more years of guarding a gate to the fae equivalent of hell and paying off my impossible tax bill so I wouldn't lose my business. I never knew where I stood with Ansel, yet wherever it was, it wasn't remotely comfortable. Christopher and I had popped into Morgan's, Ansel's bar, a few times only to be met with stony silence. Iris, his savvy bartender, welcomed Christopher with open arms and said nothing about her boss. She'd kept the conversation light and the drinks flowing, while we all ignored the man whose absence was more than felt.

"Okay, so we need people to walk in here, wallets hanging open," Christopher said, leaning back against the counter. "Let's think out of the box. Play to your natural strengths—throw a party."

"The last time I did that, my best employee was murdered, and my shop was trashed."

Christopher nodded his head. That story had been the second bottle of champagne after his arrival. "All right, so how about a virtual one? Housewives make a mint off selling overpriced cookware and essential oils that way. People can order in their sweats. Kind of love that."

"Guessing the Coven of Vesta would shun me full on for selling mass-marketed oils. They'd take away my witch card." I cracked the joke, only half sure it was one. June was wary of my introduction to the local coven, putting me off with her desire to protect them from someone so *untested*. I hated to admit how much I wanted that hesitation to dissipate, to have the chance to meet others like me, and I wouldn't mess that up.

"You don't have a witch card. Is that even a thing? What you have is a legit plant shop—"

"Boutique nursery."

"Sure," Christopher said, rolling his eyes. "And you've got some killer drink menus in progress and a great place for people to enjoy them." He gestured to the pair of tiny bistro tables he'd wedged in between the plant stands. The cheery two-tops and their matching chairs circled my antique bar. "What you need is to diversify. Plants are incredible. I mean, just look at this beast." He fanned his hand along the expansive fronds of a fishtail palm. "But they aren't the kind of thing someone buys every day. These beauties, however," Christopher said, stepping over to the vintage apothecary rack and the store of tinctures and mixes lining the shelves, "are consumed right away. And if they're good enough—and yours are, sis—the customer will come back for more. Maybe even the next day. Costs are ingredients and a bit of your time, both of which are easy to get."

I looked at the mason jars lining a lower shelf, the collection of swizzle sticks I'd amassed, and my growing collection of plant-themed mugs. The night of my opening, the part before we lost Cass, filled my mind. I'd crafted a slew of honey-themed cocktails, teas, and appetizers. The response had been resounding approval, yet all that came after that party had crushed me. "Am I stretching myself too thin?"

"Think about it this way. Would you want to be a plant shop—"

"Nursery."

"Fine. A nursery that sells bevys or a trendy lounge that sells plants?"

The strands of a string-of-dolphins brushed my cheek as I considered a drooping Alocasia. I stuck my finger up to the second knuckle to check the soil like Lotte taught me to do.

Around me, broad, dark green leaves turned their surfaces

my way. I was in constant awe of the breadth of shapes and sizes. There were plants with mammoth rounded leaves and others with pointed tips. Most were various shades of green, some run through with stripes of pink or white splotches. Many were thin and delicate, while others were thick and stiff. At the back end of the shop, Mariette, my favorite giant monstera, held court with her Swiss-cheese leaves bigger than my head. Against one side of the shop spread my wall of vining plants. A gorgeous expanse of greenery hung from, and wove around, a gridded frame I'd built from thick cattle fencing. The effect was heavenly, creating a jungle vibe. I loved this place, these plants, despite the hiccups and speed bumps that started my adventure.

But I had bills to pay.

"How do I choose?"

"The one that makes you money, my dove." Christopher was nothing if not my biggest fan and a diehard supporter. The shop phone rang. He picked it up, sunshine in his voice. "Apothecary…"

I took our mugs to the sink to wash. Not only did I like having someone around, someone I knew and trusted, but he stepped right into helping with the shop. It was the least he could do, he'd assured me, for putting him up after his life in Chicago fell apart, but I was grateful for his company.

"Mmhmm. Sounds like a lovely gathering…I'll have to ask EJ when she gets in, but I'll let you know…Yes, I think that's a definite possibility…Could I get your contact information?" Christopher wrote a number down on a piece of paper before promising he'd be in touch. When he ended the call, he held up the note. On the paper, Christopher had written *20 heads, adult birthday, boho theme.* "Should I tell her the great EJ Rookwood has retired from party planning?"

A moth that inhabited the upper areas of the shop fluttered down to land on my hand. The tendril inked under my skin sparkled, and the insect shifted its feet. As I reread the note, my brain dove into planning mode, calculating overhead, dredging up recipes that would be perfect, and listing tasks for Christopher. I sighed. "Don't think I haven't considered it. With event money, I could hire Gaven on a more permanent schedule."

Christopher tucked the note under the rubber band holding Hollis's ledger open to the current page. "It's worth a thought."

I studied the back of Christopher's head, the streaks of white shading his temples. A handful of years older than me, he was a man with a career's worth of talent, stuck as a shop helper because of cruel twists of fate. What would happen if he—and I—got ourselves together and made something of the rest of our lives? The thought freaked me out. But then again, if you didn't take hold of your destiny in mid-life, when did you?

"You book the events," I said, and he froze in place, his back to me. "Schmooze the clients. I'll do the ordering, the books. Run logistics. Makes the most sense, as I'll be in the shop most of the time. Beverages are easy, but we'll have to figure out food if we're going to run at any kind of scale. Maybe work something out with Grace to use hers after hours. Going to need licensing..."

Christopher whirled around and enveloped me in his arms. "Best decision you've ever made. This will be fabulous!"

"You say this now."

∼

An hour later, we had a stack of printed paperwork to fill out, the city's processing timeline, and a date for Christopher.

"A bit of a renaissance guy, it sounds like," Christopher

said. "Used to be with building inspections. Wonder where he'll take me..."

"What even is a comptroller?"

"He said he was *like* a comptroller. They oversee budgets and spending. Not sure a city this size has as many fancy titles."

Fifteen minutes in the city business offices and Christopher landed a date. In contrast to his luck, I'd gained a rising sense of panic at the enormity of this new business undertaking. Backpedaling on my earlier bout with bravery, I gnawed at my lip, anxious over the developments of the afternoon.

Christopher hooked his elbow in mine as we walked. "I see it on your face. Fess up. What's eating at you?"

"Can we do this? I mean, really do this?"

"Of course we can." Christopher stopped me, resting both hands on my shoulders. "What's bothering you?"

"I...it's just that...well." I inhaled and closed my eyes. The sounds of the city filtered in. The rhythmic slap of a bounced basketball along the pavement, the grinding of skateboard wheels. A horn honked, and several pigeons hooted at each other nearby. My voice added to the din. "I can't fail. Not again."

The memory of our life before Prescott flooded my senses. Cocktail parties on the thirtieth floor of a high rise. Weddings for three hundred. Bar mitzvahs with a college tuition price tag. We'd lived the glamor alongside our clients, and the crash of the business gutted me. My identity, fragile as a single mother, was solid as a planner. It kept me moored as I navigated parenting, being single, and pretending I could manage both. I'd found my footing here, only to have it ripped out from under me.

"Is this about Mr. Broken Promises who can't keep it in his pants?"

"No," I said, a little too fast. The twist of a metaphorical spoon to my gut made me pause. "Maybe."

It isn't every day a bride discovers her intended had cheated on his fiancée with the maid of honor, knowing full well his bride-to-be is pregnant with their first child. That child was Patrick, and that bride was me. No wedding I'd attended since had been worse, and that one clung to the back of my mind like a lingering cough.

Christopher pulled me close, my nose pressed against the neckline of his starched shirt, the faint scent of cologne in my nostrils. "Sometimes in life we screw up," he said, his soft voice a whisper through the trees that stood above us, their leaves flickering in the sunlight. "Other times, life fails us. Neither one, however, defines who we are."

"What do we do when the nightmares come to us?"

It had been weeks, but I still flinched at the sound of the bell in the shop, a reaction which would make Pavlov proud. I could take down the little brass noisemaker that hung above the shop door, but being caught unawares was less appealing. Here I was, stuck smack between a rock and a hard place. I couldn't be more grateful that Christopher turned up, that I'd formed a web of others who knew what was in the back of my shop, thrumming with power. When the Gentry show up, I know what to do.

If—no, *when*—the Fallen arrive, I have to be ready.

Two

Christopher popped his head in at the workroom door. "Tall, dark, and handsome is on his way. Says he wants advice on the expansion at Morgan's. Sounds like Ansel wants to add a few pinball machines. I mean, I'm a fan of the huntsman vibe he has, but a little color and maybe some new upholstery would class up the place."

"Right," I said, assessing the stack of books in front of me. I spread them out in a line of leather and hand-stitched bindings. The rainbow of muted cover colors betrayed a preference for greens, blues, and oxblood stains. Titles stood out from the covers in gold leaf, though some had rubbed off. With gloved hands, I picked up one book and smelled its bulk. I inhaled scents of tobacco, wood smoke, cloves and age. The next book I selected smelled of attic trunks: cedar, mothballs, and faded memories. "Him coming over has nothing to do with making an excuse to spy on me. Not that he'd leave town, anyway. Lotte promised she'd be back this week."

"I love that woman. So elegant. Floats through the world as though everything were inconsequential," Christopher said to himself. "Should have been a runway model."

"You aren't the only one to think so." Lotte, my first friend on Whiskey Row, had a way of flitting in and out of town. She'd hire a local to watch her artisan candle shop, taking off for parts unknown. The woman loved solo hiking, often sending a clipped text with her GPS coordinates and a cheery picture of her on a hilltop. Miles of trees were the only background. "Our neighborhood mercenary is more than smitten."

Christopher shrugged. "Puppy love is harmless—and kind of sweet. Might even turn into something. Middle age isn't a death sentence—for most."

"So you keep telling me."

I pressed my lips together and reached for another book. My fingers lifted the cover of *Direct Healing* to reveal a note etched in pencil. *To Hollis, may this serve in your tutelage.* I flipped past the first page to find the copyright information, which I copied down into a spreadsheet. Since gaining access to Hollis's veritable library in the weir room, I'd wanted to catalog the contents. The knowledge within might prove useful, knowing my uncle was a green witch, gifted in plant care and use, and his collection was vast in scope. I sought answers as to why my uncle hid a priceless relic out behind the shop and what other items had his eye. Between these studies and my shop, I had no time for puppy love or any other variety —or so I told myself.

Christopher followed behind me, dusting at the covers with an old paintbrush. He had a rusty degree from the university in museum studies before he realized the price tag of living large in a big city. The latent skills popped up in our event work now and again: vintage theme weddings, storage of a precious gown, and protecting archival-quality photo albums. Also, he was my best friend for a reason. The man teased a little, then backed off, the subtle dance of calling out a loved one but never going too hard, too long.

We stood back from the arrangement to appraise our work. Christopher turned to me. "This is just the beginning. It's going to take us ages to dig through Hollis's work, even with Lotte's help. And wait—why is Joaquin spying on you?"

"They won't tell me. He essentially said that they're looking for someone, and they're afraid I'll let them through. They've no confidence in me, zero trust, which is the last thing I need to be freaking out about, but I am, and here we are." I closed my eyes, taking a moment to release my breath and with it, my bitterness.

"Easy, dove. Remember what that doctor with the cute butt said? If you don't chill out, no more champagne."

I groaned. "Or fries."

Christopher nodded. "Or that delicious trash heap of a menu item you invented next door. Nonstop salads is what you'll get."

I groaned and set down my book. There's nothing wrong with salads, but the prospect of lettuce three meals a day was torture. With a quick tug on each finger, I pulled off one glove and then the other. I rested my face in my hands and murmured between my fingers. "I hate my forties. My body is rebelling one system at a time. Some days it's like I'm supposed to give up and let it fall apart."

Christopher read aloud as he scribbled on the notepad on the workbench. "Find...EJ...anti-aging..." He looked up at me, then added, "and crazy hot sex potions." He set the pen down, and I shot him a look. "What? Trying to be helpful."

I play-shoved him. "As though you aren't older." Christopher, as a man, was considered distinguished. His fine lines and the salt in his hair gave him the respectable, professorial energy. With a square jaw, lean frame, and an enviable wardrobe, he shaved years off his life like a five o'clock shadow.

"You don't need to remind me. I blew out those candles. The difference between us is that I treat myself like a fine wine." He stood and turned a quick circle. "I'm better with age. More desirable. Worthy of attention. I want the same for you."

"Knock, knock..." Joaquin's baritone sang through the Apothecary. The shifter was the only owner of a key to the back door, though lock picking was one of his many skills.

Whatever tenuous relationship existed between me and Ansel, Joaquin's employer, went by the wayside when I needed backup. Joaquin protected the twin portals that existed on Whiskey Row like it was his burden, not mine and Ansel's. There was no one better suited to the task. He slept in the heat of the day, prowling the streets at night. There was a past behind that heavy brow, the shaggy hair he tucked behind his ears. Lighthearted and ever-the-jester, his smile never went deep in his eyes. Whatever his backstory, he made an incredible bodyguard, stalking prey in the night. It didn't hurt that he was a shifter.

"That was fast," I said.

"I call it punctual," Joaquin said. "Shall I take a lap around the block so you can anticipate my arrival a little longer?" He lifted both brows, ever the flirt.

"This way," Christopher said. "I've got the structural maps up on the screen out front."

"What if there's a customer?" Joaquin smiled a wolfish grin. "Shall I tie on an apron? I bet I'd be decent with a trowel." He snatched a tool from my potting bench and wielded it in a pantomimed battle.

"No bloodshed," I said, fighting the urge to smile. "Sales only—please."

"Fine, fine," he sighed with mock exaggeration. "You're no fun."

"I've got an electric bill to pay," I said. "I need cash, not enemies."

"Ansel has a deal with the company. If you want—"

"No, thank you," I said, an edge to my tone. Besides the expansive bar, Ansel owned the entire block—except for the Apothecary. My uncle had refused to sell to the bar owner and had put up wards to keep him out. Hollis was a witch in charge of protecting what the shop held, and he wouldn't let a bully like Ansel push him out. Ansel was confined to Morgan's, indentured to guard the gateway to the Netherworld in a crooked atonement designed by a brokenhearted faery queen who punished him for his parents' folly. While I found moments of pity for my gruff and overbearing neighbor, I couldn't forget that Joaquin was here to do Ansel's bidding. "But if anyone comes in, steer them toward the Queen of Spades. She's a beauty with a slew of new leaves on her."

Joaquin saluted and followed Christopher.

Alone with the books, I opened one entitled *A Guide for the Solitary Gardener,* stamped with the name Stewart. On the inside, someone had written *To Hollis. Your input was invaluable, and you'll find it complements your deck. Best, V.*

I flicked my gaze to the box holding the deck of unusual cards Hollis left for me. They remained nestled in their container since I'd received them, unsure of what to do with the stack of natural designs and usual titles. Could this be the same deck? I turned the pages to the table of contents. Plant Selection, Wheel of the Year, Harvest, and Eradication of Pests seemed appropriate inclusions. Then I read: Tinctures and Potions, In Times of Darkness and Maintaining a Grimoire.

"Wait, what?" I said to the empty room. I flipped pages to inspect the section on pests when there was a shattering crash from the shop.

I ran out to the urban jungle to find Joaquin and Christopher on their backs. A monstera, its pot in pieces, lay on its side, roots sticking out in all directions, soil scattered over the floor. Christopher clutched at his elbow, laughing in the fetal position. Joaquin was a starfish, limbs flung outward, eyes closed as he chuckled.

"*Explain.*" I put my hands on my hips, attempting to convey frustration, but I had to bite at my lower lip to keep from joining in their mirth.

"He said...he said...and then I...and then we...but then..." Christopher struggled to form sentences through the laughter. He heaved between breaths, like a donkey.

Joaquin put his hand to his forehead. "Oh gods," he said, his laughter slowing. "It's all my fault. He challenged me and I took him up on it. Then the bastard tickled me—"

"You didn't...you didn't say..." Christopher remained useless at storytelling.

"We were wrestling," Joaquin said, and heaved a sigh. "I jerked my knee up to wrap one of these massive thighs around his arms and knocked the table over instead." Joaquin bent his knees, rolled onto his side, and pushed himself up. "Don't worry though, I'll buy the poor thing. I'll put it in the office or someplace. Gods know we need to spruce the place up."

Joaquin held out a hand to Christopher to haul the man upright. Christopher brushed soil off his button-down shirt and bent forward to dust more out of his hair. "Sorry, EJ. This guy is tougher than he looks. I need to get back to the gym." While Christopher was taller, Joaquin was a body hewn with a need for strength, reflexes, and speed, something Christopher's structured workouts couldn't touch.

"Forgive us," Joaquin said, capturing me with his dark brown eyes and a fringe of thick lashes. He was smitten with Lotte, I knew, and he was far from my type—whatever that was these days—but it didn't mean I missed that he could melt an admirer with his gaze. The corner of his mouth turned up, as though he read my mind. "Where's your broom?"

"It's in the back," I said, blushing. "I'll get it."

The bell at the door jangled as someone new entered the shop. "No, let me," Joaquin said, as his nostrils flared. "I'll hang out—in case." He slipped into the back before he could be seen.

Not every person who came to the shop was some evil underlord from a mythical realm. Most wanted a cute potted plant for their kitchen window to slowly kill by too much or too little water and would then come back and buy something else. Treating every customer as this unnamed enemy was bullshit I had to tolerate—for now.

Mist rolled ahead of the newcomer. This wasn't any magic on my part but a common occurrence when the dry air outside hit the rainforest of my shop. This rarely failed to obscure the customer's view and mine.

I'd thought about making it into some sort of sensory experience, like they do at the casinos in Las Vegas and department stores in high end malls. Spritz the air with aromas designed to stimulate the senses—and the credit card. The Apothecary remained a balmy seventy-eight degrees, and when I added in the need to water plants, the humidity jacked upward. The misters only added to this effect, shrouding the place in jungle-like mystery.

Near the skylights, the moths, a natural installation that had only flourished in my time at the shop, their comforting presence welcome, fluttered, resettling among the leaves. "Welcome," I called toward the visitor. "Sorry about all the mist. We're testing a new system." I waved about, seeking the switch I'd used earlier.

A person emerged from the fog, their face shrouded in a cloud of pale green hair. They turned my way, and I exhaled in relief. The Fallen were masculine entities, so far as we knew, cast out of Elysium for their failure to guard the queen's lover. Their red eyes were an immediate identifier.

This woman's peridot eyes, upturned at the corners, were stunning. A sardonic smile answered my greeting.

Fallen—definitely not.

Friendly? Not likely.

Three

A flash of chartreuse blinded me. My eyes stung and watered as I blinked, attempting to waylay tears as I fought to regain sight. There was a cooling breeze, and I coughed, gasping for air.

"Bah," the woman said, her tone dismissive. My vision swam, then returned, bit by bit, to focus on the face in front of me. She remained impassive, crossing her arms. "Hardly a green witch, let alone of the hedge. Can't see what the fuss is about."

I pressed fingertips to my temple, willing my lightheadedness to cease. "Who are you, and what the hell was that?"

"I'm Uzma, and that was a simple dispersal. You should have been able to block it."

For her part, Uzma returned my stare with an impertinent one of her own. Arms crossed, she pursed her lips, eyeing me like a half-drowned rat, spluttering in a puddle.

Glaring at the intruder—for she was no customer I would entertain—I stumbled to my abandoned water bottle on the succulent table and gulped several mouthfuls before wiping my face with the back of my wrist. I took a deep breath and exhaled out my nose, not taking my eyes off the woman. Old EJ would have pasted on a smile and asked her how I could help. New EJ waffled between the urge to choke her and the desire to learn her magic.

It had been magic, after all. A glimmer hung in the air, a faint hue of green. The fumes from her cast evaporated like smoke curls. Had she wanted to hurt me with any level of serious infliction, she would and could have done it. I'd been so wrapped up in my plans with Christopher, my guard was down, and she'd walked right up to me. This wasn't a friend, a co-conspirator. She was someone who didn't deserve my hospitality, let alone pity.

The new EJ made a decision.

"Get out," I said.

Shock colored Uzma's features. Her stance shifted as she put her hands on her curvy hips. Uzma's upper lip curled in protest. She scoffed. "You can hardly blame me for your own inept—"

"I said, get out. Leave." My pride lent more steam to my words. I flung my hand toward the door, pointing for clarity. "I'm as you said. Inadequate. You've had your fun, now go." I fumed inside. Was she a test sent by June? Or just one of the coven, eager to prove I didn't belong? It didn't matter. I didn't have to put up with the humility for a moment longer.

Uzma pressed her lips together. I watched the middle finger of her hand tap against her jeans, the itch to inflict damage calling to her. She closed her eyes in a moment of vulnerability, and her twitch subsided. Her voice was measured, taxed. "You've hardly cause to—"

"The lady asked you, more than once, to remove yourself from the premises," Joaquin said, stepping out from the back room. In a moment, he stood at my side, his voice low and seductive—dangerous, like the hiss of a serpent.

Long before the return of the Fallen, Joaquin was a

bouncer who loved moonlighting as a mercenary. He'd dealt with more than his share of paranormal threats, and a single witch wouldn't be considered a challenge. He rolled up his sleeves as he eyed the woman. "Either you can't understand her or you don't want to. Either way, I'm happy to make her meaning clear."

Outside the cracked window, crows cawed in a raucous chorus from the trees. Inside, three adults faced off. Electricity crackled in the air. The moths took flight among the vines, unable to settle.

"Call off your dog, Ember James Rookwood," Uzma said, her eyes locked on Joaquin. "Or I will be forced to show you what a proper witch can do."

"Now Uzma," a soft, lilting voice called from the door. "I told you to play nice while I parked the car."

A tiny woman brushed her way past the ferns, fronds unfurling from fiddleheads toward her touch. Black pin curls covered her scalp, a pearl barrette anchoring two in place. She wore a matching necklace with a navy and white polka dotted dress and patent red pumps with kitten heels. She clutched a matching ruby bag under one elbow and wore a pair of short white gloves.

"Now, there must be some sort of misunderstanding to clear up so we can all be friends, am I right?" With deft movements, she tugged at each finger of the gloves before removing them and tucking them into the small purse. She held out her hand to me, manicured red nails glossy in the light.

"That remains to be seen," I said, giving her hand a tentative shake. At her touch, my tattoos glowed as though the inked foliage burst with energy. We each stared until I dropped her hand.

"I'm Blythe Galani," she said, meeting my eyes with hers, of a dark mink. "Of the Coven of Vesta. I see you've met my sister, Uzma." Blythe turned to the other woman, who looked away, rolling her eyes. Blythe continued. "You must be Ember James—but it's EJ, isn't it? May I call you that?" She didn't wait for my answer before shifting her attention. The woman was a stream of speech and good cheer. "And you must be the famous Mr. Torres," she cooed. "I've heard so much about you."

"And I have absolutely no clue who you are," I said, before Joaquin could respond. The way the markings on my hand had responded to contact with this woman was disarming.

Blythe returned her smile to me. "Of course. I'm so sorry we didn't call first, but I didn't want you to ward us out or something silly like that before we even had a chance to chat."

This woman assumed I had capabilities beyond my current bag of witchy parlor tricks. The shop was warded—against my neighbor for one, and a few others—but I had nothing to do with them. My uncle was their originator, and June had strengthened them. But this sprite before me didn't have that knowledge. "And why would I do that?"

"It's not as though we'd come to just hang out," Uzma said, her voice dripping with sarcasm. "We're oathbound. Your family to ours. Our mother and your uncle swore to an alignment. Or did your family neglect to teach you that as well?"

"Oath—what?"

"Bound," Blythe said. "But we needn't discuss that now." She shot Uzma a look, and the taller sister only turned away with an exaggerated sigh. "Uzma and I came to see if you would consider helping us."

"Help you?" I scoffed, shaking my head at the audacity of the suggestion. "She attacks me in my shop without warning, and you want me to help you?" My voice rose with the humidity that filled my lungs. "And that doesn't even consider this so-called blood vow promise. Look, if you aren't planning to buy something, I need to get back to work—and some peace and quiet."

Joaquin said nothing, an unusual response to an opportunity to evict the unwanted in a furl of clever insults. Instead, he watched the women, his eyes narrowed.

Blythe looked up at me as though considering the moment. She gave a brief nod before opening her purse. From within, she extracted something wrapped in a scrap of silk.

"I had hoped to start off on better terms," Blythe said, clutching the item to her chest. "I'm sorry for that. Uzma wanted to make sure you were the real deal. It's hard, not knowing who to trust. Who will care? Still, if there is any hope you will help us, I have to try."

Uzma shook her head and started for the door. Whatever this exchange, she wouldn't serve as a witness.

Blythe handed the small bundle to me, solemn. The corners of her lips turned down. "If you are willing to talk, you can find us at the bike shop. You can send a message or stop by. June doesn't know we're here, though, and better keep it that way. But I had to see you. Priyanka was my best friend, and I can't let her be forgotten." With a last look at the bundle, Blythe followed her sister.

When the door shut behind them and their figures passed by the front window, I turned to Joaquin. "What in the actual..."

Joaquin continued to stare after the women. "Fear has a scent, and I know that one well. Lust, too. I forget about sadness, though. That one," he said, nodding his chin toward the retreating form of Blythe, "couldn't cover it with all the French perfume in her boudoir."

I made a face and gave his tricep a playful swat. "Boudoir? Have I stepped back in time?"

Joaquin shrugged, taking his attention away from the

front windows. "I get the feeling that one operates on a different temporal scale," he said. "What did she give you?"

Careful to slide the silks between my fingers so that I didn't touch whatever was inside, I peeled back the wrappings. Inside was a small ring, its adornment a metal-worked compartment topped with an oval lapis stone held in place with a tiny clasp.

"Huh," Joaquin said, squatting to peer closely at the item in my hand. "What's it for?"

I raised an eyebrow. "Poison."

∼

When I closed up for the day, I picked up the handful of pink silk and my fourth cup of coffee for the day, and carried them toward the back door.

Ringed by the backs of the dozen buildings that made up our block, the atrium was a red brick courtyard containing a few dumpsters, a bench Christopher restored to a weather-resistant glory, and a massive silvery tree, bare save for a perfect pink bud, yet to bloom.

As I crossed the worn cobbles, I fought the urge to look back at a spot in the wall, just behind the dumpster, where a loose brick can hide a wealth of trouble. That problem was one I'd been ignoring for weeks and would continue a little longer, too, if I could help it.

I settled onto the newly sealed slats of the bench, their worn wood gifted with shine and durability from Christopher's attentions. I sank into the backrest, letting a sip of the warm liquid soothe my jangled nerves. I hadn't needed to react, to fight with what little I had, but another moment of Uzma before Blythe arrived, and it may not have ended so... oddly.

Caffeine kicking in, I contemplated the ring in my hand.

Likely a woman's, given the slim fit and vintage design. The ring was exquisite, down to the filigree clasp. No work of an amateur. Inside, the band was smooth metal, without inscription. Why Blythe gave me another woman's ring and what she wanted me to do with it were two questions I let myself ponder.

The growing heat of the day brought a sheen to my forehead. I twisted my hair up in a clip. A breeze nipped at the back of my neck, doing little to ease the heat. I tipped my head back to study the branches. The tree bark was a matte gray, swirls of bark layered atop each other. Branches spiraled up toward the sky from a massive trunk.

In my ear, a faint buzzing disrupted my thoughts. I swatted in the air, unthinking. There was a pinch at the nape of my neck, and I hissed at the pain. I slapped at my shoulder, something soft and fuzzy squishing between my fingers. I withdrew my hand in which I now held the remains of a bee. Wings crumpled across stripes, a crushed body. The spot on my shoulder throbbed as I mourned the wasted life of the helpless insect.

"I wouldn't have hurt you," I said. "I didn't know."

A gruff voice called out and my back stiffened. "Are you okay?"

Ansel.

"I'm fine," I said, though I wasn't. Pain shot across my shoulder blade, down my arm, and across my back. However my body wanted to protest, it was nothing to the thundering in my head at his approach.

"Don't be stupid," Ansel said from behind me, his voice drawing closer.

I bristled and twisted to face him, readying a retort.

While Ansel was warded from my shop and confined to his territory, the atrium was definitely part of his realm. He stood there, glass in hand, a bartending apron slung around his hips. A sheen of sweat crossed his brow. Ansel tossed back his drink, ice clinking against the glass, then gave me the pitiful look one would give a petulant child. Before I could tell him exactly what he could do with his insult, he cut me off. "You've got a stinger hanging half out of your skin. Let me get it."

Time with Ansel meant one of two things: I'd get angry at what he said, or I'd radiate guilt over the distance between us. Something about him—his diehard loyalty, his effortless bravery, or sure, his mountain man build—drew me, again and again, to an aching need to know him, to grow familiar with every corner of his mind, and every curve of his body. His dismissal of my wants and needs when it came to his domain infuriated me, though. Neither of these perspectives would take me anywhere good with this guardian of a gate to the Netherworld.

I held up a hand in protest, wincing at the pain that radiated down my arm. I turned back toward the tree, as if content to go about my day, a throbbing black stinger in my neck, thank-you-very-much. "No, don't bother. I'll be fine—"

My protests fell in vain when I heard a metallic click. There was a scrape against my skin, the briefest contact, and the throbbing lessened.

"It's out," he said from behind me. Metal zinged against metal once more. "Don't worry, the blade's clean."

Without warning, an ice cube pressed against the skin on my shoulder. I shivered at the contact. "Thank you," I managed to whisper, not trusting myself to look at him as my insides warmed.

I pictured him behind me. Well over six feet tall, broader than the hull of a boat. Dove gray eyes with sun bleached hair. He had the look of a beached mermaid—were she the size of a Viking. My heart betrayed my rational thoughts as I fought the urge to throw myself into his arms and run my hand along his jaw. "I'll get something to put on it." I stood and swayed, my balance wobbling under the effect of histamines.

"Sit," he said, pressing down on my good shoulder. "You're not going anywhere for a tick."

"There's honey in the shop," I said, weakly.

Ansel's hand tensed against my skin. We both knew Hollis's—and June's—wards kept him out of the Apothecary. *Shit.*

He cleared his throat. "I've got something better in the bar."

His absence filled my senses like the heavy air before a thunderstorm.

Ever since I'd found Hollis's hiding place by the dumpsters, I'd been unable to maintain any sort of chill around Ansel. That I had, right now, the very treasure for which he searched as though his life depended on it (which it kind of did), hidden under the floorboards in my loft would enrage him to no end. The part of me that wanted to help people, to get them what they dreamed of, wanted nothing more than to hand it over. But I couldn't tell him. With the power such an object could bring, there was no telling what my brooding roommate would do. He'd threatened me on more than one occasion, tried to buy my shop out from under me to secure his rule, promised he would stop at nothing in his quest and would spare no one in his path.

Hard to say yes to a guy like that.

Every time I saw the man, no matter how furious I was with his violations of my space, his insults of my family's history, and his complete disregard for ability to function as an adult woman, seeing him shot pure fire through my insides.

Since the events of my arrival, we'd maintained a cool distance. He stayed in his shop, and I stayed in mine. The difference was that Ansel brooded over the next seven years of servitude I'd cost him with one minor mistake while I was free to pack up and go at any time.

As though I'd meant to do it. But he couldn't let that go, no matter what I said. No matter how I tried to help their cause, to find a way toward safety.

He was chained. I was free. There was no in-between.

A soft touch at my shoulder signaled Ansel's return. He rested his wrist on my skin, sending chills down my arm. With one finger, he dabbed something on my wound. The pain subsided to a duller throb, but the heartbeat continued to pound. He added more of the mystery paste, then blew on the spot. It took every nerve I had not to shudder at the sensation. I steeled myself and turned to face him.

In his trademark buttoned-up shirt, Morgan's emblazoned on the chest, Ansel stood, a white paste remaining on two outstretched fingers, the bowl of paste in his other hand. Instead of all the sensible, reasonable things I could have said, I blurted, "I killed her." Hot tears slipped down my face. The pain of the moment sank in.

"What—who?" Ansel frowned. After a beat, understanding crossed his brow. "It's just a bee. There are zillions of those things for a reason. They can't help themselves. It—she—hardly matters in the scheme of things."

"She mattered to me," I said, looking down at the mash of insect, discarded on the bench. I looked up. "Wait, what is that?"

"This?" Ansel looked down at the bowl. "Meat tenderizer. You make a paste. Mom taught me." Ansel's adoptive mother and father were former owners of Morgan's. They'd treated him as the son they hadn't been able to have on their own.

I frowned. "How did you get the stinger out?"

Ansel swung his hip toward me. A scabbard shone in the light. "With this." A hilt crusted in jewels glinted. Ansel liked to collect relics from those he vanquished. Iris told me he had a vault that could serve as its own museum. This man had used what was no doubt a priceless artifact to remove a stinger from my shoulder.

"A bit of overkill, don't you think?" I winced at the tone of my own words.

Ansel wiped his fingers on his jeans, set the bowl on the bench, and unsheathed his sword. The blade sang in the sunlight. Swirled engravings covered the metal, giving the piece a translucent appearance. "This is Blazewing. When it slices through the flesh of the disloyal, their bodies alight in flames. Stories tell of its use to behead defunct knights of the old courts."

I swallowed. Knowing he carried something that could slice off my head as fast as it had done for royalty of the past was far from comforting. "What if I'd burst into flames when you scraped the stinger out?"

Ansel shrugged. "Then we would have known the truth about you, once and for all."

"Funny that it takes you a giant blade to feel more confident when dealing with a woman."

Ansel's nostrils flared at the insult. It was harsh, but I was freaked about my proximity to such a weapon. That he wielded it as though one would use a butterknife was beside the point. I didn't like being someone's plaything.

Iris, Morgan's bartender, leaned her head out the back door of the pub. "Now that you've shown the entire neighborhood your arsenal, can we finish the keg order?" Before he could answer, she turned to me. "Oh hey, EJ. Coming over? We've got a new special..."

I gave her a weak wave, and she ducked back inside.

Ansel flipped the sword over in his hands. "In my years of experience, I've learned it's never the size of the weapon," he said. He stooped to scoop up the remains of the bee, transplanting them to the base of the tree. He covered the insect with a pile of soft sand, a makeshift grave for the departed fighter. "It's the warrior who wields them. I believe that, even for the smallest of creatures." Without looking back, he re-sheathed his own weapon and left.

My shoulder warmed, whether from his touch or the reaction, I didn't know. If only I'd known what else spread across my skin that afternoon, I could have spared all of us.

Four

"Mmhmm...we could offer this for you. My partner and I have decades of experience at top venues, and our packages are customizable to meet your size needs—"

"You enjoy saying packages too much," I said under my breath.

Christopher shot me a look before returning to the phone conversation. "I see...ah. Okay. Who was that again? Ah...all right, please keep us in mind for your future events."

"Damn." I set my ceramic cup back onto its matching saucer. Crumbs littered the napkin at my side, remnants of banana nut bread. I picked at a piece of walnut. "So, she was a no?"

"Fifth one in a row." Christopher sucked in his lower lip. With a flourish, he crossed out another line in his notebook. "Next."

We'd decamped to Second Shot, leaving Gaven in charge of the shop so we could strategize. While I sorted through the rules and regulations of running an events business in our adopted town, Christopher hunted through my meager contacts for a lead.

I read the name under the solid blue line of ink. "I remember her. She was the lady who wanted to do a corporate murder mystery. I thought she'd go for the Chicago gangster theme."

Christopher shrugged. He drained his cup and stood up from his stool. "Said she loved the opening but has already booked with someone."

"Who?"

"Some woman with a French name. Madame...something. Duvall? LeSalle?"

"Never heard of her." I pouted, bitterness coating my words, knowing full well the list of people I knew in Prescott was short. "Is she going for the brothel vibe?"

He tilted his chin. "I would have said Parisian." Christopher gestured to me with his mug. "Want another?"

"I *wanted* that party—it should have been ours!" My irrational side flared its ugly head. A few weeks into therapy, I'd learned this is a big part of anxiety. I closed my eyes and inhaled through my nose.

"Another cup it is." He looked me up and down. "While I'm up there, I'll see if Grace has anything stronger in the back." With a wink, Christopher reached for my mug and shuffled up to the front counter.

Second Shot was the sole coffee shop where the owner, Grace, was not only aware of the extranormal inhabitants of Prescott but ran with Joaquin and his buddy Yanric doing side jobs that required more than one body. I didn't ask if she had similar abilities to Joaquin, and she didn't tell me, but it was understood that we had shared knowledge that made her place a safe harbor.

Aside from the two of us, few customers occupied the

space. Grace, the owner and barista, had painted the walls a sunny yellow that warmed in the sleepy afternoon sunshine. In one corner, an artist had spread out a collection of pencils and notebooks. He hunched over his work, swapping out tools, erasing, and blowing across the page. A bomber jacket bunched up around his ears, behind which he tucked strands of limp, dishwater blond hair. He looked up and squinted past me for a moment, then returned to his work. I followed his line of sight.

Across the shop was another man, this one half lit at the window. The filtered lighting made visible the peach fuzz across his jaw, his pale lashes, and the faintest bruise at his collarbone. He read from a book of Neruda poems, tracing one finger down the text as though it were a lazy river. A worn indie band shirt clung to his torso, and a silver ring circled his pinky finger.

The artist flicked his eyes to the subject once more. I watched him bite ever-so-softly on his lower lip.

When had someone last looked at me with that kind of lust? More so, when had I last had cause to look at another as though they were some kind of delectable dessert? The image of Ansel walking away from me, an ancient sword swinging from his belt, thundered into my mind.

"Get out of my head!" I whispered to myself. The artist looked my way. I gave him a pressed smile and shrugged.

Christopher returned, carrying two fresh mugs and a concerned look. He glanced from the artist to me. The man went back to his sketches, pretending we'd had no exchange. "What'd I miss?"

I flopped back on the bench. "Just me, completely incapable of managing middle age."

My best friend rolled his eyes. "Status quo then."

Grace brought over her own shot of espresso. She plunked an entire sugar cube into the miniature cup. "It's my weakness," she said, catching my stare. "What are you two up to over here?" The brunette straddled a chair, backward.

"We're starting an event planning business," Christopher said.

Grace beamed at him. "Oh yeah. EJ told me that was your thing back in Chicago."

"Trying to, anyway," I said. "Have to land some clients first."

Christopher slid his notebook over to me, pointing at an entry. "What do I need to know about this one before I call and face another rejection?"

I sighed. "Baby shower. Western theme."

"Great," Christopher said, all exaggerated protest.

Grace volleyed her attention between the two of us. "What's wrong with a baby shower?" She downed her shot in one gulp.

"The games," I said. "And the decorations. Oh, and the guests."

Grace laughed. "So, all of it?"

The reader closed his book and stood up from the table. I watched the artist follow him out the door with his gaze. I wanted to tell him to get up, to seize the day, but I was rooted, unable to give advice I couldn't follow. The artist closed his eyes, taking a deep breath. He had the face of someone committing a moment to memory.

I turned back to Grace. "Pretty much. You've got too many groups at the same party, which always complicates things. Family plus friends and colleagues. That always makes for an awkward gathering. And Christopher hates the ridiculous games they want us to pull off—"

"Candy bar diapers," Christopher said, then swiveled his attention to his phone. "Hello? Yes, I'm calling for—"

Grace curled her upper lip. "Candy bar..."

"Yeah, it's gross. Then there are the decorations. Either

zoo animals, all the pink, or the same boho pastels everyone uses. Rarely do you get a decent theme to work with."

Grace raised her eyebrows. "Sounds like torture—for y'all."

Christopher dropped his phone onto the pad of paper. "Damn. They're booked already."

"The French tart?" I asked.

"If you mean the same name from earlier, yes." He pursed his lips. Christopher knew when I needed some regulation.

"I'll leave you two to it," Grace said, and returned to the counter. "Let me know if you need refills."

"Let's count our blessings a sec," Christopher said when Grace moved off. "Gaven landed us the art opening."

"True."

Ansel and I shared an employee and his loyalty. Gaven was an ersatz member of the Gentry, the fae established in this world and doing their best to blend in with the humans. Unlike his brethren, however, he preferred to break more rules than he followed.

Christopher slid a business card to me. "And there's this one."

I didn't have to look at the card to know what Christopher offered. "You know I can't. Ansel would kill me."

"Would he? I can respect that. We are partners. But there *are* options."

"Let's say I wouldn't end up with the biggest target on my back. Imagine the photo spread. How could we use those shots in a portfolio? The red-rimmed eyes, that waxy skin... And what if someone goes after elixir—"

"And what if it goes well? We make some money, and we get more clients."

My eyes flicked back to the rectangle on the table. The card was a deep blue with silver font, the initials of its owner outlined in a faint red. They wanted a dessert bar for a backyard movie night and a few custom cocktails. Small, intimate, and easy—especially when half the attendees wouldn't eat. This was a job we could do in our sleep, icing on top of an event planner's cake. There was just one problem.

The host, and presumably many attendees, were Fallen.

"No promises," I said. "Besides, we've got some time to decide."

"That's what everyone says, until that time runs out."

Five

"That's it, I quit." With a flourish, I tossed my bag onto the counter, followed by my keys. I dug a hair clip out from within my bag and whisked my stubborn, half-knotted tresses into some semblance of control.

Christopher stared at my entrance, the exact effect I'd wanted. Slumped onto my stool behind the sales counter and makeshift bar I'd fashioned out of an old set of apothecary shelves, he held the pose of a designer model. He clutched a black felt-tip pen in one hand, tapping the edge against his lip. One foot perched on the rung of the stool, loafers polished, pressed slacks, and a linen T-shirt that remained unwrinkled thanks to the natural humidity of my shop. Gold-rimmed glasses sat on the bridge of his nose. Somewhere in between professor and pinup, my best friend held court. "Care to be specific?" He gestured to the hand-lettered plant tags stacked atop the vintage woodgrain surface. "Just curious if I need to finish labeling the anthuriums or if we're packing bags."

I sighed, an inelegant release of all the tension I'd collected over an afternoon of frustration, humiliation, and shame. Then I did what any reasonable person would do—I grabbed a mug, poured in the dregs of our morning pot, and tossed them back. I stared at the now empty vessel, its side emblazoned with *Plant Lover* across the ceramic. There was no greater irony than this message in my hand. "I'm starting to wonder if I'm good at anything anymore. Like, why bother?"

"Oh my Emma Jane, come here." Christopher stood and held his arms out to me. We saved our pet nicknames for both the best and worst of times.

Everyone needs a best friend like mine. I collapsed into his arms, and he squeezed me, his arms a tight wrap around my shoulders. He rubbed my back, rocking me, until the tears fell. I shook in quiet sobs against his chest.

"I can't even grow something edible without messing it up."

Hands on my shoulders, Christopher held me back from his face. He cocked an eyebrow. "Edible?"

I huffed, then closed my eyes, pouting. Lips pressed together, I dropped my pants.

"What in a month of Sundays..." Christopher crouched to look at the deep scratches criss-crossing my thighs.

It wasn't my nudity that shook my staunch roommate. Christopher and I had seen each other naked—or close to—dozens of times. In our twenties, we all but poured each other into bed every other night, alternating babysitting duties after parties to which we were inevitably invited by a drunk groomsman. Plus, Christopher thought of women's bodies like he did a department store vase. Both had their place in this world, but neither belonged in his bedroom.

"June is supposed to be coaching me on intent. She said that I should be able to manifest plants when I need them, like apparently Hollis could do in his sleep." My uncle, a green witch, had a natural ability I'd yet to manifest. Thus far, without Christopher, Gaven, and Lotte, I would have a shop full of decay. "After I burnt what little grass she had and split a mesquite tree in two, I raised a blackberry bramble—at my feet. She had to cut me out of the damn thing before dousing it in gas and burning the stump where it grew."

"Huh," Christopher said. He shuffled over to the sink, grabbed a tea towel, ran it under the water, and pressed it to the worst of the scratches. I hissed, and he shifted the pressure. "I would have thought a so-called divination witch would know you'd be terrible at this."

"Funny," I said, and winced when the towel brushed another raw scrape. "It's not that I don't understand the purpose. I have drive, I want to learn—no *need* to learn, to protect myself and others. I found Cass on the floor, her body lifeless and used. I know what they did to Hollis. But others stepped in to help me. What I can't do is create hatred for something that has yet to happen. I don't want to look at the world that way. Hope is a weight that keeps me from assuming the worst. How can I pretend to fight when I have no enemy in mind? I don't know how to get that through June's thick head."

"Next time," Christopher said, handing me the towel, "at least learn to aim the blackberries."

I groaned. "What did I miss?"

Christopher struggled to stifle a grin. "Golden boy dropped by."

My heart thudded to an abrupt stop. "Who?"

"Oh, drop the act, Mother Theresa. You know damn well who. What other local farmer looks like he stepped out of Adonis's fire brigade?"

I sucked in air. "Ah, him. What did he want?"

Rowdy Beckett. A walking, talking, environmentally conscious Ken doll, he was a bit of a local legend. He ran a sizable apiary outside the city limits, pampering his bees to such a degree that they produced the sweetest honey in the county. Customers flocked from all around to buy out his farmer's market booth each week. What most of them didn't realize was that the hoard of workers he brought with him, those who manned the booth while he chit-chatted with his adoring fans, were anything but local. Customers never noticed, though, as they couldn't rip their eyes from the demigod before them. He was extranormal, that much was clear. This explained some of the incapacitation his presence brought to a social situation. I could manage a semi-coherent conversation with Rowdy, but only just. Too long in his company and something shifted within, a warmth that spread between my thighs until he'd subconsciously wrestled my every thought to his person. Some days, it was all I could do to maintain eye contact.

"Oh, you know," Christopher said. He took his seat again, coy. "Came by to drop off some honey, talk about the weather, request a pitch..."

"A pitch?"

Christopher looked up, a Cheshire grin across his face. "Apparently, he's throwing a big bash at the end of the month. Looking for some *understanding* planners, as he put it."

I frowned. There was the snag. "What does that mean?" In my short time living on this block, my scale of understanding had erupted into a catastrophic blast zone.

"Something about an old acquaintance coming back into town. He left you this honeycomb and said to let him know when we put something together." Christopher bit his lip. "So, are we going to put something together?"

I reached for the Mason jar at Christopher's elbow. A chunk of comb filled the glass container, its waxen structures seeping gooey golden liquid that pooled at the bottom of the jar. I sighed, unscrewing the lid and reaching for a spoon. "We're going to think about it—hard."

∽

"You sure you don't need me?"

"I'll be fine," I said, straightening Christopher's already perfect collar. "Have fun with—what was his name again? Gregor? Robert? Something else stuffy?"

"Neil." Christopher said, frowning. He picked an imaginary piece of lint off his shirt.

"I knew it was something stiff."

Christopher rolled his eyes. He was dressed and ready for a date—his first since arriving. He was going out with the man he'd met at City Hall and had dressed on the edge of ready and willing. He'd chosen to accent his biceps with a tight shirt and don slacks that provided a hint of package proportions to create an outfit that definitely didn't say he was crashing in his best friend's dead uncle's bedroom and yes, please, he would like to come upstairs for a drink.

In contrast to his urban chic, I was in a sundress and cardigan with gladiator sandals that wrapped up my calves. Adjustable straps and a pushup bra meant I accented the curves I'd earned while still maintaining a casual look. I vacillated between athleisure and charming shop owner, reluctant to settle on either. A part of me missed the EJ who donned sequins and pleather. Christopher always says getting dressed is a mind-fuck, and he's rarely wrong.

"You've got the labeled bottles and clean stoppers. You'll need to assemble the toasts, but I made double the chutney."

"I'll be fine," I said. "Go. Enjoy yourself." I pressed his wallet into his hands. "And if you get any action at all, you'd better tell me all about it. I need some vicarious action. Okay, well, maybe don't tell me about *all* of it."

Christopher winked and slipped out the door.

I flipped the sign dangling in front of the glass to *Closed* and leaned my back against the door a moment, breathing in the thick, warm air of the shop before pressing myself forward into action.

While the event at the Apothecary had been an unqualified disaster in that several people died after the public left, from a business perspective, people loved it. The other shop owners and I decided to keep the event going. Each month, a different business hosted, inviting the public in for a special community night. Other businesses brought some of their wares and the doors opened to draw in new customers and celebrate all that is Prescott.

This month, we were at Whipple Wines, the post-retirement love child of Brent and Bonnie Whipple. They'd built a bottle shop with a small stage and filled the place with tables. For my part, I had the cocktail mixes, spring themed, nestled in a backpack slung over my shoulders. I walked with care, not only to protect the glass but also to maintain a hold over the trio of potted plants in my arms and the hanging version that dangled over one wrist. Navigation was tougher when burdened with plants.

At the shop, Bonnie welcomed me inside. "EJ—thanks for coming!" She wrenched a pot from my grip, causing me to almost drop the others. "I told Brent you'd bring something fabulous, and you didn't fail, did you?" She eyed the Anthurium and the two radiator plants I snuggled under one arm and the bag of pitchers in the other. "What's on the menu tonight?"

"Pea flower," I said, a sheepish sense creeping in. "I know it's overdone, but people are obsessed. I thought the blue would look great in your stemware."

I'd spent the afternoon whipping up a spring cocktail collection. A gin fizz and a layered sangria, and a rose Negroni. In a twist, I'd added pea flower tincture to each, casting the beverages in hues that ranged from nautical to periwinkle.

Bonnie clapped. "I can't want to see what you brought!" She bustled me over to a side table where I set up shop, including the crisp, new business cards Christopher had printed.

Apothecary
Purveyors of plants and libations
Event curation

Within a half hour, the place had filled. People browsed the tables, taking in everything from the holiday displays and artwork to the handmaid furniture. The line for wine was ten deep, and a steady crowd gathered in front of the acoustic guitarist who glowed beneath a single blue stage light.

At my booth, the drinks were a hit. Christopher had been right about the pairings: a delicate parmesan cracker for the gin fizz, a sugar cookie made with lime zest and rose water for the sangria, and a pickled skewer of blueberries for the Negroni.

"We do parties, too," I added, when one woman squealed in delight, dragging her husband over to the table for samples.

"Phil, what about that work thing you always do? Wouldn't it be nice to have someone other than that steakhouse cater things? You know what happened to Gillian last time." She curved her hand over her mouth as though the man, rolling his eyes, couldn't hear every word she said. "Had to have been the sour cream."

"Can't," the assumed owner of the name Phil said. "They already hired some woman. Jerry said they went with a French theme."

I seethed, my every gut feeling aware of the unnamed caterer.

"Oh." The woman gave me an apologetic look and the couple moved off. She mouthed, "Sorry," when her companion had turned away.

Lotte hustled through the door, a clear plastic crate in her arms. The petite brunette had a new set of choppy bangs that dusted her eyebrows. She hurried over to me and the empty table next to mine.

"You made it," I said. "Loved your latest seasonals." Lotte's candles smelled more realistic than any others, and the shades of wax were beautiful.

"Thanks," she said. "I had to race to get here. Frankie does a great job with the shop, but I didn't know what I had left to sell until I arrived. I hope this is on theme." My friend slung her purse under the table and lifted the lid from her crate. She arranged several dozen candles by size and scent before extracting a bag of dried flowers. Lotte sprinkled dried rose petals and lavender between the candles, giving the table a romantic touch.

"It's perfect," I said.

Lotte shook out her hair, smoothed the top, then took a deep breath. "Catch me up—how are things?"

I sighed, taking in the crowd, the music, and the way my sandal straps dug into my flesh. "Could be better, could be worse. I made it here in one piece, albeit a little scratched up from my latest practice rounds with June. Christopher wants to give the planning business another go, but all the decent events are snatched out from under us by some French woman, and I don't even have the Apothecary up to speed, so I have no business starting something new, but I want to. So, so badly."

"A French woman? Sounds like your plate is full."

"And then some."

Bonnie approached, ushering someone along behind her. The woman was all pink cheeks and hair dyed a rich burgundy to match her favorite wines. "Ladies, I'd like you to meet the fabulous Miss LeGalle. She's new in town and ripe to join our little group. Not only does she make incredible body products, but she is an event planner, too. EJ, you and she likely have a lot in common."

The woman who lagged behind Bonnie stepped forward. When she met my eyes, her smile stretched outward, knowing, cruel, and calculating. The red-jeweled ring I remembered all too well glinted from her finger.

My jaw dropped.

"Oh, gods," Lotte said.

Ophelia.

Six

"Literally anyone but her!" I ranted to Lotte on the sidewalk as nervous pedestrians scooted past us, averting their eyes.

As soon as I'd flashed Ophelia a tight smile before excusing myself to tidy my display, the only response I could muster to her piranha greeting, I returned to my table. With a flick of my chin and pleading eyes, I signaled for Lotte to join me outside. Now, I was missing a sale and a potential lead because I couldn't get myself together enough to face a woman who had it out for me.

The memory of my encounter with Ophelia, when I was new and ignorant, when she tried to bribe and then threaten me, reeled in my mind. Before I knew what was in my shop, before I fully understood the consequences of my role, I knew she was a disaster waiting to happen. If Joaquin hadn't been at the Apothecary, hadn't intervened, one of us would not be here. Likely me.

Lotte, ever the cool and calm friend, dragged me away from the door. "Maybe it's a coincidence."

"That she's here? Her name is LeGalle. She's flipping French. That woman is taking all my clients—and it's all because she hates me!" I flexed my hands into claws, as though an imaginary enemy stood in front of me, grinning with that slash of red lipstick and impish eyes. "Do you know her?"

"I know of her," Lotte said, supplying a slight shrug. "We've never...how do they put it? Run in the same circles."

"How am I supposed to sit in the same room with such a vile woman?"

Lotte peered in through the glass storefront. "It's getting busy in there. Maybe you won't even notice her once you start talking to people."

We stood under a neon sign of a bottle pouring liquid into a glass with the words *Wine Time* spelled out below. Inside, the band played a cover of a Nick Cave song. "Good news. That woman with the Princess Leia hair is buying one of your plants. She's taking it up to the register. You sure you don't want to go back in?"

"Go in and hear her sweet-talk everyone? I doubt Brent and Bonnie want me to barf all over their floor." I paced the distance between a parking sign and a brick wall. In the streetlights, flecks of mica glittered in the cement. A sliver of moon hooked over the rooftops, on its patient arc across the sky. I inhaled deeply, filling my lungs with every scrap of adult-like behavior I could muster, then let it out in a shuddering breath. Eyes squeezed shut, I screwed up my face and fought the urge to run home. I thought of Christopher and our plans, of my hard and fast fall into my new life, and of the relics I had in my possession. "Fine. I'm going in but under duress."

An hour later, I'd sold my plants, given away a dozen business cards, and signed up exactly no one for a free consultation.

"I'm going home," I said to Lotte, my eyes on Ophelia. The woman perched on the edge of her table, batting her eyes at some tall, affable man in an untucked denim shirt and khakis that dripped with executive vibes. "I can't watch any more of this."

The blocks faded behind me as I walked, unseeing. A cloud hung above me, a storm brewing as I stewed.

In the square, a group of boys played with a hacky sack in the dim light. Their shouts echoed against the walls of the courthouse. I stuck to the edges of the grass, away from the shadows. Overhead, the spring leaves fluttered in the treetops, their new leaves crisp and promising. Ahead, Whiskey Row bustled with a crowd unseen on the other blocks. A string of bars, with Morgan's Publican at its center, held a historic court over the city of Prescott and its checkered past. While a bistro, a cheesy T-shirt shop, and an art gallery joined the row of establishments, at its heart, this was Prescott's raucous soul. I ducked through the crowd, going unnoticed among the revelers.

"You're here," I said, stepping into the shop. The warm damp air hit me like a wall. Christopher was back, hunched over the laptop with a coffee cup to his lips. "Things didn't go well?"

Christopher looked up from the screen and lowered his glasses on his nose. "You mean, because I'm not at his place, you assume it was a bad date?"

I considered my best friend and the string of broken hearts he'd left behind in Chicago. "Yep, exactly that."

"For your information, it was wonderful. He took me to dinner, and we chatted about romcoms, the stock market, and our favorite wines. Apparently, there are great vineyards around Jerome, and he asked if I'd like to join him for a drive out there. There was a chaste cheek peck, and I am here, by myself, trying to ignore my raging hard on in exchange for what might be the slow start to something great."

"How mature of you," I said. "What have you done with my best friend?"

"Ha ha. To keep my mind out of his bedroom, I'm working up some numbers for the pitch."

"What pitch?"

Christopher lifted an eyebrow. "The big one? For Beckett Farms."

I started for the stairs. "Oh, that." I climbed, one foot and then the other, on the black, wrought iron spiral that led up to the lofted space. "I'm going to bed."

"Don't you want to help?"

"I'll think about it later—tomorrow." I didn't want to admit that my run-in with Ophelia had shaken my confidence.

"You didn't say how your night went..." Christopher's words trailed up the stairs behind me.

I hung over the loft's railing and peered down at him. "I've met our competition," I said.

"Uh oh."

"It gets worse. Turns out I already knew her, and she hates me."

"Oh, good." Christopher snapped the laptop shut and started for the front door. "I'll lock up, and you can tell me all about the enemy. I need a new distraction, anyway."

I trusted Christopher to close up shop, grab a couple of glasses and reach for the leftovers of my recipes.. He'd double check the doors, lower the shades, flick on a lamp, and set out a tray of orange slices for the moths. Then he'd follow me upstairs. We'd built this nighttime routine in which we changed into lounge clothes and binged on old episodes of *Sex in the City* before jointly brushing our teeth.

Arms full, I took to the stairs. "She was so obnoxious! With some fake accent and this red fuck me dress. I swear even her hair was too perfect. It had to be a wig."

Christopher stood at the front window, the cord for the shade in his hands. "What was that about her dress?"

"You know the kind," I called down the stairs, shaking my head to myself as I set foot on the landing. "Slit to the hip, tight everywhere it should be."

There was a pause. "Uh, EJ? Pretty sure that woman just went into Morgan's."

Seven

I made a show of convincing myself I didn't care for almost a full twenty-four hours. It didn't work.

Throughout the night, while I tossed and turned, I shoved at the images of Ophelia that fought for my headspace. Like a lumpy pillow, I punched at her presence. She was there, her smirking visage, demanding I give her entrance to the weir. In my dreams, I was back at the winery but glued to the floor somehow. Forced to shake her hand, compelled to offer a warm smile and pretend we were fellow businesswomen, here for each other and celebrating each other's successes. Lotte poured glass after glass of cheap red wine down my throat while I overheard Ophelia land customer after customer, the lilt of her French accent a forked tongue that struck each person to whom she spoke.

I awoke in a tumble of covers, the futon firm against my aching back. My mouth tasted of cotton and bitterness.

Bleary-eyed, I ignored the pinch between my shoulders and the aching curiosity to know why she stopped in at Morgan's.

Instead, I cruised through repotting a respectable quantity

of spring bulbs into ribbon-wrapped glass jars, filling the containers with smooth, white pebbles before anchoring each bulb to a small plastic floral frog nestled in the pebbles. A church group ordered the favors for a late spring brunch, and this was an easy order to fill. But after the third bulb I handled sprouted roots, shot a stem skyward, and burst forth into a spire of hyacinth blossoms, Christopher took over. He shot a look at the glowing tattoo wrapping around my wrist and made me don gardening gloves.

My gift, a word I said through clenched teeth, was the equivalent of teenage hormones: raging and impossible to mask one minute, completely absent the next. I couldn't control something that controlled me.

Midway through the afternoon, after I'd stubbed my toe on a shelf, failed to save a file of invoices from a significant splash of coffee, spilled a bag of pearlite over the floor, and exploded my bowl of soup inside the microwave, I gave in.

I didn't want to know why Ophelia dropped by Morgan's. I needed to know.

"I'm going out," I said, brushing off Christopher's look of concern. I looped my reusable bag over my shoulder. "I'll get something for dinner."

"Dirty fries don't travel well," Christopher said. I ignored his all-knowing taunt and pushed my way out the door.

As predicted, my first footfalls were toward Morgan's. Yet as my feet met the rubbery welcome mat, I did an about face. It wasn't as if she was still in there, and even if she was, it wasn't like I would waltz in and confront her. And it wasn't as though if I asked, point-blank, Ansel would tell me anything. We had a minute level of understanding between us, and it didn't include personal secrets.

I headed south.

Blocks later, I turned onto a side street. Several industrial buildings striped the asphalt like rows of corn. Each structure was peppered with garage doors. At the end of one of the tan buildings, progressive rock steamed out of a massive, open door. Out front, a group of teens crowded around a half dozen bicycles resting on lifted stands. A woman with one side of her head shaved, the other in a curly mop of purple, lectured as the teens worked on the bikes. The woman wore a black tank top over loose-fitting canvas pants with one leg rolled to the knee and a thin flannel tied around her waist. As I approached, she appraised me with soft, sable eyes. With a nod, she granted me entrance into the shop.

I ducked through the wide opening, my eyes adjusting to the interior. While the outside was abuzz with youthful voices, the inside was dark and quiet. Several bicycles sat in various states of assembly, their shapes casting eerie shadows under the two shop lights. Faint notes of jazz trickled down the back hallway, and I followed the mournful voice of Billie Holiday. I passed a conference room, storage, and a small kitchen, and headed for the dim recesses of the hallway as the music swelled.

"Hello?" My voice echoed through the shop as I passed drawers of nuts and bolts, a barrel of discarded handlebars, and stacks of wheels. There was a rack of used bike jerseys with a sign that said *Free to a good home, ask to try on.* "June?"

I approached the hallway, tiptoeing as though on the hunt for a tiger. The depths of this warehouse were unknown, and it wasn't like I'd called first. I'd come blazing into a witch's territory without permission, an aggressive act in the world of magic, but I was desperate. I would tread with care, avoiding an upset. The thing about approaching a big cat, though, is that they've smelled you long before you spot them.

"You have thirty seconds to explain yourself before I singe the hair from your head."

I froze, breathing in every word of that warning.

"I have a target," I said, keeping my hands where they could be seen. Without looking down, I knew the tattoo on my hand glowed with intent. "I don't want to kill anyone or anything, but I want to make them...stay away from me. For good."

Words choked in the voice behind me. "And this couldn't wait for the next time we train? I've already committed to witnessing your endless inability to show any worthwhile skill."

The words stung, a barb in my side, yet the warble behind them betrayed something akin to emotion.

I turned to find June, transfixed.

The upright fire of a woman, well into her crone phase of life, had the rounded shoulders of the burdened. Her typical thick rope of a silver braid lay limp over her shoulder, frizzy and unkempt as though she'd slept on it. She wore a black T-shirt half tucked into a pair of black jeans, her boots scuffed. Around her neck hung a cord strung with a wire-wrapped black stone. Dark circles shadowed her eyes. Her skin was dry and wan, lips papery like husks.

"What happened?" For in that moment, she wasn't June, the powerful divination witch, leader of the Coven of Vesta, she was someone old enough to be my mother, haggard and worn, as though carrying the weight of the world on her shoulders.

June blinked, as though assessing the sincerity of my words. She looked away, gathering her thoughts, then returned to me. Her nostrils flared, a brief return of her fire. "Priyanka was killed."

"Who was she to you?"

June didn't wait for me to catch up. "Our last hedgerider. She had more talent than you possess in that cursed pinky finger."

I bristled at the jab, but June continued.

"She was out on a hike, near Thumb Butte, scouting out a place for our moon rites."

I nodded. "I've been there. It's a beautiful spot." A spot that would now be known as the last place the woman had been alive. A slew of natural dangers came to mind: fell from a cliff side, eaten by a cougar, stung by a rattlesnake. Lotte had walked me through the risks of each, prepping me to be careful on our own hikes.

"Priyanka drowned," June said. "In a flash flood."

I frowned. The butte loomed over the city, covered with trails for catching the sunsets. I might have been from a city, far from the trials of living in a high desert, but I'd seen no valleys nor low spots in which water could gather—and besides, it hadn't rained in weeks. "But how is that possible?"

"Indeed," June said. "One of our sisters works in the coroner's office. Priyanka's lungs were filled with water. Yet her own equipment, her clothes, and everywhere around her was bone dry."

"But that's...impossible."

June's eyes turned to steel. "Is it? Like people who shift into beasts, rips in space that allow travel, and a race of beings who seek to regain control of other realms?"

I'd forgotten my first lesson with June: never underestimate the world around me as it wasn't designed for my safety or benefit. "I'm sorry, that's horrific. What can I do?"

June had been clear: I wasn't welcome to join the coven, not yet, and possibly never. She and Hollis were from the same age, yet it had been clear their alliance was one of mutual purpose rather than deep friendship. June guarded her group, her clan, with a ferocity that had no bounds.

Yet, Blythe and Uzma, two of her followers, stepped out from under June's watchful eye to seek me out.

June opened her mouth, no doubt to deliver a harsh

rebuke, a chastisement that I was the last person able to help, when the instructor appeared in the hall.

"We've got a customer, and she doesn't want my help."

⁓

"Ah, June, *darling*." The woman's voice dripped with sugar. "It's been too long. How are you?"

I remained in the hall, a shiver running down my spine. I knew that voice.

June's shoulders straightened. I could see her back from my angle. Her response was clipped. "What do you want?"

"Why, a bicycle, of course. Seems I'm going to stay in town —for now. I need something to get around, and they just look so...fun."

"We don't have anything you want."

Ophelia tsked. "I'm sure just about anything will do. I'm easy to please. Maybe one of the bikes with those cute baskets —" The simpering voice cut off. There was a pause, and Ophelia spoke again, her voice lowered. "You aren't alone."

"I don't think we can help you, Ophelia," June said. There's another shop in the valley."

Ophelia chuckled, a soft sound. She peered around June. "Come out, come out, little mouse. I won't bite."

I hated her taunt, despised how it grated in my ears.

June intervened. "I think it's time you go."

I summoned every ounce of hatred I could muster and stepped out into the shop. "Sounds like you aren't wanted here," I said, committing to more strength than I felt. "Seems to be a pattern. If only you'd learn to take a hint."

Ophelia's upper lip curled. She flicked her gaze toward June. "Scraping the bottom of the barrel for membership these days?"

I wanted to slap the woman, feel the sting of her cheek

under my palm. Instead, I dug my fingernails into my palms, willing my breathing to slow and my head to quit its buzzing.

"For your information, EJ is one hell of a hedgerider. From the original line."

Ophelia grinned from the corner of her mouth, a predator's pause before the pounce. "Oh really? And let me guess, you're her mentor. That's adorable. Funny how she exudes all the power of a marshmallow."

"Is that an official provocation?" June's words boomed.

With a flick of her hand, Ophelia turned her back to us and sauntered toward the open door. Those in the class stopped their tinkering to watch her exit. "No, not yet. This cat is going to enjoy playing with her mouse a little longer." In the sunshine, the teens backed away from the woman as she left.

"So, you know my target well, I take it," I said. We faced the door, watching as the students returned to their tasks. Wheels came off the bikes and were set aside.

"I do," June said. Her eyes stared down the street.

"What *is* she?" This was a question that haunted me from weeks before. Joaquin stood up to her, but he, too, was wary of the woman. I needed to know who I dealt with if I was going to activate whatever lay inside me in time for our next altercation.

June's eyes narrowed, her mouth a thin line. "La Damme Violette."

Eight

"La what?"

"No one you should ever come against in a dark alley."

June instructed me to stay away from Ophelia. She refused to answer any of my questions and told me to save them for our next practice session.

"But what do I do if I see her?"

I couldn't help the whining. I'd wanted to take action, to be on the offensive, yet I ran from Ophelia like prey from a predator.

"Nothing," June said. "You don't do a godsdamned thing. If you have any sense of self preservation, you will leave her be. At least for now." June approached one of the student bikes. She picked up a lost bolt and handed it to the student.

"But you said I was from an original line...what does that mean?" I followed June out into the dying afternoon light. Three crows flapped into view, alighting on the branches of an elm tree, the lone greenery in the industrial parking lot.

June stopped, her shoulders tense. She glanced around, checking if the others listened, but their instructor had gathered them near a big shop refrigerator to pass out drinks. June whirled on me. "Part of facing down such an enemy is looking bigger than you actually are. It's a survival skill. Start using them."

∼

I all but stomped down the sidewalks, pounding my frustration in a staccato rhythm that did little to assuage my irritation. Everywhere I turned, I was dismissed, ignored, or otherwise pushed aside. The women's websites decried this time of life, the shift from the mothering phase into a place where we faded into the background, forsaken in the interest of the young, the fresh, the bouncy.

Ophelia's grin surfaced in my mind, a sneer aimed to disarm. She couldn't be long out of her twenties, yet June spoke of Ophelia as one speaks of an ancient force, one wrapped deeply in the arms of time.

If June wouldn't give me answers, I would get them elsewhere.

"Fetching my hiking boots," I said, taking the stairs two at a time. Christopher and Gaven stood over the table of orchids. Gaven held a Cattleya orchid, its epiphytic roots splayed in the air, exposed. I snatched my shoes, pack, and a hat before going back out the way I came. "Be back soon!"

At Lotte's, I found Joaquin on the sidewalk, staring up at a hand-lettered sign posted in the window.

"Every time I come by, she's gone. It's like she knows," he said, without turning to look at me.

I deflated. In Lotte's elegant script, she apologized for the need to close early. My plans were shot. I turned to Joaquin. "That you like her?"

Shock split his face like a lightning bolt. His dark ember eyes sparkled, then softened. "It's that obvious?"

I nodded.

He sighed and turned back to the door. "Thought she might want to play a round of darts. Got quite an arm on her. Now I'm just a man with an afternoon off and no woman on which to spend it."

"I'm no Lotte," I said, offering a smile. "But I could use an escort, if you're free."

∽

Joaquin's motorcycle hugged the curves up to Thumb Butte. I heard my father's voice in my head the whole ride, expounding on the vulnerability of a body with no cage to contain it, the physics of anything that went wrong. Still, I smiled into the wind, savoring the ride. I'd been on the back of this bike before, trusted its driver, and maybe, for just a moment, relished in the risk.

I'd mentioned the hike, explaining that I needed to see something. With a lift of his eyebrows, Joaquin understood this to be no ordinary walk in nature, but a mission. You can give the mercenary the afternoon off, but you can't take the adventure out of his drive. Within ten minutes, we were on his bike, headed up the mountain.

June said I needed training in self-preservation. I could think of no one better to provide that than someone who made his living staying one step ahead of his enemies. In Joaquin's line of work, one error could equal the end of the game—and his life.

Of course, it didn't hurt that he was a were. His other form, a giant, wolfish beast, took more than a little time to get used to, and to be honest, the shift continued to take me by surprise.

We dismounted at the trailhead. I untied the bandana from around my hair and re-knotted it around my neck.

Joaquin locked the helmets in his panniers and followed me onto the trail.

The sun hung low, flirting with the edge of the horizon. Faint puffs of clouds flitted at the edges of the sky, promising little in the way of shade or moisture. Rabbits hopped everywhere, their spring population burst on full display. Joaquin caught each movement, his eyes darting to the bushes as the mammals ran from our footsteps. A hawk soared overhead, its pattern ambling toward the idle observation, yet with a sharp dive among the rocks, it proved otherwise.

"All right, we seem to be the sole human occupants. Care to tell me why you wanted Joaquin Time? Not that I'd blame anyone for that."

For a man who'd seen the darkest of life, Joaquin was rarely without a jest. "I needed an expert," I said, smiling. "And the fates directed me to you." As we walked, our eyes on the trail, I filled Joaquin in on my encounters with Ophelia.

He sucked in air. "That woman. Never knew when she'd overstayed her welcome"

"June called her Damme something—what does that mean?"

"Have you ever heard of white women? Often confused with witches, but they aren't always."

"I think so."

"Old Feelie is something akin to that. But she is the woman in violet, a nod to her roots."

"What...is she?" To the west, the sun began its dive. Where it contacted the horizon, a shimmer betrayed the boundary between earth and sky.

"A member of the Bandorai. The only one left, I suspect." Joaquin pointed out a coyote, slipping through the sage. Its scrawny silhouette slipped through the brush, silent and hunting. "From a long line of powerful women who bent the will of the world their way through dynasties, kingdoms, and every human downfall we know."

"Bandorai?" I tucked the term away on my mental list to research. Preferably with a bottle of champagne and a bottomless plate of dirty fries. My stomach rumbled.

Joaquin reached into his pocket and handed me a piece of jerky. I didn't ask about its origin but chewed the snack with gratitude. He shoved a second piece into his own mouth. "Female druids. Priestesses tasked with maintaining the balance between nature and man's ambition."

A candy wrapper, caught in the breeze, tumbled over the soft earth of the trail. I toed it, checking for stickers or spiders or who knew what. Finding it to be no more than a piece of trash, I picked it up and stuffed it in my pocket. "If it's true that they've died out, that would explain a lot."

"There are many with that opinion and calls for the old ways to return. You aren't alone in drawing a correlation between the state of the world and the lack of its earliest caretakers. And there has been a resurgence of the ancient means. But with the good..."

"...come the others, like the Fallen," I said, and left the mention of our mutual experiences hanging between us. "So, June is right."

"About?" His eyes met mine, probing.

Joaquin walked out of any woman's dream of a dark and dangerous bad boy. Black, thick hair, the kind which only looks better with the silver highlights of middle age, paired with deep brows and fathomless eyes, gave him a rakish look. Far from the football player physique, he was a born wrestler. All sinew and tension, a jaw that cut like glass. We were friends, and that was all we would ever be, even if he and Lotte never found each other—but that didn't mean the energy of such a companion was lost on me. For a hot second, I stared back at him, then shook my head, as though I'd been staring into space, instead of at this gorgeous man.

Despite what Christopher said, I wasn't dead on the inside, just...hibernating.

"That I should stay away from her. At least for now. That she's powerful."

Joaquin cocked his head at me, assessing. "Don't count yourself out. But maybe, for now, follow her advice. I know it can be—do you smell something?" Joaquin's pupils dilated and he froze in place.

I blinked, waiting for him to reanimate, but he remained silent, watching. I turned my attention toward the landscape in front of us, yet saw nothing. As though moved by an inner drive, I reached for the leaves of a juniper, grasping them between the fingers of my right hand. Within the plant, there was a vibration, a warning of a force moving our way.

"It's not her," Joaquin whispered. "I think we should head back."

The sun's last light sent rays of orange and purple through the sky. Joaquin's pace increased, and I picked up my own to keep up. I lowered my voice to the softest of whispers. "Who?" I dared to ask, an owl eager in the approaching twilight. I wanted to know why the trees stretched toward me, why the grasses sprouted under our feet as we made an escape.

Joaquin shook his head in a signal that we wouldn't discuss what was happening here. He changed the subject. "Ansel's got a storyteller coming in tonight, an old friend. You should stop by."

I tasted fear, then, recognizing his desire to appear as though we'd come out for an idle hike as regular humans, the casual inhabitants of this wild land. "I doubt he'd want me there."

Joaquin rolled his eyes in mock exaggeration. "Oh, you two. He's oddly protective, that's all. Not a fan of newcomers.

And who can blame him? They stir up trouble, and he's too grumpy to have to change his ways." He winked at me, a measure of assurance.

"A storyteller sounds like something I would enjoy. Maybe I'll see if Topher's up for it."

"Stories have so many sides," Joaquin said. "Part entertainment, part moral, part warning, part history. I've always loved them."

"Do you know any?"

"I'm no professional, but I know a few."

"Such as?" Our casual talk eased my grown dread, softening it at the edges. As night slinked in across the valley, the shadows closed in around us. The bike was in sight, as we'd left it, and I fought the urge to run.

"There once was a king who, along with his brothers, ruled the lands and seas as giants among the earth."

A hundred feet stretched between us and an escape from the desert pressing in around us. "And then what happened?"

"Some say the humans they created ruined everything. Intended to be playthings, humans fought for control of their realm, failing to heed any of the brothers. The five of them fell out, each retreating to their own corners of the world, bent on waiting out the time of man until they could begin anew, creating a world once again. Yet the brothers grew restless, each not trusting his brethren to uphold their part of the bargain. One brother has returned in defiance of his king, on a quest to seek his inheritance."

"Which is?" Sixty feet. Our footfalls were soft and insistent on the sand. I kept my face forward, refusing to seek something that wasn't there amid the growing dark.

"A realm of his own, having freed it from the destruction of human rule."

"This realm?"

"This one...or a bigger prize..." We made it to the bike.

Joaquin extracted the helmets, handing me one before donning his own, anchoring it in place with a chinstrap.

"Elysium?"

Joaquin shook his head and mounted the bike. "Nether," he said, then started the engine. "Think about it. Souls to command, room for endless expansion. All one would need is the crown."

My gut twisted. I thought of the royal object, wrapped in velvet, nestled under a board in my loft. "The same one Ansel wants," I said. Joaquin didn't reply. It wasn't a question. "What happens next in the story?"

Joaquin appraised me. "That part isn't written yet."

I blinked, unnerved under his stare of assumption. If I dared infer anything, his look suggested I could have something to do with a wayward prince attempting a hostile takeover of the kingdom of the dead. I climbed behind him, wrapping my arms around his slender middle. I shook, trembling from the build of pressure.

Joaquin turned his head toward me, his lips a deep pink below the face shield. "Have you got Little White?"

I pictured the dagger tucked in my pack with my water bottle and compass. I nodded.

"Good. I've got an idea."

Behind us, puddling outward across the blacktop as we drove off, water seeped outward, seconds too late.

∼

At the cemetery, he slowed to a stop. "I can't go in," he said, dismounting. "Consecrated ground and all. But you can. Through the gate."

"...to do what, exactly?"

"Make a weir."

"Make a—what!?"

"Try it. Just a minor cut with Little White. See if you know where—and how. You feel like everyone is counting you out, I get that. I can smell the pain of rejection on you. So, prove them wrong."

I frowned, my brows drawing together. I was tempted, and I could think of no reason—other than possibly getting sucked into another realm or time—to not try.

I opened the heavy iron gate and stepped onto the grass. Green surrounded toppled headstones and the more recent marble behemoths. I walked until the pull of an old oak called to me. I set my palm on its bark for a moment, searching for something.

I withdrew the blade from my back and unsheathed it. The metal glinted in the remaining light. Without allowing myself to freak all the way out, I jabbed it into the space in front of me and dragged down.

There was a tear, followed by a swoosh of air. I opened my eyes to find a dark slit in the space in front of me, a sucking sound coming from within.

"Oona's stars!"

Joaquin shouted from outside the fence. "I knew you could do it! Now try closing it up."

I regarded the gap in front of me, squinting at it. Did one un-cut a rip in a realm? Instead, I reached out with my hand, the one marked by my experiences, and brushed at the opening. It closed, then, as though zipped shut. Without knowing why, I pressed the side of the blade to the former opening, as though sealing it.

I staggered back to Joaquin, winded. "How did you know I could do that?"

"I didn't. But I saw someone else do it with a much bigger blade than yours, so I figured...what could it hurt?"

"What could it hurt? I could have been sucked in." My jaw went slack. "Or let someone else out."

Atop the church, the three crows had joined a row of pigeons, watching us. One cawed, insistent. I stared at the space in the churchyard where moments before I'd cut a hole in my existence.

"Then we would have known," Joaquin said, chuckling at the blade, still in my hand. "That everything June says about you is true."

NINE

I shelved my lessons with Joaquin as an official act of self-preservation. June would be proud of this decision, except there was no way I would tell her—or anyone else—what I'd learned to do. My fingers still shook from the memory of what I'd done, their tips numb.

When Joaquin dropped me off, I raced upstairs, shoved the blade in my underwear drawer, and pretended I'd had a perfectly normal evening.

It crossed my mind that Joaquin would tell Ansel. In fact, I had little doubt he would. I didn't want to think about what Ansel would do with this information, how it would infuriate him that this incompetent witch—me—was born with every silver spoon he needed. The walls would radiate from the storm within Morgan's, Ansel's anger stirring up the air, crashing against the confines of his servitude—something else that was my fault. The more I thought about it, the more I dreaded my next encounter with Ansel.

I would have to do the mature thing and completely avoid him—forever.

"How fun, a spur-of-the-moment hike with a hot

bouncer. Sounds like an adult film in the making. Too bad I know you better," Christopher said, his tone wary. "The least you could have done is pick up dinner on your way home from gallivanting in the desert with Mr. Leather and his crotch rocket."

"Don't twist the guilt spoon too tight. You know you like takeout—and the way Joaquin dresses."

"That I do," Christopher said, setting a stack of crates next to a table. He consulted a list in his hand before filling the crates, checking each off as he added it to the collection.

"What are you up to?"

"So, I take it you forgot about the festival this weekend?"

I smacked my hand against my head. "I'm a complete idiot." On a whim, we'd signed up for our own booth at an arts festival, considering it a way to dip our toe into the market scenes.

"Too much time with a motorcycle between your legs must have addled your brain."

I nodded, his teasing fair play. I would tell him about the weir, but over the wine tonight. For now, I needed to be a better friend and business partner. Or at least, that's what I told myself for an excuse. In truth, I needed my own time to process, to consider what had happened and what I would do with it. "How can I help?"

Christopher consulted his list. "I've got the plant inventory set. We need a tablecloth—plastic is far too ugly. Oh, and maybe a curtain, too? And those battery operated lights you've got draped around Marietta."

I looked from my friend to my cherished giant monstera, wrapping her way up a cedar plank covered in moss. "Did anyone come by while I was gone?"

Christopher moved around me, selecting more plants for the crates. "Gaven came by to see you. When I told him we'd be at the festival tomorrow, he made an idle suggestion that I think is pretty brilliant."

I peered into the crate at Christopher's feet. There was a straw hat with a wide ribbon around its middle, a pair of fake glasses, a banner of leaf cutouts, several leis, a watering can, and a plastic crown resting atop other random items unearthed from my boxes of still unpacked belongings from my Chicago life.

"Toph—what exactly is going on?"

"You'll see."

~

"Okay. Gaven is brilliant." When I saw the finished effect of Christopher's handywork, I had to admit the manifestation was fantastic.

We'd claimed our allotted booth, a spot between a man who made custom cutting boards from gnarled wood and a woman who'd brought a collection of jewelry and mobiles made from vintage silverware. Beyond our corner were dozens of other tables and booths, the creative side of Prescott on full display for the Family Arts Festival.

Opting for a booth had been a small business risk. If it was a success, we'd consider a more permanent presence. If it was a failure—the fate I assumed—I'd only be out the money I paid Gaven to watch the shop.

I yawned and stretched, our call time far too early after another restless night. I'd dreamed I was walking through town, Little White in hand. The streets were crowded, and I kept cutting weirs each time someone bumped me. Soon, the square and surrounding buildings were full of gaps, a soft vacuum sound audible over the crowds. While everyone continued with their days, oblivious to the issues I'd caused, hands appeared through the openings. Disembodied fingers tugged at the edges of the gaps, opening them wide enough to allow a hoard of Fallen to climb through. When I'd shouted into the night, Christopher came out to check on me, certain I was under attack.

Now, he whistled under his breath as he plucked at the dry ends of a bird fern and fussed over the new stem of a Ginseng Ficus, his latest project. "It is awesome, isn't it?"

Christopher had turned the table sideways, creating space to the side. We'd borrowed Grace's van to haul the plants, decorations, a side table, and a huge wicker chair to the market. The furniture anchored the back corner of the booth. A basket next to the chair held the hat, glasses, and a few other items. Plants surrounded the chair. A black bamboo fanned out behind the chair, medium Dragon trees stood at the sides, and a collection of various philodendrons nestled at its feet. Above the chair, strung from the frame, was a sign that said *New Plant Parent*. He'd wound Mariette's lights around the string, giving the entire booth a festive energy.

"I love it."

Christopher handed me a polaroid camera. "You're on the hook for the pictures."

We did brisk business for the first hour, capturing a couple who purchased a fern, a yoga instructor who wanted peace lilies for her studio, and several customers who'd selected from the rainbow of pincushion cactus. Most took us up on the picture, exclaiming over the image as it surfaced within the white frame.

"This is great," the yoga instructor said, smiling at the image. "She's my first enormous responsibility."

Only one older man scoffed in offense. "Ridiculous. It's just a plant," he said, escorting his wife toward the cutting boards.

The crowd swelled at the event, as residents made their

way to the market. Several of the Fallen slunk through the crowd. Their red-rimmed eyes, vacant look, and hesitant walk caused them to stand out. As they passed us, I tried to picture them before they'd lost their existence to the elixir. Beings once considered exceptional and perfect, reduced to wander this world, awaiting passage to the next. One of them, a blonde in a pink T-shirt patterned in hibiscus, stopped to touch one of the mobiles, the blaze in his eyes urgent and probing. When the piece spun, its fishlike shapes dangled at various heights. I stepped around a dwarf lemon, inching closer to the guy in pink. Muscled, lithe. Like a mountain climber or a surfer on spring break. Someone gorgeous and godlike until destroyed by the cage designed to hold him. When he turned my way, his eyes found mine, and I looked away, guilty.

"Smile!" Christopher snapped my picture before I could rearrange my expression. He handed me the photograph.

"Did you know," I began, waiting for my portrait to show as I waved the film around in the air, "that every year, there's a World Naked Gardening Day?"

"I'm listening." Christopher followed my gaze to the departing backside it followed.

"People post pictures of themselves—in the buff, with their plants—on social media. Everyone celebrates."

Christopher rested his chin in one hand, considering this new information. "Are you thinking what I'm thinking?"

"We're going to need a sign-up sheet."

∼

The next morning, we'd solicited the name of one volunteer, a bookseller. He'd purchased the orchid showpiece, proclaiming it would be added to his collection, misted and kept warm with the utmost care. When I approached him with the idea of the calendar, he'd all but leapt to sign up, asking how soon the shoot would take place.

"Should I come to you, or will you come to me?"

"I guess we haven't thought it out that far," I said.

Christopher stepped in. "We'll be in touch with the details," he said, handing the man his picture and ushering him out. "Meanwhile, consider which of your plant friends you'd like to feature."

When he'd gone, I breathed a sigh of relief. "Adorable but kooky?"

"One can hope." Christopher dusted off the chair, replacing the purchased orchid with another from a crate behind the table. "I can tell you without calculating that we are selling through our inventory."

"What if we donate the proceeds to charity?"

Christopher frowned. "Then we drown in debt?"

I waved the camera in my hand. "No, from the calendar. We solicit a group of sexy locals with a lot of contacts. We make the calendar, they help advertise, we get more business."

"I'm following you. So, we're looking for people willing to take part, who love plants and know a lot of people."

"Book Guy is great. He's the only shop in town. We should get a firefighter because, duh, but who else?"

Christopher and I brainstormed a list. We were poring over our contacts when Blythe slipped into the booth. Christopher raised one eyebrow, then busied himself in the opposite corner of the booth. "Hi," she said, waggling her fingers. "I came to see if you got anywhere with my request."

I thought of the ring tucked away under my floorboard. "I...uh...haven't had the mental space to explore."

Blythe nodded, then chewed on her lip. She clasped her hands together, brushing a thumb against her palm in a circle. "Priyanka used to do it for us—before she turned dark and fearful, then died."

I swallowed. "How did Priyanka...do it?" I didn't know what *it* was and needed something to fuel my hunt.

"I don't know," Blythe said. "She would lay her hands on something—or someone—and just know."

"I'm not sure I can help you," I said. Disappointment was evident in her eyes, and I stumbled on with my excuses. "I've never done this work before. And I don't have the ring with me."

"Please," Blythe said, clutching her bag. "We are out of time." She undid the clasp on the vintage leather purse and rummaged inside. From within a wallet, she withdrew a ticket stub, the kind used for a raffle. "This was her drink ticket," she said, handing me the small blue stub. "Would it help?"

I accepted the small rectangle and closed my eyes, holding the paper tight in my hands. I'd just begun my routine to shut out the sights and sounds around me when I sensed someone behind Blythe.

"Whoa, wait!" Christopher's shout broke my concentration. "You can't bring her in here!" He dropped the outer curtain, anxious at the attention from the other booths.

Uzma pushed past him, the arm of a pink-haired woman slung over her shoulder. The woman's head lolled when Uzma paused. Her clothes were sopping wet, making damp circles on Uzma's clothing. She eased the woman off her shoulder. "No time," she said, brushing Christopher off and turning to Blythe. "It's Kim. I found her behind the booths."

Blythe knelt to check the woman's vital signs. The woman stared into space, her skin a sickening gray. I recognized this from the dancers at Bryce's club. Joaquin called this *the afterward*, when someone was so high on elixir they were past the point of communication.

"Who gave it to her?" Blythe's words trembled. "And why is she wet?"

I thought of the desert, the unnamed prince.

Uzma shook her head. "Don't know. Found her like this."

Blythe turned to me. "Can you help us?"

I reached for the woman's hand, and Uzma shrank back, dragging her friends away from me.

I frowned at Blythe. "I can't do anything if I can't touch her." This was true. I wasn't sure I would be effective then, either, but I'd promised to try.

Blythe nodded to Uzma, who set her mouth in a line. She didn't flinch when I reached for the woman's hand but glared at my every move.

There was a shudder as a flood of emotions raced up my hand. The woman dancing, sweat pouring down her back. One of the Fallen up close to her, smelling her neck. She looked into his eyes, searching, as he wrapped his arms around her waist. Then there was flame and fire, exhaustion and thirst. A face above her, a hand reaching out. A waterfall that wouldn't stop. The woman shook, as though responding to a chill. "It's okay," I said, a weak offering. She turned her head to face me, choked up water, and with a soft sigh, she was gone.

Blythe wailed a soft moan.

I released the woman's hand. In her touch, I'd seen her life, the moments before her death.

"Gods," Uzma said. "You *are* a ferier!"

Ten

"A what?"

Uzma crouched to lay her fingertips over the woman's eyes, closing her lids, while Blythe shook with soft sobs. "Ferier. You usher the living into the realm of the dead."

"But all I did was—" I began an explanation I couldn't finish. What had I done, exactly? I couldn't say. Regardless, there was a dead woman in our booth with a market full of people around us. "And who was she?"

"Another victim."

"Tell us what you saw."

"Are you mad? Hand her to me," Christopher said. His emergency mode kicked in. "Not sure about Prescott, but where I come from, finding the body of someone in a booth is a great way to get yourselves arrested. Tell me where to take her. You can catch up later."

"To June," Blythe said.

"She just left on a delivery. To Cottonwood." Uzma pulled Kim's hood over her face and swore under her breath.

"We could take her home," Blythe said.

"How will we explain the fact that she's dead to her roommates?"

"We have to go," Christopher said. He peeked around the front flap of the booth and gave a smile to someone outside. "We'll reopen in just a couple." He let the plastic drop and turned to face the sisters. "I'll carry her, but we need a plan. Now."

"Take her to Morgan's," I said, piping up. "The back way. They'll know what to do."

Christopher shot me a look. "Are you sure about that?"

I nodded, not sure in the slightest.

My best friend regarded me, then shook his head. "All right, I'll carry her."

"I'll drive," Uzma said.

Blythe scrunched up her face as she released the woman into Christopher's arms. Uzma lifted the back flap of the booth, and Christopher ducked out, the petite woman in his arms. With her body curled toward his chest, anyone passing by would consider her drunk in the arms of a friend, not dead in the clutches of a stranger.

Blythe pressed the heel of her hand to her forehead. Tears fell from her eyes in fat drops that trickled down her round cheeks and fell into her lap.

"Tell me what you saw, please."

When I finished her request, I watched her, uncertain of what else to say. I didn't understand what I'd seen or what to do with what I'd learned about the woman. "I'm so sorry."

Blyth rubbed at her eyes with the back of a hand and sniffed, then released a shuddering breath. She looked at me, her eyes welling up once more. "Don't be," she said. "I hated her."

"You...wait, what?"

"She broke my locket and went after Uzma's ex. The only

reason we found her was because I sensed major terror from one of our sisters, and Uzma found her."

I frowned. "I...don't understand."

Blythe sighed. "I'm empathic." She used the hem of her dress to dry the wet spots on her cheeks. "I absorb emotions and can transmute them into energy and will—unless they're too strong, and then it's like a flood to my senses. Like right now, you're deciding whether to pity me or be furious that we deprived you of your business partner."

"The market closes at two. You've got one hour to figure that out."

~

"You will explain to me why a witch and your *friend* brought me a body in the middle of the day."

Christopher and Uzma had returned to the booth before the market closed, silent and chastened. Uzma collected Blythe and left, promising to send word if they learned anything about what happened to Kim. Christopher helped me dismantle the booth, packing the remaining plants into the rented van. When the door shut, sealing the two of us within the cab, he spoke. "You-know-who wasn't happy. Says he wants to see you the minute you get back."

Now, with Ansel in front of me, Christopher's words became palpable. Ansel fumed. His eyes darkened, and a mist filled the room, blackening and billowing into dark gray clouds. The hair on the back of my neck stood up as the room bristled with electricity. Overhead, the silver sculpture of a stag gleamed in the growing tempest. I knew Ansel wasn't all human. Half fae, his birthright that became a yoke around his neck. What I didn't know—and had yet to brave in conversation—was what the entirety of his power entailed. Shackled as he was to this place as a guardian, I had a few years yet to find out.

I stumbled through a rapid explanation. "The woman died in my booth, in the middle of the market. Her leader was gone. We needed somewhere to take her."

"Coven business is none of mine," Ansel said, his voice sonorous.

My hand fluttered against the skin of my thigh. I pressed my lips together. *You are a drop, floating on the sea of calm. This is only a wave, and you will travel on.* I lifted my eyes to his. "Maybe not. But we all understand that if a human figured out any small piece of what's happening here, it would help no one get closer to their goals, right?"

Ansel didn't answer. His upper lip twitched.

"I know," I said, steadying myself, "that you may have dealt with a similar problem before. You seemed like a logical choice to help us all."

Ansel chewed over this statement. "You know, this wouldn't have happened without your side business. Sending him over here, too. What does he know?"

"What he needs to know, and nothing more," I said, unsure if Ansel would be satisfied with that response. I wouldn't show my hand for Christopher's safety and my own.

"He's booking with the Fallen, you know. Throwing parties so they can play at normalcy." Ansel glared at me, nostrils flared, one eyebrow raised. "He won't let them in, will he?"

So, Ansel knew. I hadn't hidden the fact, nor had I broadcasted the details. Of course he would find out. It had only been a matter of time. "No. He won't."

Ansel pushed back from the bar. He shifted his jaw as he paced behind the massive mahogany structure. Its wood gleamed from polish, rows of glasses sparkling from their shelves behind him. He grumbled, stomping off toward the kitchen. "Foolish humans."

Was this the end of our interview—Ansel questioning me, nothing coming of it, and us returning to a fragile impasse? While it was tempting to accept the closure, I failed to stop myself from blurting. "But what if he's right?"

Ansel turned around. "Who?"

"Christopher. My *friend*."

The air in the room grew cold, and I shivered. My taunt had irked the man. He cocked his head, waiting for me to continue.

I sighed. Every conversation with Ansel alternated between hot and cold. There was no middle ground, no place where I was safe to have thoughts that might contradict him, no opportunity to seek compromise.

"Why are all the Fallen automatically considered evil? What if some are okay, and we're treating them like some kind of trash to be taken out when they are just lost. Existing isn't a crime. Couldn't there be some way to let them stay as long as they behave? Dance their asses off at the night clubs, go to brunch on Sundays, and shop the Black Friday sales. There's more than enough room for everyone."

"So, their need to steal blood from others in order to stay alive is fine with you? Or have you forgotten how your own employee died?"

Cass. My heart sank, my feet became lead weights on the floor. Attacked in the shop on our big night, one of the Fallen had used and discarded Cass, her life forfeit and disposable.

"They aren't all like that," I said, my conviction wavering. The image of Kim came back to me. I needed to know who attacked her and why. There had to be more to her story. "Rowdy works with all of them. Gives them somewhere to live and a job to do while they wait. You don't see his workers out causing problems. They stay on the farm."

"Been out to see Beckett, have you? All that honey must have gone to your head. Did your Rowdy tell you what they do with the Fallen who don't comply with his vision of Utopia? There's a place for those who won't conform to his dream for the future."

I frowned, parsing together Ansel's meaning. I'd seen the Fallen at Beckett's. Sure, it was far from a joyous place, but no one was suffering—were they? "I just think—"

Ansel snapped. "Oh, *you* just think? You, who's been here all of two months, have a thought about how we, those who've been living in this madness for decades, can solve the problem? *Fascinating*. Please, do tell me what it is. I'm sure it will instantly solve all our problems." Sparks lit his pupils from behind. His hands curled over the edge of the bar top, knuckles white.

"Hey," Gaven said, striding into the bar. "Sorry I'm late. Helped Christopher tie ribbons on fifty of these tiny boxes. Each one has a little air plant inside. Those tags are a nightmare, EJ, but I've got the hands of a pianist." He wiggled his fingers. "Got 'em done." Gaven turned to Ansel. "Want me on dishes or expo?"

Ansel spoke through gritted teeth. "I want you to escort EJ back to her shop. Then I don't care what you do. I'll be in my office."

∼

"Wow. Okay, I've kind of got to take the brute's side on this one."

"What?"

I'd finished telling Gaven the story of our afternoon. He scratched at his chin. "I mean, you made your problem—and a body is always a big problem—into his problem. He's never been a fan of that."

I opened my mouth to retort, then closed it again. Gaven had a point. I'd complained over just as much at the Barber wedding last year. The father of the bride wanted to invite his secretary-turned-girlfriend to the rehearsal dinner since he was paying. The mother didn't want the woman there. She gave an edited list to the doorman. The result was a shouting match and a toppled platter of oyster shooters. "I didn't have anywhere else to take her. What was I supposed to do?"

Christopher walked out of the workroom, a clipboard in his hands. "G-man," he said. "What's new?"

"EJ was just catching me up on your afternoon."

"Yeah. That wasn't awesome," Christopher said. "But in other news, I'm going to have to call a vendor. Our order's messed up. I'm going to need a proper latte for this one—want anything?"

"No thanks," I said. Christopher pointed to Gaven, who shook his head.

"Back soon." Christopher held the door open for a couple on his way out.

The man wore a pair of pitch-black sunglasses and a button up shirt the color of spruce needles tucked into a pair of ill-fitting jeans. He had his arm around a woman who wore a pair of cutoffs and a black tank top. She carried a small suitcase in one hand. The man steered her toward the counter and plunked down a small stone. Its red and green hues swirled within. He was fuzzy at the edges, as though outlined in a soft glow.

I ignore the man in favor of watching the woman. She kept glancing at the door, as though unsure if she should be there. Her grip tightened on the handle of her bag.

The man knocked his fist against the countertop. On his pinky was a thick, gold ring, the diamond symbol from the graveyard carved onto its surface. "Passage, please?"

"For one...or two?"

"Two," he said.

"But..." I began. "Uh...isn't she, well...not like you?" With all the new entities in my life, I still stumbled over how to refer to differences without calling them out. I'm sure I sounded like an imbecile to this otherworldly seeker.

"We've made it more than once," the man said with a wink. "Makes her woozy, that's all."

I grimaced at Gaven. He shrugged, so I pocketed the stone. Gaven ushered them to the back of the shop.

When Gaven returned to rejoin me, I decided to share my newest trick. "Did I mention that I can rip holes in the realms?"

Gaven's eyes went wide. "You what?"

"It worked," a voice called from the hallway. The man stuck his head out of the door to the weir room. "She made it. Anyway—thanks!"

We watched him disappear back into the room before Gaven spoke. "Okay, catch me up. Holes in the realms. Gods, EJ, that's wild. How? When? Did June teach you to do that?"

"She didn't..."

Gaven's phone rang. "Hey, Joaquin...Uh huh...yep...How many of my bones?...Got it. I'll be right over." Gaven shoved his phone back in his pocket. "Ansel will turn me inside out if I don't get back over there, so you know what this means."

"That his sunshine personality is in full effect?"

Gaven snorted. "No, that I'm coming over after my shift. I'll bring snacks, you'll provide the entertainment. I've got to see this."

∼

The ring of a video call never ceases to sound distant, like a bugle blown underwater.

There was a tone of confirmation as the face of my son

filled the screen. Reddish brown hair plastered to his forehead, white earbuds in place, a shadow of stubble across his chin. He scratched at his scalp. "Hi, Mom—how are you?"

Patrick. My affable goofball who loved reading Tolkien, playing lacrosse, and carving gravy canyons into his mashed potatoes. The kid I moved mountains for, working long after he'd gone to bed so I could afford decent schools, math tutors, and a stack of college applications to make his dreams come true. I'd had him too young, then spent his childhood making up for that. He was the kid who loved building with blocks but struggled with seeing numbers on a page. With a diagnosis came support, and then in high school he took off like a rocket toward his dream of becoming an architect. Now he was a graduate student at an elite design school, almost finished with his first term. I missed him something fierce. Our schedules over the many time zones would sync up at least once a week, leaving me with all the joy and heartache of watching your baby bird fly far from their nest.

Behind Patrick, the screen showcased the tiny apartment he shared with three roommates in the Monmarte neighborhood. The living area was a comfortable chaos of books and laptops, coffee cups, and wine bottles. The space led into a cramped European kitchen in which one of Patrick's roommates stood over a tiny stove. Weak light streamed in through the window over the sink, the sunny blue of the Parisian sky visible through the panes. The ache for his hugs, the game nights on our ancient couch, and the loss of just having him around squeezed my heart. I fought the urge to blubber into the phone, burdening my son with all my secrets. Instead, I tuned into his life.

"Not as good as someone within walking distance of a fresh croissant, but I'm getting by. How are the fellas?"

Patrick looked over his shoulder to check the room, then

leaned toward the camera and mouthed the words. "Emile has a girl over."

"Oh my," I said, drawing out my response. "Do we like this girl?"

Patrick shrugged. His shaggy hair, in need of a fresh cut, was tucked behind his ears. "He met her at the labs. She seems all right. We just don't think he knows what to do with this kind of attention. Like I had to tell him to make her coffee and eggs...or something."

I smiled, remembering the challenges of being twenty-two and navigating adult slumber parties. "Sounds like he's got some coaches to help him out. Don't forget some fruit on the side."

Patrick looked over his shoulder. "Emile, you can use my last banana." The man at the stove gave Patrick a thumbs up, coupled with a sheepish grin, and my son faced the camera once more. "Now tell me about good old Whiskey Row. Shot up any bad guys yet? I fully expect everyone to be riding horses and spitting into brass buckets when I visit this summer."

"Uncle Christopher showed you too many cowboy movies," I said. "And they're called spittoons. But it's going all right. We had a booth at the art fair, which was more fun than I thought. People loved having their pictures taken with their plants. We're going to turn it into a fundraiser. You know, like those firefighter calendars, but with people in the buff, holding their plants. Christopher is downstairs setting up for the photoshoot."

"Sounds fun," Patrick said, and I beamed from the approval. "But don't send a copy if you're in it, okay? I don't care if the French would be cool with that kind of thing."

"No calendar for Patrick, got it."

The jury was still out on whether I'd have to pose. We'd been light on sign ups, but Christopher was optimistic. If everyone showed up, we could do a full calendar year.

Maybe eighteen months. We'd bickered over whether it was better to run a calendar that started in January or June, landing on the latter since we'd be marketing them in May alongside the makeshift holiday. Our first handful of volunteers was due in an hour, appointments spaced to allow for privacy.

Patrick looked over his shoulder, then back at me. Soft curses could be heard in the background as a smoking pan was carried from the stove and dropped into the sink. "I'd better go. I think Emile burned the eggs."

"Better help him out. Talk soon? Love you, and good luck!"

When the screen went dark, my mood fell alongside. When someone is the light of your life for so long, it's gut wrenching to lose them, even if it was to fortuitous circumstances that took Patrick halfway around the world. Had I stayed in Chicago, I'd be hurting just as much. Probably more, with all the reminders of our former busy life around me. Here, I had the cushion of my own adventures—on a good day.

"Do you think this snake plant would hide a full package?"

And this just might be a good day.

At the foot of the stairs, I approached Christopher with a wary eye, considering him from all angles. He held the plant, a smaller specimen in a six-inch pot, below his belt. I rested my chin on my hand and tapped a finger against my lips. "I think that might depend on the package. Can you give me more specifics?"

Christopher cocked an eyebrow at me and pursed his lips. "Put your money where your mouth is, toots. Maybe you should interview everyone about their size needs."

I rolled my eyes. "Let's put out a selection and let folks pick." For the calendar, we'd offered our shop as a back up location as Christopher suggested that not everyone who wanted a garden had one.

For the photoshoot, we'd closed the shop Monday afternoon and papered over the windows, allowing light in but keeping prying eyes out. Christopher hung white sheets from the ceiling beams and aimed the dozens of grow lights to approximate proper studio lighting. As he adjusted, a rubber plant sat on a stool in the center of the room as his mock subject. Christopher consulted it through the lens of his phone's camera as he shifted his equipment into place.

There was a knock at the front door.

"Must be our first victim," Christopher said, glee in his voice as he reached for his phone.

I'd been so lost in my nostalgia I'd neglected to preview our schedule. We'd agreed that a half hour should be plenty of time for people to sign our makeshift volunteer form, undress to their comfort, pose for a few shots, and get put back together in time for the next appointment. I planned to run interference should anyone show up too early—or late.

I patted my pockets in search of the list of folks coming by. "Who is—"

Joaquin breezed in the front door, shrugging out of his jacket. "Where do you want me?" he asked with a wicked grin, canines on full display.

I stumbled over my words as he tossed the jacket onto the coat rack, then reached behind his head to tug his shirt off over his head. "I...uh..." My heart beat in my ears, blurring my focus. Yes, this man was the other half of a complicated-something to my friend Lotte. No, I'd never thought about dating him or anything remotely close. But I'd be a liar if I didn't find all my engines revving up for this first shoot. "You can put your...okay then," I said as he discarded the shirt off to the side. Christopher remained silent, allowing this show to play out as it may.

Joaquin had the muscles of a triathlete—sinewy, tight, and designed for endurance. His skin was a deep ochre, mottled with scars. He unbuckled his belt, adding it to the shirt, and dropped his jeans to the floor. A nasty, jagged line snaked across one thigh. Black hair dusted his body and heat animated off him. He reached for the band of his shorts, and Christopher jumped in, holding up a hand he could definitely see around.

"We've got a variety of plants for you to choose in order to...um...accompany...your picture. Take your pick while you're still...well."

I remained silent, my mouth hanging open. Joaquin caught my eye and winked. He chose the spiral cactus, setting it on the stool, then dropped his jeans to the floor. Christopher gave me a knowing look, and I erupted into a coughing fit. I stumbled over to the sink, eyes watering.

"Okay," Christopher said, attempting to regain control over the situation. I gasped at the sink, reaching for an abandoned cup of coffee. "You can take your pick of positions." I choked on my next sip, and Christopher ignored me, barreling forward. "We can try a few, see what you like. There's the stool, of course, the big palms, or you might like the tropical garden."

Joaquin proved a competent model. He followed Christopher's suggestions, beamed a gorgeous smile, and looked good —really good—in the proof shots we showed him. "Can you send me some of those? You know, once you've made your choices?"

"I'll touch them up, and we'll send them all your way. A tiny token of how much we appreciate this."

"Naw, thank you, mate," Joaquin said, half dressed. He clapped Christopher's shoulder. "Haven't had that much fun in far too long." Joaquin climbed back into his T-shirt, pulling the fabric down over his chest.

"Thank you," I said, unable to form much more in the way of a sentence.

Joaquin winked again. "You're welcome." At the door, he paused, one foot still inside. "Let me know when you shoot next year's spread."

"Wow," Christopher said, when Joaquin left. "If the rest of the afternoon is anything like that, I may want a career change."

The next few appointments were far from brazen, yet each made for a great shoot. There was a man with an incredibly long beard who asked to be captured peeking out from behind Mariette's leaves. A member of the Women's League held two golden barrel cactus plants aloft in front of her mastectomy scars, lips red and hair curled like a 50s pinup girl. A woman in her eighties held a macrame plant holder filled with a healthy Inch Plant, its purple leaves a beautiful cascade against her soft, papery skin. The bookseller ended the afternoon by accessorizing his orchid shoot with his fluffy orange cat, a natty pair of Clark Kent glasses, and a vintage gardening book.

"These are fantastic." Christopher pulled up the images on his laptop.

On the bigger screen, the colors and joy of our volunteers popped. Excitement built up in my gut. "I love them all. Do you think we'll have enough?"

Christopher nodded, tweaking some of the filter settings. "I've got email submissions, too." He flipped open his laptop. "Here's one. Jane and Tarzan."

I peered over his shoulder at a couple in a greenhouse, clutching the first lettuce harvest of the year. "Cute. Have we had anyone—different—submit?"

"If you're asking me if there are any of the Fallen, the answer is no. Not yet, anyway."

The bell at the front door tinkled. Without looking up

from the computer images, I called, "I'm sorry, we're closed today for a photoshoot."

"I know," came the voice of satin and sandpaper. "That's why I'm here."

At my shoulder, Christopher spoke up before I could say a word, his voice cold and clear. "I would have thought you received my rejection email."

I blinked, staring at Christopher. He'd received an email from Ophelia and had said nothing to me. This couldn't be good. "What have I missed?"

Ophelia simpered. "A decent volunteer for your little project. He only rejected me because you couldn't handle it, I presume." She looked at Christopher. "Am I wrong?"

"Wrong isn't the first word I'd use to describe you," Christopher said through his teeth.

I considered my options. I wanted to kick her out, banish her from my shop. Attempt my own wards to keep her far away. But was I to hide from this woman everywhere, my own friends masking her existence, forever running like a coward? I steeled myself instead.

"Fine," I said. "We'll shoot you. Take your pick of plants."

Christopher eyed me like I was a mad dog, losing my connection with reality.

"Couldn't hurt," I said, a complete lie.

Ophelia selected a few of the plants before peeling out of her black jeans and purple top. Underneath she wore a matching set of lace lingerie—because of course someone like her would never stoop to the laundry day mix-and-match. With a toss of her hair over her shoulder, she stepped into the lights. "I'm ready."

As Christopher completed his adjustments, Ophelia remained motionless. Only her lips moved as he tried different camera angles, tilted a light to shine on her curtain of satiny hair, highlighting her berry-stained lips. "Ember James Rookwood. I hadn't wanted to come here, to visit this dinky little town again. But the more I thought about it, the more I realized I had unfinished business."

"I didn't ask you to move here."

Ophelia shifted on the stool, nestling the plants in her lap. "You cost me something that day, Ember James. Something more precious to me than anything in this pathetic little life you pretend to enjoy. You will pay for that."

"Impossible," I spat. "I don't have a clue as to what you are talking about."

"It's no matter," she said. "I'll take what is owed."

Christopher pulled his phone away from his face. "I think we're done here."

"We are," Ophelia said, collecting her clothing. "For now."

But I wasn't. "You can't go around forcing people to do what you want."

Dressed once more, she smiled at me. "Of course I can. That's exactly what I do." She turned to collect a moth that had settled on the wall of vines, paying witness to the afternoon's activities. "First, I have to determine what *you* hold most dear." The insect crawled on her palm, adjusting its wings. She closed her eyes and touched it with the tip of her finger. The animal caught fire. As it burned, faint images of those I'd lost, Mom and Hollis and Cass, flashed in my mind, and I saw stars. I gasped, reeling, as the insect blackened into dust. When it was gone, she blew the bits from her palm. "So much was taken from you, Ember James. Seems we have some things in common. Too bad for you, the count is nowhere near finished."

I watched her, horrified. June and Joaquin had been right. This woman was dangerous—and she hated me. "Tell me what you want, Ophelia, then get out."

"Oh, but you see, what I want is to *take*. To rend and leave in ruin. And that involves time—and anticipation."

Eleven

The sting of Ophelia's words followed me for the rest of the evening and well into the next day. I couldn't shake the idea that she lurked around every corner, watched me from each parked car, and otherwise studied me, like a spider caught in a jar, for my weakness.

Christopher was over it.

"Realistically, what can she do? So you denied her travel through your little pit stop. That's no different from that night at the Kitten Club when you downed three hurricanes and proposed to half the boys in the place, so the bartender cut you off. You didn't curse his stuffy ass. You came back the next weekend and tipped him something fierce."

"I did. But I had to. Those were the best hurricanes."

"And you," Christopher said, pressing the camera to my chest, "have the best weir on the block. I say let it go. She'll get over it, or she won't. Otherwise you will be too busy with your fabulous life. You won't have time to care what she's done."

I closed my eyes. "I hope you're right." Christopher hadn't heard what I'd caught in Ophelia's voice. The pain, the desperation, that raw hunger for justice. Either that or he had far more faith in me than I had in myself.

"Now go. This one wanted us to take the picture at their place. I'd go, but I'm seeing Mr. City Council again for brunch."

"I'm half the photographer you are, but I'll give it my best."

Christopher pressed a tote bag into my hands. "There's portable lighting, a sheet, and a little greenery just in case. If their plants are rubbish, you can slip behind the building and grow it into something impressive."

"Magic some vines. Got it. Where am I going again?"

"Beckett Farms," Christopher said. His smile reached from ear to ear. "The owner's waiting for you."

∼

The taxi dropped me off at the front gate. Across the wooden arch stretched a sign indicating I was in the right place. Beyond the gate stretched a dirt road. On either side, as far as the eye could see, were fields of lavender. A soft hum filled the air and lifted into the cloudless sky. I opened the gate and walked.

I'd considered begging off the job, telling Christopher to reschedule when he could attend, too. But then I considered that for this temporary gig, Ophelia would be miles away, and I could think of something else.

A golf cart appeared ahead. One of the farm hands drove with Rowdy in the passenger seat, a giant dog sitting on the bench in the rear.

"Hi," Rowdy said, his perfect teeth white and welcoming. "Thanks for coming out here."

"Thanks for having me." *Not your best work, EJ.* "This place is beautiful," I said.

The edge of Rowdy's smile kicked up. "Can I give you a tour?"

"Sure." The driver hopped out of the cart. I shrugged my tote bag higher on my shoulder, unsure of the protocol. Those warning videos they showed us as teens played in my head, the ones about not getting in vehicles with strangers, bringing a buddy to all social situations, and the one they should have made—be cautious when near any members of the fae. Rowdy slid over and patted the passenger seat.

As Rowdy drove, shifting his gaze from the fields to the road in front of him, I studied him. He wore a loose, short-sleeved, button-up shirt with tiny cow skulls on it, navy print on hot pink, with a pair of cutoffs. He'd shoved his feet into a pair of worn, brown leather sandals and a braid of grasses ringed one wrist. A rash of stubble across his cheeks and reflective sunglasses anchored over his face. His un-bleached hair gave him the look of a surfer on Mission Beach, awaiting the next tidal shift.

"We've done some incredible things on the farm. It's nice to have someone to share them with," Rowdy said. His eyes met mine in the rearview mirror for a moment. "Not everyone will come all the way out here to see us."

"That surprises me," I said, thinking of the hoards of admirers crowding his booth every weekend.

Rowdy shrugged, then reached back to pat the dog. "Some of us flirt with ideas, others make them happen."

I was quiet, letting his words sit in my mind. He reached forward to turn on the radio. The soft melodies of decades old country music filtered through the tiny speakers. Overhead, the cloudless sky was a blue ocean. The fields rippled onward, a rainbow of flowers dotting the expanse.

We approached two big barns, mirror images of each other. The two-story buildings had crisp metal roofs, dozens of windows, and imposing garage-style doors. "The one on the left holds our farm equipment, stalls for our rescue donkeys, bottling, shipping, and...additional storage. On the right, it's kitted out like barracks—for the farm workers. The greenhouses are on the backside of the house. Long-term plans include guest accommodations. They'd be open for people after a more short-term stay in a peaceful spot."

Here was the line that separated Rowdy from the other extranormal in Prescott, the unspoken reason his world existed outside the city limits. I thought of his employees who scurried about the booth, filling orders and restocking shelves. Red-rimmed eyes, hunched shoulders, and silent movements. This was the line drawn between Rowdy and Ansel, Joaquin, Gaven, Iris, and all the others who opposed the invasion of these other beings into their city. If they, unhesitating in their efforts to eliminate any Fallen who crossed their paths, chose not to form an offensive and storm Beckett's Farm, there had to be an excellent reason. There was also the question of the storage facilities on the farm. Rowdy sustained a workforce reliant on a fae drug. How was this happening? And since I had it on solid authority that no one would bother to tell me, I aimed to figure out why this afternoon.

For now, I chose the safe route. Or to be completely honest, to ease into bravery. "Rescue donkeys—what do they do for beekeeping?"

Rowdy laughed, warmth emanating from his mirth. "Not much. Stubborn as rocks. But we love them. Rescued most from a pack outfit that closed up shop, picked up a few others here and there. They're our pets at this point—or more accurately, we're their staff. The boys love 'em, treat the furry beasts like babies. Not sure who rescued who at this point."

Whatever I thought alone time with Rowdy Beckett would be, this wasn't it. He was easygoing, human-like, and affable. "Then it's practically a sanctuary."

"That's what my accountant likes to call it," he said, and took a sharp turn at the back of the first barn. "Wait here."

While he entered the barn, I did my best impression of being casual and relaxed. I crossed one leg over the other and bounced my foot. The back of the first barn had shelving full of boots on one side, a clean whiteboard on the other. There was a concrete pad with a hose and a row of sharp tools magneted above the spigot. The end of the other barn featured a deck filled with lounge chairs, an outdoor fan, and a foosball table. Party lights hung from the rafters and a baseball glove lay idle on a table. This space was decorated like the back yard of a fraternity, aimed west toward the sunsets.

Idle, I scanned the field in front of me. In the middle, I spotted a host of white boxes nestled in among the plants. Above and around them buzzed a faint black cloud. A shrouded figure moved around what I assumed housed the hives.

"Here we go," Rowdy said, climbing onto the seat. He handed me a laptop, a tablet, and a handheld radio. "Let's go see the bees."

As we drove off, the figure from the field stood to salute the cart. Rowdy nodded and kept driving. I couldn't discern the features of the worker, but I knew what I would see. Where those aware of the extranormal presence in Yavapai county saw a dangerous invasion, Rowdy saw a workforce.

Acres ambled by. The crunch of the wheels on the dirt road added to the heat of the day lulled me into a submissive state. I would have sat in the passenger seat all afternoon. But when we reached a field awash in orange, Rowdy slowed the cart to a stop. He reached into my lap for the equipment, and I froze, both wanting and fearing him touching any part of my body that was suddenly an incredible traitor to the professional-esque job I'd been sent to do.

Rowdy flipped open the laptop and opened an app. The

screen lit up with dozens of squares on a grid, each glowing. He clicked on one. This brought up a screen crawling with numbers. "We've been able to install some pretty great sensors on the hives. They allow us to track the heat and humidity, even how much honey is produced. We have alarms on the hives so if anything goes wrong, we are out here troubleshooting in minutes."

I leaned in to look at the display, my shoulder brushing Rowdy's arm. He smelled of orange groves and cut grass. This close, his irises appeared to pool as though molten gold served as their source. "That's incredible."

Rowdy grabbed the tablet and the radio. "But this is even cooler. Come on."

I followed him out into the field. This one had bright pops of orange interspersed between the lavender. "California poppies?"

Rowdy nodded. "The bees love them. This way, when the lavender's out of season, the poppies pick up the slack."

"Does that change the honey?"

The corner of Rowdy's mouth turned up. "There's only so much control I attempt to hold over the bees. Too much, and they'll revolt, leaving me without their company. They appreciate a gentle management. I try to let them know what a good thing they have here, so they've no cause to leave."

I wasn't sure we were talking about the bees anymore.

I followed Rowdy into a field, the soft shush of the plants against our legs a signal of our approach to any critters hanging out around the bushes.

Over a short hill, stacks of white boxes appeared. They surrounded a pole atop which was some sort of equipment—weather-related, I guessed. Rowdy tapped at the tablet and handed it to me. "The key to bees is to treat them with respect. I won't promise you'll never be stung, but I can say that if you give them proper respect, you decrease the likelihood that will happen." From the back of the cart, he pulled netted hats from under the seat and long-sleeved tan jackets. "We won't get too close, won't need to, but these should provide you with any assurance you need."

I tucked the tablet under my arm as he guided me into the jacket, like a gentleman escorting a lady home from the cinema. Hat firmly in place, Rowdy donned his own jacket and moved toward the bees. He lowered his voice to a whisper. "A little closer now. All right, let's see that screen. Aim it at the bees."

I lifted the black screen to face the hive, and its surface lit up in a wash of color. Rainbows of intensity covered the screen, the shapes a geometric shading of those ahead of me. The hives themselves glowed with reds and yellows, the fields softer with shades of greens and blues. Around the hives flew dots of yellow, circling before disappearing within the prisms. "It's the bees!" I took another look. As though an X-ray of the hive itself, the lifeblood within those containers throbbed with energy, the screen a map of its inhabitants. "It's beautiful."

"That it is," Rowdy said, peering over my shoulder. "It's another tool we have to check on the hives without cracking them open and disturbing what they have going on. This way, the bees trust us to let them do their thing, and we give them the space to make the magic happen. Our honey is different because our care is different. My investment is different."

Rowdy held my gaze a minute longer than my insides needed to pool like warm honey at my feet. The soft buzzing in the background, the sticky-sweet scent of honeycombs, and the proximity of his body lulled me to a supple status I both wanted and feared him knowing.

"This is impressive," I said, gesturing to the tablet and the hives behind it.

"We work with what nature gave us, and it strengthens us,

together. I'm uniting the forces at play, not trying to change what is into something else entirely."

Big, puffy clouds crowded into the skyscape. Songbirds flitted about, singing to each other across the field. Rowdy stood near his bees, dedicated to the success of this ecosystem in which he operated. The pull of his confident explanations tugged at my insides. I squinted at the fields, seeking a coach for how to navigate a conversation in which I wanted to ask about everything, yet knew I had to walk with careful footsteps. A weight on my shoulder reminded me of my original purpose, the motivation for my visit. I needed to reorient this visit, get my bearings.

Rowdy beat me to it. "Time for that photo shoot?"

"Sounds good," I said, handing back the tablet.

"Great." There was that million-watt smile. "I've got just the spot."

Back in the cart, Rowdy drove us farther out, moving beyond the farm rows, their stripes guidelines against the earth. Near the edges, the dirt path opened into a field coated in wildflowers.

The barns were tiny dots in the distance. We were alone, save the flora and the surrounding fauna. Rowdy brought the hand radio, jamming it into the back pocket of his jeans, but left the other tech. As before, I stepped in his footsteps, not wanting to crush more of the precious plants than necessary. Wildflowers carpeted the land, stretching out to meet a grove of desert willows visible in the distance. We made our way to the center of the field, a slow wind through the native color on display. Poppies, desert marigold, and lupine grew among the native grasses, soft color pops blanketing the surrounding earth.

"How about here?" Rowdy paused and turned to face me. "This is where I garden."

"Uh..." A breeze tickled the stems around our feet. Blossoms bobbed among the tall grass—tall, except that it would fall short of covering much more than Rowdy's ankles. "That makes...sense."

Rowdy unbuttoned his shirt, and I blanched. To mask my discomfort, I turned away and dug into my bag for the camera. I looped the device over my neck and took a few shots of the empty field to check the lighting. When I turned back, the camera fell from my hands.

Rowdy sat in the grass, legs crossed. A soft tangle of wheatgrass blocked the crux of his body. I dragged my eyes back up to his face. He noticed.

"Will this work?"

Invited, I ran my eyes over the bare skin kissed by sunlight, adopting the stance of an artist framing the shot.

A soft, golden fuzz covered Rowdy's arms and thighs, the same shade as the scruff of his face. He lifted his knees, resting his forearms atop them, shooting me a look of feigned innocence. I bit my lower lip, catching onto his game, yet wanting to play.

"I think so," I said. "But I'll let you know after I take a few shots." I lifted the lens to my face and snapped the shutter several times to break the silence.

"Any positions you'd like me to assume?"

I lowered the camera. He gave me an impish grin, one eyebrow cocked. "Just be yourself," I said, and retreated behind the camera. Heat from the sun's afternoon rays combined with Rowdy's flirtation lit my every cell on fire. A line of sweat trickled down my back. I needed a distraction. It was as though he could see into my mind through the other side of the lens and could read every sex-starved thought fighting for air within.

If Christopher were there, the teasing would be merciless.

Camera pressed to my eye, I exhaled in a slow and steady release. My finger pressed the shutter like it would bring me release. "It's warm out here," I said, plucking at the front of my shirt. Christopher's lessons about Gestalt design principles fought against my reptilian brain that wanted only to ogle the subject before me.

A crackle from the radio shook us from the afternoon's stupor. Rowdy reached for the handset and twisted the dials.

"...north field...DWV..." came through the speaker.

Rowdy pressed a button. "Be there shortly."

He stood, and I looked away but not before I snapped a mental picture for later. "What is it?"

"Pesticides," he said, stepping into his shorts. "Not ours."

We rode in silence. I knew next to nothing about beekeeping, but from the lack of expression on Rowdy's face, whatever happened had to be serious.

We once again approached the farm buildings, Rowdy slowing at a field in which a few of his workers bent over a hive. Two held their own devices, verifying data, while another held a jar topped with mesh. Rowdy hopped out a second after parking. I hurried after, unsure if I was wanted, but unwilling to miss out.

Three Fallen, waiting with solemnity. One held the jar out to us.

"Poor little thing," Rowdy said. He peered inside the jar, then handed the container to me. Inside was a bee, clinging to a small leaf. In place of its wings were mangled objects that could serve a few purposes, none of which were flight.

"She'll never be airborne. What is a life for a creature such as this without their proper attire?"

Rhetorical question or otherwise, I pitted the bee I held within my hands. The others gathered around us, as though mourning the loss of flight and purpose were the animal's just due. I thought of the stories Joaquin told of the great blackened wings of the Fallen, stark evidence of a forsaken status. As if in pity, one of the Fallen at Rowdy's side shrugged his shoulders back.

"Better show me where," Rowdy said. "We'll try cleaning the combs, and..." Rowdy glanced back at me, as though deciding how to phrase his next directive. "Send up a night brigade."

One worker took out his radio and muttered into it.

"Will you be able to save this one...and the others?" I asked, worried I knew the answer.

"We'll try," Rowdy said, reclaiming the jar. "This won't be ignored." As he spoke, a dozen others approached in two rows of six. Weapons strapped over their backs, they moved as a unit, fanning out at the crossroads toward the different fields. Behind them, others marched out of the barracks, streaming into the barn where the din of activity was audible out in the sunshine. "If there's one thing we don't do here, it's use pesticides. For the bees to be sick, someone else has spread poison, and we'll find that source. We take our role as stewards of this land seriously, and I do as its leader."

More Fallen poured out of the buildings and fanned out through the fields. Many were armed, all searching for the source of chemicals that killed one of their treasured members.

Rowdy followed my gaze as even the three who'd alerted him to the find joined the search for any clue about who—or what—caused the devastation. "I am not so unlike your friends, if you think about it. I, too, want the Fallen where they cannot harm life but work toward a better place to live. Where I differ," Rowdy said, as the fields filled, "is that I hope to coach integration, a communal understanding, whereas your friends want only extermination. Tell me, EJ," he said, locking eyes with me. "Which of us is in fact the destroyer?"

Twelve

With Christopher's snores sounding from the bedroom, I wedged a fingernail file under the loose board in the floor of the loft. I caught the edge of the board with my thumb and lifted the board up and out of the way. Stealth and silence were my goals. I probed the shadowed space below the flooring until my hands found the velvet-wrapped lump below. I left the leather-wrapped grimoire in its resting place and withdrew the sack printed with the emblem of a liquor brand and cinched with a neat bow of gilded cording.

I untied the loops to reveal something that was never meant for me to hold. Heavy with gold and dripping with diamonds, the Crown of Immortality, also known as the Circle of Stars, is an ancient fae relic. I'd been told it was the key to the Netherworld, the means to control the land beyond the living, the path to an eternal life—and I held it in my very mortal hands.

"What am I doing?" I whispered to myself. Creatures who can command the forces of nature, those who claimed to be my friends and associates, and those who were definitely neither, would give anything to lay their eyes on this crown, let alone hold it. Rumors of its location swirl around the four realms, with all aware of its existence desperate to find the crown for themselves. I thought of Rowdy's words, his insistence that all creatures in nature figure out how to coexist or perish.

Here I was, in some ridiculous spat with a French witch while harboring an object with the power to command an entire realm—if I believed Ansel.

Which I didn't. Why should I? He admitted to wanting the crown for himself, and was desperate to find it. Sure, it could be the key to his escape from indentured servitude under his boss, a mysterious Sharon, who was after the crown herself. He could seek the crown to pacify her and earn his own freedom. Or he could be after its control for himself as the ultimate escape. End the curse and become king of the souls below. Each of these options seemed impossible. But then what? And where would that leave the Fallen on Rowdy's farm?

First, I had yet to settle on the idea of a Netherworld. Very much alive, I had no evidence that this was a place, let alone a kingdom. True, many things that shouldn't have come to take up residence alongside this new life of mine, but there had to be a limit somewhere—hadn't there? Second, why would my uncle have the crown hidden at his place—and how did he get it in the first place?

~

"Been a minute," Iris said. "Was beginning to think you were too good for this place."

"Never," I said between bites. The cook that night at Morgan's had piled my fries with blue cheese, red sauce, and some kind of sour cream drizzle. The effect was a salty-creamy magic that didn't quite pair with my standard champagne order, but I wouldn't complain. I'd yet to meet the chef, but they knew me by my order.

Morgan's was packed for a Tuesday night. Besides the regular dart tournaments, they'd added a trivia night. Joaquin perched near the pool tables, reading questions off a tablet to a handful of eager teams competing for a free round of drinks.

"What is the first prize reward at the Wife Carrying World Championships in Finland?"

A saucy patron called out to the players. "Your mom!"

"My mother, may she rest in peace, wouldn't let you kiss the sole of her boot."

One player joined in. "Get 'em, Joaquin!"

The heckler ducked his head back into the booth with his buddies, and Joaquin read the next prompt.

A focused quizmaster, Joaquin continued the game. "The mystery author, Agatha Christie, was known for sitting in her bathtub and eating which fruit?"

"So, where's the big man?" Iris topped off my water with a cracked plastic pitcher.

"I could ask you the same thing," I said, a wry smile on my face. Ansel had remained elusive since I'd been stung, as though limiting his exposure to me, still. "But if you're talking about Christopher, he's gone over to Lotte's. They're going to scroll through trending social media accounts looking for inspiration."

"Sounds...sweet?" Iris, a friend to everyone, was herself least interested in fitting in. She stuck to an edgier appearance. Blue-streaked hair, white cutoffs, and a cropped sweatshirt gave her the air of a college student majoring in communication. "And if you're talking about Ansel," she said, and gestured with her eyebrows, "he's upstairs." Iris leaned closer. "There's a rumor that the crown's been seen nearby, and you know him. A dog with a damned bone."

I matched her tone, lowering mine. "*The* crown?"

Iris nodded, her eyes on the patrons, as though one might be a covert operant. "Everyone is after it."

"Everyone?" I was a parrot, eager for a treat.

"Joaquin was approached multiple times in the last few weeks to go after it."

"But don't they know—"

"That he works for Ansel? They do now. He finds a polite way to say no...after he collects what information he can. Gentry, Fallen...everyone."

I paused, my next fry aloft in my hand. "What about Ophelia?"

"That French train wreck?"

I snorted as a deep voice boomed from the stairs. "What about her?"

Iris shot Ansel a look. "Our friend here was asking about the *movie* everyone wants to see. I let her know that just about everyone seems interested in seeing it. You know, the one about the hero finding ancient treasure?"

"Ophelia has no interest in that *movie*." Ansel pushed past Iris and made his way to the computer terminal. He punched buttons with his back to us. His long hair, twisted and held in place with a pencil, hung past his buttoned collar.

"You seem really certain about what Ophelia wants," I said.

"I know what she likes," Ansel said through his teeth.

"Isn't she the woman who was pissed you wouldn't let her through the weir? She sounds like the desperate sort," Iris said.

"That's her," I said.

Ansel shot me a look of irritation. He held a stack of receipts in one hand. Mist filtered into the bar through the clearstory windows. Clouds formed above the heads of those gathered in the bar. Droplets splatted on the bar, on the back of my hands, and plinked into my glass of champagne.

"Turn that off," Iris hissed. "There's people everywhere."

Ansel's expression hardened. A muscle above his upper lip twitched. He ignored me and turned to Iris. "We've been given more than enough reason to think this person is a far bigger deal than one of the *Bandorai*." Ansel spat out the last word as though it were a vile taste on his tongue.

Iris's eyebrows peaked at the mention. "You left out that tidbit before."

I ventured a question. "What does that mean?"

Iris ignored Ansel's glare to answer my question. "Bandorai. A female Druid...of sorts."

"So, some mother-freaking-god of some ancient shit? Pretty sure anyone like that would be interested."

Joaquin set his empty pint glass on the counter, interrupting us with a heavy clink. Iris chose a fresh glass from the rack, filled it at a tap, and slid it his way. "God is overdoing it a bit, I think," Joaquin said, and took a sip. He licked at his upper lip. "More like a royal understudy. Fancier than those blokes in Westminster with the robes, but definitely less powerful than La Llarona."

"She must have been sobbing about something convincing up there," Iris said, gesturing toward Ansel's office. Ansel's nostrils flared and a thunder clap startled the patrons. Iris didn't blink. "You had her up there for hours."

Electricity hummed in the air. Nonchalant, Iris brushed past Ansel to wait on a new customer.

"Better get back to the teams," Joaquin said, spinning on his heel. "Or literally anyone else."

Ansel returned to the computer. He remained silent as my blood boiled.

"Why don't I get to know?" Ansel continued tapping into the computer, so I restated my question to his back. "No one tells me anything of substance. How am I supposed to help if I don't know anything?"

Ansel rolled his shoulders back. Tiny ice crystals dotted the edges of the mirror over the bar. Iris, returning from the kitchen with plates in hand, spotted the shift in atmospheric conditions, and hissed. "Enough. Someone will see you!"

"You see?" I wasn't letting this go. "Everyone is loyal to you to a fault. I'm the one who's risking my business, my livelihood, to take part in this chaos you call a plan. I'm learning as fast as I can, as much as I can, and I would like some credit!"

Over Ansel's head, the aloe Joaquin had picked out sat on the shelf. I held it in my gaze, staring hard. I extended my hand in its direction, pulling my fingers toward me in a wave. Tendrils popped out from the soil and stretched outward, reaching for Ansel. The new stems entwined in Ansel's hair, wrapped around his hands.

"Stop," Ansel said, and ripped his hands free from their binds. He leaned over the counter, his breath warm on my cheeks. My heart thudded in my chest. I froze my face in a mask that held my fear deep within my heart—I hoped.

"Save your party tricks. What we have is something big. Something that could wipe all of us out. This isn't some weak janitorial reject from Elysium. You and your lack of useful skill are a liability, not some asset. So no, neither I nor any of my associates will bring you into our confidence. Until you can show me you're a force worth facing, my job is to keep you safe in your cozy little world where you play witch." Ansel stormed off, leaving the bar for his office at the top of the stairs.

I saw the remnants of my vines tossed on the counter in his wake. What he called my "trick" had taken weeks of practice. Maybe he was right. I was too far behind, too old and encumbered by responsibility to jump into something new. Too afraid that my comfort would be dislodged if I took risks.

Or maybe he was a selfish ass who didn't know who he was messing with.

I tossed back the rest of my glass, left some cash on the

counter, jammed the last few fries in my mouth, and pushed my way out to the atrium, not caring who saw me.

Red brick surrounded me in a lopsided polygon framed by the walls of each building edging the block. Ansel's domain—all except for the Apothecary.

I crossed the cobblestones that remained from Prescott's earliest days, as well as the more recent cement patchwork. I stood in front of the great silver tree, taking one deep breath after the other, holding back tears. My father, ever the practical man, once told me that getting upset over a bully is like worshiping them. I felt that in this moment, directing my ire to the upstairs office window in Morgan's.

I shook my head to clear the image of Ansel from my head. I banished the piercing gray of his eyes, the scent of whisky at his collar. With a deep breath, I steadied myself and looked at the tree.

In the upper branches, the same three crows sat, blinking their beady eyes at me.

"Hello, fellas. Don't mind me. Just out here trying not to lose my shit."

One crow hopped down to a lower branch, bent forward, and cawed at me. The bird bent to brush its beak on the branch, back and forth, then pecked at the wood.

I reached out for the branch. As soon as my fingers touched the bark, the crow flew off to an upper branch. Between my fingers, the branch swelled. As I watched, a nub formed. This initial burst of green spiraled upward into a bud, identical to the one I'd made several weeks ago.

I pulled my hand back, rubbing the tips of my fingers together. The same crow—at least I thought it was the same one, hard to tell with black birds—cawed again. At the animal's command, I reached for another branch. At my touch, it too budded out. I reached for a third and then a fourth. My creations remained tight purses of their contents, yet their existence was proof I could do something. What, I didn't know. I needed to talk to someone who believed in me, a person who would help me, not get in my way.

I plopped myself on the bench, champagne swimming in my mind. I pulled out my phone, determined to get questions answered.

Thirteen

"So, you didn't burn my number," Blythe said. She'd been quick to respond to my text to meet.

I'd figured Second Shot was as safe a spot to meet as any. Grace was loyal to Joaquin—they ran in the same mercenary circle—but she wasn't a snoop. I assumed the attitude that if I was out in public, it would be like I had nothing to hide. That I, one hedge witch, was meeting with another witch. Perfectly typical—for the extranormal.

We met in the late afternoon; the morning rush was long gone. To her credit, Grace spared a curious glance for the two of us, then headed for the kitchen of her cafe. Blythe and I were alone with our iced mochas and agendas. The smell of baking wafted out through the doors to the kitchen.

"Figured I ought to at least listen. I still think I'm the last person you want trying to help you, but I'm also ready to be wrong about everything. That's become my norm in this place."

Blythe smiled, revealing a chipped tooth. Today she wore a tiny silver nose hoop that complimented her elaborate caftan covered in paisley whorls of red and white. "For someone who is new to all of this, it seems like you have things under control."

"Ha," I said. "In my attempt to stand up to a bully, I wrapped a vine around his hand."

"That's a good start. A warning."

I closed my eyes and shook my head. "A tiny one. It tore like cooked spaghetti. Then, as pissed off as I was about the whole thing, I manifested a dozen buds—none of which would bloom. That's me. That's my half-assed witchcraft, if I dare naming it to begin with." I detailed my irritation with Ansel without mentioning the crown. "The only one who tells me anything about the Fallen is Iris, and she's walking the line between truth telling and irritating her boss." I ended in a huff, the release of having someone to gripe to a relief.

Blythe studied me for a moment. "You've been at this all of what—a few months?"

I nodded.

She leaned back in the booth, her shoulders squaring against the wooden slats behind her. "You're going to have to cut yourself some slack. Most of us have years to practice before utter chaos descends upon us, if it ever does. Do you have any idea how many Iowa witches spend their lives fussing over the corn crops for lack of anything better to do? Here you are, new to it all, and of all people, you seem to manage better than most."

There it was, the reflection I'd heard dozens of times. *You're so good at handling stress, EJ.* What I was good at was hiding my freak outs. Losing it in the middle of a wedding—or when your husband walked out on you—wouldn't help anything, I'd always told myself. Meanwhile, I learned to stuff my feelings down deep into my gut until I either forgot about them or they ate me alive.

"Not sure I have much of a choice. Until everyone quits trying to crash my shop, I've got no choice but to stay involved. That's why I called you—I could use a little coaching."

Blythe pouted, her painted lower lip puffed out. "And here I thought you wanted to help me."

"I do," I said, and did a self check on my intentions. I wanted to help her. Despite her brash sister, Blythe brought kindness and concern, something few had spared me over the last few weeks. "I hoped we could work out a trade."

Blythe's eyebrow, perfectly waxed into a dark crescent, lifted. "Oh?" She smelled of roses and honey. Her lacquered nails clutched her glass as her red lips sipped at the striped straw nestled among the ice cubes.

"It's a poison ring," I said, watching her expression.

She released the straw and nodded. "We know that much. It belonged to her mother, who was also a coven member. A powerful green witch—like your uncle."

"You want to know why it's empty," I said, letting my words settle like a dropped ring into a lake.

Blythe's eyes snapped to mine. "You know?"

I nodded in a slow and deliberate movement. She wouldn't like what I had to tell her, but it was her right to know. "I planned to tell you regardless of whether you would help me."

I'd taken the ring out to the ancient tree, tucked myself into the bench, and held the piece in my hands. With my eyes closed, I sat with it in my hand, patient and open. I hadn't known the witch who owned the ring, but in my hand, it warmed. When I guided my thoughts to its owner, a chilling breeze danced over my hair, a sadness behind it.

"She took its contents," I said. "All of them." This was the message the wind brought me. The ring's owner carried magic within the jewelry itself, and when she needed it most, the power was there, at her fingertips. "Before he tried to drown her with his kiss."

Blythe swallowed. She looked down at her lap, pressing her lips together. A fat tear rolled down one cheek as she clutched at her hands in her lap. She took a shuddering breath and met my gaze. "Was it quick?"

"I think so," I said. "She was gone as he began."

Several more tears streaked Blythe's cheeks. She dabbed at them with her napkin. "Thank you."

"Of course" I had the urge to reach out and hug this woman, this ersatz sister, but the timing wasn't right. The need to comfort was deep in my soul and something to consider at other times. Part of my former job, yes, but could also be part of my new identity. Instead, I set my hand on hers. "I'm sorry."

Blythe took a steadying breath, releasing the air through her lips. "Thank you. I'll let Uzma and the others know. They'll appreciate your trust, as well. And," she said, sniffing, "what can I do for you?"

I'd considered this moment, unsure of what I would say. I wanted to ask a million questions, get the background of every change that came my way since Hollis's death. My hands itched for instructions, my brain for guidance, and my heart sought sisterhood. Yet, I wouldn't risk pushing Blythe, or even Uzma, away. I needed them far more than they needed me.

"I want to know...or rather, to understand...well, it's like this. I don't know if I'm supposed to feel a certain way. How will I know what to do with whatever it is I can do if I don't know what to begin with?"

This had bothered me over the last several weeks. More than the secrecy of the others, it was that I didn't have some innate understanding of how to conduct myself. Shouldn't someone with something extra know exactly what to do with that power? I was a witch without a way.

Blythe reached across the table to take both my hands in hers. She rubbed a thumb over my tattoos, examining the intricate weave of the plants. Then she sat up a little straighter, closed her eyes, and smiled.

As she did so, it was as though a warm liquid poured from her skin into mine, its heat spreading from my hands, up my arms and through my torso, and into my heart. Within moments, the tension that gripped my spine released, and I was lighter. Somehow, peace settled in.

"Witches, those of us with the wisdom to know the world on a more intimate level, aren't here for other people, nor are we here to help ourselves. We are the force that seeks balance in a chaotic world, knitting fate together with nature, and monitoring all that comes from that marriage."

"That's...beautiful," I said, my insides soft, yet a small yearning deep from within pushing me to ask for more. "But what do I do?"

Blythe squeezed my hands, a brief gesture of assurance. "You can see your gifts for what they are. Learn them, use them. When you find fear, defeat it. No one controls your future, or what you will do with it, like you. Soak up knowledge like the forest floor soaks up rain. Trust yourself. Take leaps. Say yes. What you seek has been inside you all along."

∽

"Get your tartan on, I'm ready."

"My what?"

After accepting Blythe's invitation to meet again and giving the woman a big hug, I'd rushed back to the nursery. Gaven, covering for Christopher, who was managing a retirement party in the ritzy Hassyampa neighborhood, blinked as though I'd slapped him with my words.

"Whatever it is you wear when you go home. I'm more than some random fortune teller. I'm a godsdamn hedgerider, and I'm going to do something about it."

"Oh. *Oh.* Okay. Are you sure? Should we let someone know..."

"We go—now," I said. This was in part because of impatience but also because if I hesitated, I would cave into fear. *When I'm afraid, I will conquer that fear.* Blythe lit the fire of courage under my feet, and it was time I did something with the flames. "To a graveyard, if you can swing it."

"Um, right. I'll just lock the door." Gaven hurried to the door and flipped the sign and the deadbolt.

I shoved one arm and then another through my lightest jacket, then opened the door to the weir room. Gaven followed me inside. He squatted down in front of the low shelving under the window and pulled books from their resting places. As he shifted the ancient tomes, a collection of Hollis's that was fragile and leather-bound, stuffed with mystery, a soft vacuum tugged at the air within the tiny room. Book by book, Gaven revealed a gaping hole leading into a blackness that had no place in the shop, yet here it was.

"Whatever you do," Gaven said, wrapping my arms around his waist. He slung his own around me and held me tight, like a gangly teenage boy hugging his mother, rather than a several hundred-years old member of the Gentry escorting a mortal witch. "Say nothing when we get there."

Later, with experience, came my sophisticated description of weir travel. Like those chutes at the bank, somewhat, or an amusement park ride in which your body is whooshed through a tunnel, lights flashing around you. My insides jellied and there was a momentary roaring. The shift was as though time and space engaged in a tug-of-war with my person, then spat me out, bored and in search of another plaything.

But that first time, my words were brief.

"Holy shit," I said, when we landed on a soft patch of grass.

Gaven made a guttural sound to remind me of my place.

I'd said the words into his shoulder, but the minute he released me, I understood his caution.

We stood at the base of a tree leaning over the wall of a church. Moss clung to old stones, the edges crumbling into the grass. Slabs of headstones carpeted the graveyard, some upright, others toppled. A small group of silver-haired people shuffled toward their cars. Heads bowed, some held flowers and their boxy purses, while others clutched hats in their hands. A priest patted them on the back, ushering them into their cars.

One woman looked up, as though surprised she'd only just noticed two figures clinging to each other near the wall. Her eyes narrowed, studying our presence, until a man placed a hand on her arm and tugged her toward the circular drive.

When the yard cleared, Gaven whispered, "You did it, EJ."

"Where are we?" I stepped toward the short wall of the graveyard to take in my surroundings. Grassy fields, cloud-laden skies. Longhaired cattle peering at us over a fence. Rows of white cottages lining a road in the distance.

Gaven pointed to the lake that stretched out below us. "Loch Gairloch," he said. "This is...well. Where I'm from. The area anyway. And this," he said, turning to the building behind us, "is my old church."

"It's beautiful," I said. "If haunting."

A small building, its profile remained imposing. With tall spires and a bell tower, the vintage building was nothing short of serious. I pictured the stained glass windows, a vaulted ceiling, and velvet lining the pulpit.

"We shouldn't stay long," he said, eyeing me as though he were a physician assessing my health. "I'm not surprised you made it, but I've no idea what the effects will be."

I inhaled the heather growing in mounds everywhere. A babbling brook nearby trickled its way through the grasses. I'd just arrived and was hesitant to leave.

"Over here," Gaven said. "I have to visit an old friend before we go."

I followed him back to the corner of the graveyard, to the base of a yew tree. On the way, he snapped a rose off a bush lining the yard. He set the blossom on a grave nestled at the base of the trunk, its stone facing west.

On impulse, Blythe's guidance echoing through my mind, I set my hand on the headstone. *Henrietta Lancaster.*

"Retta," Gaven said, a sad smile on his lips. "I brought her food in the famine. One of eight children, none of whom ever had enough. One day I returned to find that she, too, had joined the rest of them. Couldn't save her in the end."

"How tragic," I said, chastened by his words.

"She was a good friend," Gaven said. "Would listen to me talk for hours. Never batted an eye at my adventures and gave the best advice. I still tell her my secrets to this day. I like to think she is still a willing audience."

At our feet, several other Lancaster sites fanned outward. I read the names on each. "James Richard, beloved son. Charlotte, daughter, with the angels now..."

"Poor things," Gaven said.

I paused at the last family stone. "Bartholomew Crane, husband and father...what does this part say?"

Gaven stepped up to the marker. "Mu tha thu airson a bhith buan, na teid eadar an tè ruadh agus a'chreag. Essentially, 'if you want to live forever, don't die.'"

"All those letters for that?" I stared at the words, willing them into patterns I could recognize.

"Well, literally the end bit means don't get between a redhead and a cliff, but you get the idea."

My fingers traced a shape carved into the stone. The maker had carved a diamond, arrow tips on each point. I thought of the ledger I'd found among Hollis's things. He'd drawn that very symbol all over the pages. "What is this symbol?"

Gaven stepped up to the stone. "It's a compass rose, the sign of the Order." Gaven ran his finger along the lines. "Those who ruled the realms are tasked with maintaining the four interests. Each point refers to a cardinal direction, a different court."

"Why would that symbol be here?" I stared at the stone, willing its presence to make sense.

Gaven shrugged. "This is an old church. There are many secrets within—and without—its walls."

I set my hand on the stone, as I'd done with the ring. I closed my eyes to the beautiful land around me and opened my thoughts up to what might come.

Nothing.

"This grave is empty."

∾

"You can tell—how?"

We'd done what anyone would do when they discovered an empty grave with an unusual symbol carved into the rock. We went to the nearest pub for a pint.

"I've learned that I can associate objects that belonged to the dead. That stone never covered a body, so there's no one there." I slid my empty glass along the rough-hewn table. We sat in one of the tiny booths that lined the room. A grimy window let in the weak afternoon light. The place smelled of fried fish and old vegetables.

"So, Retta's father wasn't buried with her?"

I shrugged. "I guess I could check all the graves, but the way that woman looked at me, I don't think today's the day for that."

"Don't I know you?" A man leaned into our booth, bleary-eyed, his ire directed at Gaven. He closed first one eye and then the other, as though studying my friend for identifying aspects. "Wait a minute, I remember you. You're the one who left my Agatha!"

Gaven stood up, pushing his chair back. "I don't know any Agatha."

The man pursed his lips, lowering his brow to glower at Gaven. "You do all right. Wouldn't let me touch her for a month. And here you are, come sniffing around again. Well, you can't have her back, you spineless git!"

The man swung at Gaven, who ducked. Gaven turned toward me and mouthed the word, "Run!"

Without waiting for further direction, I sprinted for the door. There was a crash behind me. Wood splintered and glass shattered. I skidded out the door and headed for the lane. My lungs heaved, unused to anything faster than a brisk hike with Lotte. After a pathetic block, I slowed to a stop, bending at the waist to heave forward.

Gaven caught up to me. He was grinning ear to ear. "That was fun. Tripped him just as he was about to catch me, the lumbering idiot. He'll be hurting in the morning." Gaven brushed off his pants and regained his breath. "It's not my fault his old bird dog wouldn't stop following me when I rescued her from a trap. C'mon," he said, "there's one more thing I want to show you."

Sitting along the seaward edge of the old lighthouse, we took in the weak sunset at Rua Reidh. "Outstanding," I said.

"I'll never tire of this view," Gaven said. "Much has changed since my time, but some things never will. Up here, I'm king of the ocean, the Blue Man himself."

I kept my eyes on the water, searching. "Speaking of kings—any word on the crown?"

He looked at me. I continued to face the water, uncertain I'd be able to mask my secrets.

"I assume you mean the Circle of Stars. No, there hasn't

been. But...there sure are rumors. What I wouldn't give to see the set of them."

"Set?"

"The four. One for each of the realms." Gaven drew the same diamond in the sand with a stick.

"If you had all of them, would you be the ruler of everything?"

Gaven tented his brow. "Have you ever tried to wear four hats?"

I nodded. "There was this hot-air balloon wedding in the city. Christopher was sick and our boss was having a personal crisis with her ex, so I got stuck with this wedding. When the balloon man passed out from food poisoning brought on by his chicken salad, there I was, hundreds of feet in the air, serving as emergency pilot, preacher, and counselor all in one until we could get the thing back to the ground. Not my best moment."

The sun dipped below the horizon, and Gaven stood. He held out a hand to me and hoisted me up. "Shall we head back? That priest should be knee deep in his supper and old reruns of Absolutely Fabulous."

"I must have missed the weir. How do we get back through?"

Gaven winked. "Yet another secret my Retta keeps for me."

Fourteen

It had been that easy. Yet the moment remained surreal, as though I'd made it up in my head. As though hours before, I hadn't been across the seas in a foreign place, then back again.

Back in the Apothecary's safety, I couldn't stop pinching at my skin. Tiny confirmations that I was here, present, and whole and had memories from a graveyard, with Gaven.

Beneath Retta's gravestone was the weir. Gaven himself had moved the girl's body, knowing she'd wanted to rest near the loch's edge, not in the sadness of a forgotten yard. Now, in the safety and comfort of my existence, I mourned the girl I'd never met, the one who hadn't lived long enough to meter out her own life in successes and failures, fumbled decisions and incredible coincidences.

"How are you?" Gaven peered down at me as though I were a patient waking from anesthesia.

"Like I just had a massage from the inside out. And there are six of you somehow. But I think I'm okay. Does it always feel like this?"

"Wouldn't know," Gaven said. He took hold of my jaw and tilted my head back to squint into my eyes.

I studied his face, the effervescent visage of a young man. Black, shaggy hair, so silken it shone with blue. Peridot eyes rimmed with thick, short lashes. A long, sharp nose that fit the lanky frame of his body. If I hadn't known he was a centuries' old fae, he could have been a second son of mine. Instead, he was an ethereal being with far more experience than I, assessing his fragile human friend for travel damage.

"Ah—is this your son, then?"

Dale Tindal, a stack of paper under one arm, elbowed his way into my shop. He ran the printing shop, a hodge-podge of services squeezed into a tiny shotgun-style building on the north side of the block. Like many, he'd inherited a business from his family. As the digital age gobbled up the need for printing presses, he'd shifted again and again, meeting customer needs.

Gaven released his hold on me, and I stepped back. "Gaven is my employee," I said. When Dale's eyebrows lifted at my response, I continued. "And he is like a son to me. Especially with Patrick an ocean away, I need someone to fuss over."

"Aw, Mom. I like that."

Having decided that there was nothing inappropriate going on, Dale continued. "Brought the proofs you wanted," he said, handing me the stack. He rocked back on his heels. "Have to say...many are quite...well. Let's just say that I think you'll have no trouble finding customers for your little project. In fact, sign me up for one."

I looked at the first image. Joaquin, cheeky and impish, the corded muscle on his frame assured. He gave the camera a come-hither look that would translate across any language. "These came out well."

"I took the liberty of printing out a few so Christopher

could make sure this is what he wants. There were so many good ones."

"Thank you," I said, tucking Joaquin and the others under my arm. "I'll call you when we get it together."

Dale dipped his head toward me and left.

"You know I'm not leaving until I get to see those, right?"

I rolled my eyes at Gaven's insistence and took the images over to the kitchen area. While I brewed a fresh pot, the scent of chocolate and hazelnut in the air, Gaven helped me tack the photographs above the sink. They stretched into the back hallway, the images bright in the gloom.

I glanced at the first few. There was the sexy Joaquin, his russet skin gleaming in the lighting. Next was the stunning—however prickly—Ophelia, her creamy skin in deep contrast to the cactus she held. The men's choir, standing behind the hedge in front of the performance hall, their director with a pitch pipe slung around his neck. Christopher in his glasses, a retired sheriff who loved snake plants, and the garden society, each member snuggling their favorite plant of the year. The owner of the Christmas shop held a miniature tree, and the couple who owned the bistro down the block sat in their garden, a sumptuous brunch on a tiny wrought-iron table, peace lilies in their laps. Near the bottom of the stack, she found the images of Rowdy, a golden man against a sunny spring day. In his images, the soft stems of the wildflowers did their best to mask the shadowed places on his body, as though they didn't want to release him from their caresses.

"No way," Gaven said, reaching for the proofs. "Why wasn't I invited?"

He held up a picture of Iris. She'd donned a long, blue wig that draped over her breasts and gathered over her belly. Surrounded by mesquite trees and a tan brick wall, she stood behind a prickly pear, her tattoos in stark contrast to her pale skin. A strip of black leather wound its way up one arm, and she wore silver gladiator sandals on her feet. The image was stunning in every way, yet what caused the two of us to stare was the snow at her feet and atop the plants, a thin white blanket covering the scene. Iris had her face lifted to the sky, as though welcoming the icy weather.

"But how...oh." When the bulk of our interactions stemmed from my penchant for champagne and her complaining about a grouchy boss, it was easy to forget she, too, was extranormal. "I think we have our December."

"Merry Christmas," Gaven said, grinning. "Can't wait to tease her about it."

"Don't you dare," I said, giving him a playful shove. "I can't afford to lose my models before I've sold a single calendar."

"Are these the images you want to use?"

"Christopher wanted some proofs to help decide the layout. We might frame these and auction them off, or just sell them here in the shop. There are so many. How will we narrow them down? And what if we can't sell any of them?"

Gaven lifted the next image. "I'm no expert in this demographic," he said, eyeing the image from top to bottom, "but I'd wager you've got your interest bases more than covered." He handed the photograph to me with a wink.

I looked at the image and my eyes went wide. My insides, having been pressed by weir travel, were again a puddled mess, my belly warm with desire. "But when—how?"

Gaven shrugged, and I looked at the image again.

Ansel sat on a garden bench, as diffused sunlight graced his tawny skin. His hair was up in his treasured sloppy bun. A strand of ivy wound around his neck and draped over taut pecks before trailing downward. He held a pair of trimmers in one hand; the arm draped over a bent knee. In his other hand, he held a rose, its pink petals divided by his nose as though he couldn't bury his face deep enough in the soft folds of its aroma.

"Should I leave you alone with that one?" Gaven's question hung in the air as I stared at the picture with undisguised lust.

I shook my head and looked away. "I'll leave them until Christopher gets back to help me make some choices. But I've got to get back to potting."

With unmatched reluctance, I forced myself to turn from the images I knew would haunt my dreams.

∼

"You have a smell about you. Fresh water," June said. As a divination witch, she used the old practices to her advantage.

I shrugged. "We repotted several dozen succulents—people are obsessed with them—and I trimmed a shelf of polka dot plants. Bet you're smelling that."

June pressed her lips together. "I can't help you if you aren't honest with me."

I met June that evening for a practice session. She wanted to see what I could do and planned to show me some defensive moves. When she got within four feet of me, however, her attention shifted.

"Why would I have anything to hide?" The moment the words were out, I thought of the crown. When Gaven left, I'd unearthed the thing again, desperate for a place to hide it. I considered burying it in Mariette's pot, beneath her long and stringy roots. Yet this seemed too exposed. I considered destroying the object but worried that to do so would cause further harm to myself. My itch to be rid of the thing stemmed from the danger it held but had been spurred by the image of Ansel from that afternoon. The way my body responded to his, bare and lush, meant that I couldn't hold out for the better. While I considered what to do with the crown, I wanted to wear myself out through training.

"You seek absolution," June said, readying her stance. "But I am no priest."

I faced her, stretching my hands. She'd wanted me to use my newfound vining ability to disarm her and practice restraints. I itched to make this happen. "I seek only what's rightfully mine," I said. "My family's legacy."

After our practice, in which June had evaded my control far more than she succumbed to any of my amateur attempts to restrain her, I found a dozen texts. Then my phone rang.

"Gaven told us about your adventure," Joaquin said. "Boss wants to talk strategy."

I hadn't asked Gaven not to spread the news of my ability to use the weirs (though still a single instance), but I hadn't sworn him to secrecy either. "No thanks, I'm busy," I said, and hung up. I expected the phone to ring again, either Joaquin with a sugared repeat question or a blustering Ansel, insistent I head next door as it wasn't as though he could come to me. But my phone, and the shop, were silent. Christopher was on another date, leaving me alone with my thoughts—and the crown. I'd kept so many in danger because of that thing. I could give it to Ansel and be done with it, yet all I wanted after finding evidence of Christopher's photo session with Ansel was for my heart to stop pounding.

At my sales counter, I paged through Hollis's journal, a ledger of sorts he'd kept at his side. I looked for more images—like the symbol I'd seen in the graveyard or anything else that could explain the weir connections.

The bell at the door tinkled. A small man in a sleek navy suit entered the shop. He strode up to the counter and plunked down a gold nugget. "Glad to have another friendly face here," he said. On his wrist was the same image as from the gravesite, tattoos in luminescent ink. "Your uncle was such a good man. Even until the end."

"You knew Hollis?"

The man bowed. "As the queen's escort, I know all the watchers—well, the ones who are left. It was a big part of my job...well, until...anyway. Hollis became a little edgy at the end. Wouldn't stop talking about Death. Asked me if I knew the guy one day. With a wild look in his eye, hair sticking out at all angles like a scrub brush, Hollis grabbed me by the collar and said, 'Avoid him at all costs. He brings only destruction.' That was the last time I saw him, poor man. Nasty business."

"And did you—er—do you...know Death?"

The fae shook his head. "I did what Hollis said. I avoid the guy at all costs."

While he didn't know Death, I knew someone who did.

∾

"So, I take it the flesh wound was an excuse."

I'd closed the shop early, bought a bottle of expensive French bubbly from the wine shop, and contacted Joaquin. He had a contact I'd needed.

The moths were aflutter in response to my rushing about. They would settle on one of the vines only to stir at the slightest breeze, taking flight about the windows before alighting on a new leaf. It wasn't until my guest arrived that they committed to the massive leaves of a bird of paradise, the moths' wings folded and peaceful.

I held up my finger to the Nurse. "I have one," I said. "Cut myself on a nasty thorn from the euphorbia. Nothing an Epsom soak and a Band-Aid didn't sort out though."

The Nurse glanced at the stack of treats, the bottle in its chiller, and two of my favorite short-stemmed coups from my growing glass collection. Christopher went on weekly scouting trips to thrift stores to add to our collection. "So, not entirely false pretenses," she said, a smile playing about her lips.

"Lucky for me, Joaquin didn't ask questions."

The Nurse, sporting a cropped cape over a slinky evening gown, made her way over to my makeshift bar and perched on the stool. She hung her small, beaded medical bag—containing what had to be vials of the Angel's Share, otherwise known as fae elixir—on the hook I'd attached to the end of the bar. Her sun-streaked hair was half up, skewered by a slim wooden stick with a gem on one end. She wore sky-high heels she crossed at the ankles. The snake of her silver stethoscope wrapped around her neck. "While I can't say I'm sad about a girl's night, don't sell that man short. I've seen him sacrifice himself a dozen times over for just about anyone in a moment of need. He can't help it. It's like a curse."

"He's saved me a time or two," I mused, dropping a few enlarged crystals of honey into the bottom of two glasses. I squeezed a half lemon between the two, then poured champagne over each with a steady hand. We watched the bubbles rise and tumble over each other in the glasses. I handed her a glass. I lifted the other. "To Joaquin, then."

"To Joaquin," she said, and we clinked glasses. She sipped, then smiled. "This is good, really good."

"My take on a Bee's Knees," I said. "I get the honey from Rowdy…you know of him, yes?"

"I know of him, yes. I can't say we are well acquainted." The Nurse cleared her throat, then drank again from her glass. She left a faint print of lipstick on the rim. "Well then, if I'm here on other pretenses, let me know. I admit to being a long-time lover of intrigue."

I considered this woman in my shop. She seemed at home and yet entirely out of place all at once. Like an antique vase in a modern apartment. Her speech, too, had a different music to the words, as though in a tempo I'd yet to hear but recognized nonetheless. I knew next to nothing about her: not her past, what she did with her days, or even if she had a name. She could have been fae, a succubus, or some other creature that could snap me out of existence with the wink of an eye. Yet somehow, we were kindred spirits, drawn together by our situation. It was up to me to find out how close those interests lay.

"I was hoping you'd tell me about Death." When I said the name, her eyebrows shot up over the top of her glass. "What was he like?"

"Was?" Her tone was teasing.

"Was…is. I guess one can't be Death and have time bound placement."

I realized then that I, who only a year ago would have been obsessed with the latest Dior cuts, which florist used fair trade flowers, and how to get the llamas dressed in formal attire not to spit on all the guests, was now courting favors from unknown entities in my tiny plant nursery. The world was a strange place, and I was its puppet, never the opposite.

"No," she said, shaking her head. "One cannot."

I held out the tray of brownies to her. "I'm not after details of your sex life or anything—"

The Nurse snorted and set the glass on the bar top. "I can assure you we never knew each other…carnally. There was a time once when maybe…but that is all in the past." She selected one of the squares. "But when I knew him well, he was dashing. Confident. Observational. At one with the forces that shape the worlds. And lonely, so very lonely."

"I can't think how Death could have many friends."

"He did, though. Does still, I'm sure. People are drawn to him, no matter where he goes. Even the most stouthearted have that flicker of possibility, the draw of inevitable closure that tugs at their conscience. Sure, they don't know him—not his real identity—but something in their core calls out for him. Yet over time...well, he is Death, after all."

I nodded, as though this was a normal conversation to have in my shop on a Wednesday afternoon.

"So...you met in...?" How did one delicately ask a relative stranger if they'd been to hell—Nether—for a date?

"He rescued me from a life of drudgery, though I didn't appreciate our friendship back then. To me, he was a man of contradictions, of great power. I failed to understand that, with me, he just wanted to be normal. A man."

"I can see how his—job—would make it difficult to be normal."

The Nurse nodded at the glass in her hand, a smile at the edge of her lips. "Eh, it's not as they describe it in books...or movies. He's tasked with balance, not individual decisions. None of that black cloak and scythe kind of thing. More like... paperwork. Reviewing numbers."

"Sounds like business," I said.

"It always did to me."

"If it's not too forward...what happened?"

The Nurse plucked a crumb from the fabric pooled in her lap and set it on the edge of the plate. She reached for her bag and withdrew a slim golden cylinder. Cap off, she applied the lipstick with the expert fingers of someone who no longer needs a mirror. She snapped the cap back into place. "Oh, you know how marriage goes." She brushed off my question like another crumb on her gown. "Interests diversify, societies go to war, and you..." Something akin to nostalgia crinkled at the corners of her eyes. "Grow apart."

"I'm sorry." I, too, knew that song.

She bit at her lower lip, the fresh slick of red smearing onto her teeth. "If you're going to ask where he is, I wouldn't know. Travels to this realm and the next, aimless and uncaring. A bit of an unrepentant gambler at this point. A wife worries, you know. Even if...well."

From behind the bar, I unearthed a worn, leather-bound book. I'd retrieved the tome that morning, treating Hollis's grimoire with tender care. With my fresh eyes of experience, pieces assembled, and I was eager to share my interpretation. "My uncle was obsessed with Death. Hollis believed he'd found the key to immortality." I opened the book to a two-page entry in which Hollis had drawn a gigantic tree, its branches spreading across the deckled-edged paper. Exotic birds peppered the upper limbs. Fist-sized flowers tipped the ends, each containing a jewel at its center. Below the ground, roots stretched, anchors in the soil of time, fungi expanding outward from the trunk. The Nurse bent to examine the drawing. She traced her finger along a branch. I inhaled a steadying breath and took the risk I'd been talking myself into for most of the day, terrified I'd find out something I wanted to know—and that I wouldn't. "Hollis traveled the world seeking this tree, bringing my mom and me many treasures back from the adventures. This was a passion that took over his life, to where he neglected his business. When my mom died, we heard from him less and less. I think he let this quest take over his reality. In the last few entries, he drew this symbol over and over again."

"The Order..." the Nurse whispered.

Who or what she was remained a mystery, yet her awareness was a hint, however small. "He thought they had something to do with it. The separation of Death from life."

"No doubt they do, the bastards." The Nurse's words were barbed.

"If the realms need Death and life to maintain balance, who—or what?—is in charge now?" This was a question I'd asked others and received little in the way of an answer. Lotte told me it was too delicate a balance for any one entity,

Joaquin said himself so long as he remained topside, and Iris replied that control is an illusion.

In contrast, the Nurse stared out the window, her gaze vacant. "No one. The loss of the crowns put an end to the fighting. Now, allegiance is held in secret while those in search of power seek proof it is theirs to hold. The first to source any will have a field day of laying waste to the rest." She turned a trained eye my way. "What has any of this to do with you?"

I balked at her assessment. "I...guess it doesn't. But—no, it does. Whether anyone around here likes it or not. I've had my shop infiltrated, been almost killed, lost people I loved, coven members missing—"

"The witches, too?"

"Yes, and this insane woman is after me with some vendetta I don't understand."

The Nurse lifted a manicured eyebrow. "One of the witches?"

"No, well, not quite. Her name is Ophelia—"

She frowned. "That doesn't sound like Feelie."

"I assure you, it's her. There was one time I didn't let her use the weir. She was acting like she owned the place. Bossed me around and it was the wrong day for that. Even tried to toss some ring at me like I'm desperate. Well, I'm not, and I didn't know—"

"Ring..." The Nurse covered her mouth with her hand. "Oh, Hector. No wonder. The poor thing." She stood from the stool and reached for her bag.

"Wait." Was she leaving to lend a shoulder to Ophelia? Look for Death? Or was she off to peddle her wares elsewhere? "Please, before you go, can you tell me about the card?"

The woman paused the gathering of her belongings to study the card. In it, Death, personified, stood in a garden of roses, the scythe over his shoulder. On his head was a crown and at his feet, a great black bird. He held his hand out as though in invitation.

The Nurse took the rectangle of cardboard and stared at it as though it depicted an old lover. "This is French," she began. "A tarot card. He was fascinated with their meanings, picking up decks here and there. This was one of his favorites, hand drawn by a blind artist who did caricatures along the Seine over a century ago. He adored the artwork and sought her out the next day to commission a full deck. In her place was a new artist, one who painted garish river scenes. The painter said the young woman had been attacked in the night, her purse stolen, her belongings smashed and trampled along with her frail body. Police dragged her away, the man said, and no, he didn't know where. Death went on a killing spree that night, taking out every vagrant he could find, in search of those who'd harmed his muse."

"Did he find them?"

She shook her head. "Exhausted by the carnage and grieved by loss, he occupied a house of sin for a month, drinking, gambling, and who knows what else."

I pictured the damage such a loss would inspire. "Was this before you two..." There was no polite way to ask how old she was or how long their relationship had lasted.

The Nurse nodded. "Before we married, yes, but I knew him then."

I swallowed. "I assume he made it out alive...er...okay."

"He did. Came to me a wreck. He'd dragged himself out of a drugged stupor, sailed back across the sea, and slept for a week before he roused himself. He'd wagered the card and lost it, the very object which inspired the wrath that led him to the destruction."

"If my man came home from a bender, blaming it all on a card and a Frenchwoman, I don't think I'd be as supportive."

The Nurse gave me a sad smile. "These are dark times,

when the balance is upended. Death as I knew him grew wary, short-tempered. The world screamed for him at the same time as it pushed him away. He grows tired in times like these, knowing it's his duty to right the realms again."

"How so?" I pictured Death, a rakish skeletal figure, swooning around the streets of Paris, lamenting the loss of sanity around him and finding an innocent artist who spared him judgment to bring him joy.

"In Death, there is quiet."

I looked down at the card in my hand, then up at her. I handed the card to her. "If you see him again, please give it back. Tell him I'm sorry for his loss."

"I will," she said, her tone solemn. She tucked the card into her bag and withdrew a smaller one. "This is my number, should you need me, or if you just want to chat. I enjoyed this. It's not often anyone calls to talk."

I smiled and nodded.

"And remember what I said of Joaquin. He's a yang in search of a yin. A woman need never fear a man like that."

"But what about Ansel?" The question slipped out before I considered the implications, the inferences she would make.

The Nurse's face darkened. "He's a halfborn torn between his past and an unknown future. Any woman knows what that brings out in a man. Tread with care, but trust in the sands of time."

I locked the door behind my departing guest and made another Bee's Knees. I tossed a light shawl around my shoulders and headed out to my beloved bench.

Everywhere I turned, each of my problems bloomed into a bigger issue, woven into thick layers of complexity. I couldn't hold their enormity within my powers. I needed help, guidance, yet I was far from trusting anyone—at least not with all of myself. With each feeble attempt to right my world, it only descended further into chaos.

But what choice did I have? Curling up into a ball and hiding from reality was tempting but would make me an easy target. The best way to keep living was to not die. As a human, I was vulnerable. As a take-no-shit mother, I was a force to be reckoned with. My magic, what little I could muster, was icing on the cake—and I was hungry for more.

Fifteen

"Again."

I narrowed my focus to the center of the glass jar in front of me. Within lay a small object, inert and waiting for spring.

"You're hesitating. Just do it."

I ground my teeth. "You want me to center myself, so I need a minute. I'm not a machine."

June huffed, crossing her arms. The coven leader, decked out in a pair of coveralls and work boots, leaned against a table saw. "And I'm not getting any younger."

"Neither am I," I muttered to the jar in front of me. *In-two-three-four, out-two-three-four...* With my mentor quieted for the moment, I could seek that thread of intention. Faint, but present.

Over the last few weeks, I'd become faster at locating the source of my ability, but my resolve still waned according to my environment. June's deep-seated irritation and impatience rattled me. Shaken, I was useless.

I let out my last deep breath and focused my energy. I gave thanks for life, sending love into the jar.

The seed inside wiggled, then split. A green shoot, like an errant tongue, whipped out and twisted upward, forming a spire. Roots spilled out of the casing as the stem shot up, thickening. One leaf and then another popped outward as the little plant cleared the lip of the jar. Within seconds, the roots wrapped up and over the rim, clinging to the sides in search of earth, while the stem expanded into a thick tube, sporting leaf after leaf. At its top, a bud formed. It was a bud of green sepals which exploded into a yellow and orange sunburst of petals, studded with hundreds of black seeds that swelled within their matrix.

"Stop!" June stood between me and the massive sunflower. Soft pattering signaled the drop of the flower's seeds onto the concrete floor. "I said, keep it small!"

"But why?" I watched the flower drop its petals, one by one. They fluttered to the ground like brightly-colored teardrops. "How am I to fight off otherworld creatures that attack me if everything I do is so restrained?"

"What you lack," June said, "is *control*. A witch of your age should choose her weapons—and her battles—with care and concentration. You are equal parts surprised by and afraid of what you create. Anything you've done to protect yourself so far has been a lucky accident. I'm surprised you haven't gotten more people killed the way you operate. You're as reckless as a goat in heat."

My pride stung as though slapped. "It's taking too long. I want to *help*."

"You'll help us by getting a hold of yourself!"

"Then give me something to do that makes sense." I was whining, but I didn't care. "I need a task I can believe in. Sprouting microgreens isn't exactly inspiring."

June frowned at me, then scanned the shop. She strode over to a bike on a stand. On one side of the handlebars, severed cables hung loose, a missing brake handle balanced on the seat. "Fine. Fix it."

"But I don't know—"

"You wanted something useful to do, and I need these brake cables fixed. Make it happen."

I pressed my lips together in an attempt to keep my frustration bottled. Without another word, I approached the bike. The handlebars hung like horns off a bull. The complex strands of cable arched in a curve, disappearing into the mechanics. "This isn't a living thing. What am I supposed to do about a bike?"

"You wanted a problem, a real one. How will you fix it?"

"But I—"

"See? You've no idea what to do other than flail about, pitying yourself." June strode toward the back of the shop, a dismissal. "If there was some sort of magic button to come into one's power, we all would have pushed it. You're either willing to do the work or you're not."

June was right. What little I'd done had been reactive, impulsive. I hadn't the slightest clue what I should do, which made me dangerous—and pathetic. It was reckless to think I could harness my abilities in the heat of a moment. I wanted to be useful, needed to, in fact. But there was desire and there was application. I only had one of the two in spades.

I reached for the handlebars. Brake lines were a concept I could follow, but their actualization was something I left to the professionals.

I touched the tip of the handle, resting my finger on the rubbery grip. Frustrated, I hung my head, seeking my next move. Out of the corner of my eye, I watched a tendril extend from my fingers, a manifestation of my tattoo. The tiny sprout twisted up and outward, reaching back until it stretched down to the brake pads along the wheel. I stared as a second tendril joined the first, winding its way to join the end of the other.

"Look," I said, calling to June. I pointed to the bike. "I did it!

"You made wiring out of plants. I don't see how that—"

"Test it," I said, interrupting with far more confidence than I held.

Glowering at me, June hauled the bike off the stand, set it on the floor, and mounted the saddle. With a wobbling start, she pedaled the bike in a tight circle. The brakes squeaked when she squeezed the handles, and the bike stopped.

I looked down at my hand. I'd sprouted a new tattoo. A sunflower, its bright head of gold and auburn, was flush against my skin, joining the other ink.

At the door to the garage, Uzma stepped in. She stood with her feet apart, arms crossed in front of her chest. "Why didn't you tell us you think it's her? We deserve to know." This question, hard and curt, was directed at June.

"What's me?"

"Keep your voice down!" June hissed the reply, like a dragon protecting its hoard. She squinted over Uzma's shoulder, into the darkness beyond. A lone coyote howled into the night.

Uzma pointed at me. "You think she's the living vine—don't you?" The pitch of her voice rose with each word.

"Wait—I'm what?"

June shook her head. "No. I'm just working with her—"

"That would explain it," Uzma said. The woman wore an oversized bomber jacket over cargo pants. A knife was tucked into her belt. She paced the garage, thinking aloud. "You wanted to test her. Find out what she's capable of, so you—"

"Silence!" June's voice split the room.

Uzma froze, her back to June. She whirled around. "No, I won't be quiet. If there's any chance she's the one we need, *everyone* needs to know."

I waved my hands at them to regain some attention. "What are you talking about?"

The women ignored me. Uzma said, "It's the prophecy, isn't it? I *knew* it."

I looked at June, and when she didn't respond, turned to Uzma. "What prophecy?"

"Of course you didn't tell her. Why would you? Wouldn't want to risk the little kingdom you've built," Uzma said, smirking.

"You know that isn't true." June's voice was ice, her eyes steeled against Uzma's accusations.

"I'm telling her." June opened her mouth in protest but Uzma spoke before the older woman could get a word out. "A living vine will stitch anew what became four crowns back into two."

"The what and the who?" I was lost, and more than a little tongue-tied.

Uzma shook her head slowly at June. "I'm going to help her."

"Like hell you are."

"Watch me." Uzma grabbed a hold of my arm, dragging me toward the exit.

"She can barely do anything." June called out. "Untrained, she's dangerous. You could get killed."

"We have no choice," Uzma said at the doorway. I shook my arm loose from her grip, but she paid me no mind. "We're getting nowhere without her."

"There's always a choice."

Uzma put her hands on her hips to square off with the older woman. "This one is no longer yours to make."

Sixteen

"So, there are four crowns?" I studied the complex drawing on the floor of June's shop. Uzma had made quick work with a grease pencil, outlining what she understood to be true. I puzzled over the images, sorting out facts as they came my way.

Uzma stood back to appraise her work. She'd drawn a compass rose, a diamond at its center with a circlet at the end of each cardinal direction. To these shapes she'd added what had to be the jewels, Xs and stars of varying sizes. "Each with its own role."

"That's quite the collection."

"It's said that the crowns were made by Goddess and Green Man. They sought to balance power among their creations. Allowing too much to rest on any one head would spell a downfall. They were distributed among the most worthy of their natural lines, to be passed down in succession."

"I get it. They played favorites."

"Pretty much," Uzma said. "Their most treasured of creatures, the firstborn, received the crowns and were tasked with ruling the realms."

June ran her tongue under her lower lip before speaking. "Leave it to the fae to screw that up." Reluctant but unable to stop the younger woman, June stood by while Uzma debriefed me.

"What happened?" A breeze blew into the shop. The hair on my arms stood up as an owl hooted in the distance.

"What always happens," June said, throwing up her arms in defeat and walking back over to her workbench. "Corruption."

Uzma watched June walk away before continuing. "Essentially, the longer each ruler wore a crown, the more they considered themselves the one true ruler. As their lives went on—and on—this grew in intensity until the four courts were at war."

I shook my head. "Don't tell me this is where I come in."

"Get over yourself, girl," June called from the back of the shop. "You were mere stardust back then." She flipped on an overhead light. The bulb blazed above the table.

Uzma stooped to draw a bower, its height draped with tendrils. Threaded between them, she'd drawn what appeared to be a vine, its ends linking the four directions. From this thread grew leaves of several shapes and sizes. "Not you," Uzma said. "But I'm guessing your—our"—she shot June a look—"ancestor. Goddess and Green Man grew a vine to link the fortunes of one crown with the other, effectively balancing the stability of each vine on the other. This meant that no one ruler could take from another without knowing consequences. The prophecy came from this balancing."

"But what makes you think it's me...or anyone? Wouldn't it be a plant?" The familiar squeeze of my chest shortened my breath. The flutter of wings beat against my lungs from the inside, and I struggled to get air. *Easy.* I closed my eyes and exhaled a long, slow breath.

"It was at this time that the first witches came to be. Many claim they were made as an answer to the power hungry firstborn. The witches knew of the prophecy, were the first to write it down and pass it along the lines. Green witches are the most closely related to the first witch."

"I'm a hedge witch, though," I said. "Allegedly. Wouldn't that exclude me from this situation, even if the so-called vine is, in fact, a walking-talking person?"

Uzma glanced at June. The older woman's shoulders stiffened, but she refused to look up. "Hedgeriders became the intermediaries between the firstborn and the witches. Peacemakers."

I opened my mouth to talk, but words caught on my tongue refused to tumble out.

"See?" June tossed a wrench onto the table. "If she were the vine, she would know this to be true. She would feel something. *Do* something. Not sit here like a stifled bump on a log, waiting for answers to be handed to her. She would *know*. I'm only training her as a favor to Ansel and as a protection for us. Without basic skills, this one is dangerous at best."

Uzma bit her bottom lip, considering June's words. "Maybe. Maybe not. But if we're as desperate as you say we are, shouldn't we follow all the leads?"

I couldn't wrap my head around Uzma's words. June's dismissal fit. It couldn't be me. That I was any part of controlling multi-realm chaos was ludicrous.

"I've tested her," June said. She came around the corner of the table, hands on hips. "Or are you accusing me of not living up to my duties?" Uzma said nothing. "I didn't think so. The crowns are lost. If the prophecy is true, if we find one, we find them all. Until then, there's no reason to think the legends of the living vine are anything more than wishful storytelling intended to avoid war. As I've stated, repeatedly, the way we protect ourselves, our sisterhood, is to find the crowns. When witches control the relics, we become that very vine, able to prevent the Fallen, the Gentry, and even the Order from ever hurting another one of us again. If you want to make a difference, you will give up on those who only waste your time"—here she gestured at me—"and focus on what will make a difference." June stormed out through the giant doorway.

I looked back at Uzma. Her lips were pressed in a straight line, her eyes on June's retreating form. Without looking at me, she said, "Take me to Ansel."

∽

"What is *she* doing here?"

Iris threw a bar towel at Ansel. "Do you really think EJ would come here, given all of your warm commentary about her kind, if she didn't have a fantastic reason?"

"Thank you," I said. "And she's right. It is a good reason. This is Uzma. Uzma, this is Ansel, Lotte, and Joaquin. Gaven's in the kitchen."

Ansel grunted at her. Lotte smiled, and Iris nodded.

Joaquin, per his typical style, held out his hand, flashing a wide grin. "Pleased to meet you."

Uzma frowned but shook his hand.

"I think we are going to need the coven," I said. "Or at least Uzma and her sister, to help us find the crowns."

"Crowns?" Joaquin's eyebrow kinked upward. "As in, plural?"

"You told them!?"

"There are four," I said, ignoring Ansel's growing anger. I saw Lotte give a slight nod of her head. "I'll let Uzma explain."

Ansel's stony stare focused on me. "I am not talking about ancient relics with anyone. Should such items exist, some of us," he said, looking at me, "would have the sense to keep this knowledge to ourselves."

"You've talked to me about one. I'm a witch, too."

"That was different. You're a...well. You can...It doesn't matter. I only care about one crown, and whenever I get my hands on it, the last thing I'm doing is to call a meeting and tell everyone."

I stared at this stubborn man. He behaved like a child, pouting over a toy he wanted to keep for himself. "She's offering help. Can't you see that?"

"Witches," he said, the word rolling like a handful of pebbles in his mouth, "should stay in their lane. Monitor the seasons, do something about the environmental shitshow that humans have created. But when it comes to beings with far more power in their pinky fingers than you'll ever have, leave that to those of us who share in the blood of their ancestors." With his final proclamation, Ansel headed for the stairs.

Uzma fumed. A corded muscle in her neck flexed, and her hands balled into fists. "We will not sit back while your kind do nothing," she called. "Someone is taking my sisters."

"The Fallen," said Joaquin. He'd listened to their sparring match, and only with Ansel gone did he weigh in.

"Maybe," Uzma said, turning to him. "And maybe not. The Fallen take anyone with pure elixir in their blood, it's true. But that's not the case for my sisters. Witch blood is tainted, like an antidote."

"It contains a deadened version of elixir?" My high school biology knowledge kicked into gear.

"It will have an effect," Uzma said. "A lethal one."

Seventeen

"But what are they doing with the witches?" Iris stepped in to transition our conversation from a total standoff to something that could translate into productivity.

"Killing witches. They might also be torturing them to get information, but we aren't sure." Uzma filled in what I'd seen of Priyanka and Kim's demise.

"Ophelia arrived when this started," I said. "Could it be her?"

Lotte shook her head, the soft dark curls of her hair brushing her cheeks. "As a Bandorai, that wouldn't make sense."

"I don't follow." The longer I stayed on Whiskey Row, the more extranormal I met and the more difficult it became to keep them straight.

"She's like a witch," Iris said. "She has focused abilities and uses tools—including words—to bend the universe her way. Why go after those adjacent to herself?"

"Competition?" I slid onto a bar stool. Iris set a glass filled with soft yellow, bubbling liquid in front of me. "To get back at me?"

"But you aren't in the coven. That would be careless. There's only one of her."

"Thank the gods," I said, and sipped the champagne. The bubbles tickled my tongue.

"Something has changed, shifted," Lotte said. "Something —or someone—bigger than Feelie."

"Why does everyone insist on using that cutesy nickname for a woman who wants to murder me?"

"Sorry," Lotte said. "It's just...well, some of us knew her from...before."

I huffed. I didn't want to think about an Ophelia people liked. A reasonable, affable woman. Someone Ansel liked and then some.

Joaquin set a black boot on the brass foot railing and leaned into the shiny bar. "What do you propose we do?"

Uzma turned her attention to Joaquin. "So, you're in?"

Joaquin titled his head back and forth, as though reconsidering his position. "Boss has his reasons, as most of you know." He gave me a look that said *and needn't share with our new friend.* "He may not agree with you, but he'll want to stay involved in anything to do with the crowns. Better to take part from the beginning."

"All right," I said.

Uzma jumped in. "We need info on the crowns. Their last locations, who had them—anything. We've tried our records, but there's little beyond the prophecy."

"We've been checking our networks," Iris said. "but nothing's solidified yet. Essentially everyone is looking everywhere they can. But there's one group I haven't tapped into...yet."

Joaquin smirked. "The Gentry."

"It's not like we're all best friends," Iris added.

"If you ask them, wouldn't that point fingers back to

Ansel?" I remembered his words of warning. "And who would you even ask?"

Iris shrugged. "They do come in here now and then. We are the only—what does Christopher call it? Oh yeah—*extranormal* bar in town. I'll frame it like he's just heard a word and is curious, like it's any old bounty. If he said nothing, that would be weird."

"Could I read the prophecy and any of the related texts?" Lotte's voice was soft, thoughtful. "I might dig out some nuances."

Uzma regarded the other woman. "Can you read in Latin? These texts are older than dirt."

"She can," Joaquin said, his puppy dog eyes wide and adoring.

"I'll bring them to you," Uzma said. "I'll have to borrow them, somehow, but let me figure that out."

"We've got Prescott covered," I said. "But what we need could be realms away. Who is doing that research?"

"Me," Gaven said. He entered the bar, a smattered apron wrapped around his waist, headphones around his neck. "I've got the weirs and the Gentry covered. At least, I'll ask around."

"We'll check the black markets," Joaquin said. He looked down at his feet before meeting Uzma's eyes. "Check for any witch products."

The wrinkle between Uzma's brows deepened. "You think they could be..."

Joaquin gave a little shrug. "Until we know what happened to them, I think we need to stay open."

"I'll stay here and do my usual nothing remotely helpful," I said under my breath.

Lotte, ever the calming presence, reached out to give my arm a gentle squeeze. "You've got a *shop* to watch and Christopher to protect." The gentle emphasis reminded me of my duty to the back room of the Apothecary.

"You can watch Ophelia, too," Iris said. "Just in case. It is quite a coincidence that the most powerful Bandorai comes to our podunk town and witches disappear."

I thought of that day when I was out with Joaquin, the presence among the sage. I didn't think it was Ophelia—did I?

Joaquin pressed his hands together and held them to his lips. "Bases are covered. The key," he said, turning to face Uzma and me, "is that no witch should be out on her own."

"Then I'm going with Gaven," I said, resolute.

"Don't think Boss will like that."

"I've done it before."

His eyes went wide. "A ripper *and* a walker?" He spun toward Gaven. "Why didn't you tell us?"

Gaven shrugged. "It was just one quick stop, to my village. Like a high-speed plane. She basically twisted my arm into it."

My heart warmed that Gaven had kept the secret between us until now. I wasn't sad he'd said something, given the look of awe on Joaquin's face. "And there's no one else here who has," I said. My words challenged the others, leaving little room for a response.

"But what about the weir?" Joaquin hadn't followed Lotte's earlier turn of phrase.

Uzma blinked. "Weir?"

So much for keeping things quiet.

"*Weirs*, technically," Iris said.

"Christopher knows how to manage the shop," I said. "*All* of it. He'll be fine when I go."

"And I'll stay with him when she does," Uzma says. "My sister, Blythe, too. Apparently, we have some new stuff to learn."

Iris addressed Uzma. "You'll need to be oathbound, witch, that you won't say anything. You and your sister."

"Not these again. Will someone, literally *anyone*, please explain them to me?"

Joaquin stepped into the conversation. "It's when a witch swears on something with their life. Should they forfeit, they die."

"How do you know about those?" Uzma adopted a chilling tone, her question wrapped in an accusation.

"Stick to the topic at hand. We can't have you telling the coven about anything you see or hear here," Iris said. "Seems only right."

"I'm not saying no to the oath," Uzma said, her words guarded, "but I'm going to have to tell the coven I'm up to something or they will tell me nothing, and that will get us nowhere fast."

"Fine. You will tell them small bits of information we agree upon."

"Done. I'll tell them I got a job with EJ. We can only get so many hours at the bike shop anyway, and we're always complaining to June about that. This will explain why I'm there when EJ is out."

"It's settled then," Iris said. "Who will cast the oath?"

"EJ," Uzma said, without hesitation.

"You want me to cast something when I can barely grow a lily pad in a jar? And what about Blythe?"

"If anyone can, it's you," Iris said.

"She means," Uzma said, "you're the only one who can, so you have to."

"Oh. So, what do I do?"

Uzma approached me. "She needs something to bind with. String?"

Iris came out from behind the bar. "I've got register tape." She handed me the roll of paper.

Uzma scrunched up her face. "I suppose that will work."

"I'm going to need a little more direction."

Uzma rolled her eyes and held out her right hand to me.

"Wrap my arms and say the words: *I bind your secrets tight to mine. What I hold dear, wilt too be thine.* Got it?"

I nodded, knowing every emotion other than confidence. My hands shook as I wrapped the paper around Uzma's hand, the beginning of a mummy costume. I repeated the words, my hand resting on the end of the tape. My tattoos glowed and an oak leaf wrapped itself around my middle finger.

"That was cool," Uzma said, watching my skin. "Priyanka couldn't do that."

I shook out my hand, uncomfortable at the scrutiny.

Without further comment, Uzma nodded at us, then ducked out the door of Morgan's.

"You okay, sis?" Joaquin regarded me, concern tight in his jawline.

"Okay? All I have to do is find four crowns, identify an unknown yet likely godlike entity, and throw a huge party in less than a month. In Chicago, we'd call this a typical weekend —minus all of what I just said."

∽

On Sunday morning, I hauled Hollis's grimoire, his ledger, and a few books over to Morgan's. I'd fallen asleep deep into my search, tiny tabs of colored paper sticking out from between the pages and to my face. I'd wanted coffee and a breakfast I didn't have to make.

The bar was dead, and I had plenty of room to spread out. Next to our abandoned plates of eggs, Gaven unrolled a map of the world as I knew it. I wasn't certain the crowns were even in this realm, but Gaven seemed to think so. "If they were in the fae realms, they would have been discovered. The Gentry do not have the same powers here, so it's the perfect place to hide something you want to stay lost."

Iris peered over my shoulder. "But where do you look on a great big planet?"

I'd spent the greater part of the evening combing through Hollis's notes, checking for hints. I tapped Europe with my pencil. "Sent us postcards from all over the continent, especially in the months before he died. On his last visit, he brought my mom some perfume. She said it stank like bad decisions."

"Definitely French," Iris quipped.

"There's also a lot of quotes from Shakespeare and some sketches..." I trailed off. The texture of the paper underneath my fingers warmed. I paused, letting the connection settle. The vine along my inner wrist glowed when I traced Hollis's sketch of an armless sculpture of a woman.

"Neat trick," Gaven said.

"It's new," I said, unsure of what I saw myself. "Kinda handy, though."

"Paper is made of trees," Iris said. She picked up our empty plates. "And Hollis is dead, may the gods bless him."

I grimaced. "June says I may work with bones one day," I said, and shivered.

"What would Hollis have wanted with the crowns?"

"Maybe nothing," I said, neglecting for the thousandth time to explain what lay hidden in my shop.

Uzma slid into the booth next to me. "I have to agree, knowing him as I did. At least not for personal gain, but he wanted them managed." She tapped a finger on the page. "This is a containment spell, magic so that other magic cannot be used. And look at this page. It has the diamond of the Order and four sections. There are some notes here," she said, holding the paper closer to her face.

Iris returned. "Do we think Hollis knew anything useful?"

I nod. This was as close as I was comfortable getting to the truth. "He knew of their existence, and enough to focus his efforts."

Gaven pulled out his phone. "I've got notes in here from when I covered the shop for him. I can get more specific."

Ansel clomped down the stairs. When he saw the occupants of the first booth near the kitchen, he froze. I thought I saw a look of surprise, followed by a look of longing. This was replaced by a scowl. "I approved of none of this."

"We know," I said.

Ansel turned to me, and I shut my mouth. "If you find anything, you bring it to me, not to anyone else. You *owe* me."

Uzma looked at me, lifting her eyebrows as though to ask why I would tolerate this from anyone. I volleyed my irritation to Ansel. "Why do I owe you?"

"You're the reason I'm still here, remember?"

Great, another failure I'd have to share with Uzma. "I'm doing this to protect my shop, my friends. Not because I owe you or anyone else."

"Famous last words."

∾

When the time came, I was eager to travel through the weir. Like a skydiver, I was hooked.

A week had passed since we'd had the debrief over brunch. A perfectly mundane week with no sightings of the Fallen, no missing witches, and nothing from Ophelia. I saw her, once, riding past on her bicycle. She had one pant leg rolled up, a helmet strapped to her head. To anyone else, she was a stylish environmentalist, one of the many moving into Yavapai county for the year-round sunshine and dry air. She'd be on her way home from her job as a project manager, returning to her rescue mutt named Rocket and a girlfriend who worked in finance. Funny how much we assume about women in their middle decades. They can seem so harmless, their lives too mundane.

When the truth was anything but.

Friday morning had Christopher and I each puzzled over old texts, seeking advice.

"Might need to say no to this one," Christopher said. He consulted his computer screen before scribbling down some numbers on a pad of paper.

"What is it?"

Christopher had been adding events to our calendar, no more than two a month at first. His laptop depicted a lush garden, boughs of white flowers and ribbons draped around the celebration.

"Regency wedding," he said. "I don't know if I can get swans anywhere near this town. And they want grass but don't want to pay country club prices."

"What about the botanical gardens? Don't they have peacocks?"

Christopher sucked in a quick breath. "You're brilliant. I'm on it." His fingertips curled over the keyboard as he typed with newfound fury.

"Any luck?" Uzma dispensed with small talk from the moment she entered the shop.

I watched the moths flutter about on the breeze that blew in with her, adjusting to the shift in energy. "None. I've been through this book a dozen times, and nothing sticks out."

Given the very real limitations of traveling on my finances —even with the potential of skipping air travel—throwing darts at Europe and visiting everywhere didn't float as logical choices. "How about you—anything?"

Uzma flared her nostrils. "June is stubborn about sharing, but that's to be expected. She got miffed when I asked to see one of our old texts. It's a book from Priyanka's family. She said I needed the family's permission before I took anything. I'll keep working on her."

"How's Blythe?"

Uzma avoided my gaze. She reached out for one of Mariette's leaves, stroking the sleek, green surface. "Not good," she said. "Curled up in her bed, afraid to step out of the house."

"That has to be hard to watch."

"Not much I can do, though," Uzma said. "I've known her all my life, well enough to have learned that grief is complicated. There's no A to Z. It's a rollercoaster of reminders."

I thought of my losses, and the memories took hold. I closed my eyes, acknowledging the pain that was always just below the surface.

Christopher sat up straight, as though he noticed Uzma for the first time. "Oh, hey there. You wouldn't know how to turn a peacock into a swan, would you?"

"No," Uzma said. "But I could sure try."

Christopher beamed at the witch, then turned to me. "I like your new friend."

∼

Gaven stopped by after a shift at the bar. He had a special knock after dark, a one-two, three-four that let me know it was him at the back door. He held up a bag of fries and grinned. "How's the trip planning?"

Uzma was long gone, and Christopher had yet another date and I was left to my own devices. All I'd consumed was a mushy apple and a handful of nuts, so this offering was well received.

"It's going." I rummaged in the bag and pulled out a few of the golden sticks, dripping in a dark red sauce. I took a bite. "Ooh, a little spicy. I like it."

"Gouchang," Gaven said. "Kimchi, too."

"Thank you," I said, reaching into the bag to extract the container of fries. "This will be a solid distraction from my continual failures. I've narrowed things down to exactly nowhere, but I have identified at least a dozen places I'd love to visit someday when I win the lottery."

Hollis's ledger lay open on the counter, its edges ragged. I'd turned its pages again and again, in search of guidance, yet found a string of disconnected thoughts and drawings, interspersed with business notes. I abandoned my hunt to scarf the fries. Gaven pulled the book closer to himself, reading from the notes. "Only vaulting ambition, which o'erleaps itself and falls on th'other."

I paused my late night nosh. The words hung in the air, waiting for the connection. "Where is that from?"

"Macbeth," he said, tapping the page.

I examined the fry I held between my fingers. "The Red King..."

"Killed his cousin for the crown," Gaven said. "Not the finest of my countrymen, but not exactly out of order for the time."

On the page beneath the quote, Hollis had sketched the familiar compass, this time with only the top and righthand arrows in place. There was a circle with several triangles ringing its circumference between the two directional points. "Gaven, where was Macbeth born?"

"Round about the center of Scotland. Why?"

I smiled. "Am I wrong, or is that very spot northwest of here?" There was a flutter in my belly that spoke of hope.

"It is," Gaven said, holding my rapt attention. "But this is a quote from long after he was born, and in fact, foretells his death."

I bounced on my toes in anticipation. "Well then, my brilliant friend, where is the dead king buried?"

Gaven grinned. "In a darling abbey that houses more than one crown, I'd wager. I'll get my tartan."

Eighteen

"It's so...beautiful."

I stared at the shoreline at my feet, soft sand sinking beneath my shoes. A pastel rainbow of tiny pebbles spread out before me, wrapping the coast. I shivered in my thin rain jacket. I'd discarded the bulk of my winter gear when I left Chicago, saving only a few of my favorites. My wool peacoat, a down parka, and this bright blue wonder that did little to block the cold at the higher latitudes.

It had been months since I'd seen anything that counted as a body of water. I thought of Lake Michigan, its expanse stretching out like a gray field in front of the city, snow blowing up from its surface in the winter. A stark picture compared to the gentle undulations of the impossible blue ribboning outward from this island.

"It is," Gaven said, standing at my side. His hair blew in thick locks around his forehead. He'd donned a square-cut olive coat, the collar turned up, and dark jeans that disappeared into hiking boots. He could have faded into the scenery, a shepherd tending to a flock, combing the moors or tracing the lines of his heritage across the sea. Here on this island, a short crop of rock and grass, he was in his element. "Been a fair time since I was here."

"Doesn't seem…occupied." We'd taken a bus from the Portree weir, again greeting our small church, then a ferry from Oban over to the island with a collection of tourists. Those around us snapped away, capturing dozens of pictures they'd never view again if only to select the one to prove they'd been there, that they had traveled the world. When we'd disembarked from the ferry onto an island of three square miles, their voices quieted, eyes on the abbey.

"Might be a hundred people in the village," Gaven said. "Maybe a few more. All living on some of the oldest rocks in the country."

We shuffled forward, ducking around a couple consulting a map, a relic belying their ages. At a white-washed stand, Gaven bought us each a coffee and a biscuit. "I keep a bit of cash for my travels," he explained, handing me a steaming cup.

There was something about weir travel—weir walking, as Gaven called it—that left me famished. As though the distance took its toll despite the shortened time. I flipped open Hollis's notes to the page with our quote and the compass rose. The weight of error passed upon me, then, the coffee bitter on my tongue. I'd dragged us halfway around the world, risking who knows what of my life and limb, on a few scribblings of a possibly mad old man.

I rubbed a thumb over his words, missing my uncle. How like him to lay out a goose chase in cryptic messages and vague directions. Underneath the quote, he'd drawn a man in a crown, the image filled in with heavy, black ink.

We followed a group as they made the trek to the abbey, their tour guide's amplified voice guiding us toward the stone building. Her jacket bore the logo of a tour company, her hat pulled down tight over her short bob. She was wrapped in a great, purple scarf, fringe draped over her shoulders. In one hand was a staff with the Scottish flag at the top.

"Welcome to the Isle of Iona, one of the most spiritually significant places in Scotland! Iona has a long and fascinating history, and today we'll explore one of its most iconic landmarks—the Iona Abbey.

"The abbey was founded in 563 AD by St. Columba, an Irish monk who came here to spread Christianity. One of the most important things to remember is that the Abbey you see today isn't exactly the same as the one from St. Columba's time. The original monastery was more of a simple wooden structure. Over centuries, it was rebuilt and expanded in stone. Most of the current structure dates from the 12th century, when it was transformed into a Benedictine abbey. The abbey faced many challenges throughout its history—from Viking raids in the early Middle Ages to the dissolution of the monasteries in the 16th century. But it endured and was beautifully restored in the 20th century."

Gaven and I kept a few paces between ourselves and those at the back of the tour. The abbey loomed in front of us, stone crosses rising from the grassy surface in front of the building.

"This island is considered a sacred burial ground. Many Scottish kings, including Macbeth, are said to be buried here, along with Irish and even some Norwegian royalty. These ancient graves link the island not only to its religious past but also to its political history..."

At the entrance, we fanned off from the group. Our plans got us this far, but I was out of my element. On a small island where nearly every corner was exposed, its prime places crawling with tourists, we needed to strategize away from an audience.

Above, three crows cawed from their perch atop St. Martin's cross. Bedraggled, a few feathers sticking out of place, my constant companions watched us. Had they flown all this distance?

"Remind me of Odin's ravens," Gaven said, watching the trio. "But there are three of them. Do they ever let you pet them?"

"Not yet," I said. I racked up unexplained oddities like a traveling circus. One bird scratched under a wing with its beak. "So, where's Macbeth's grave?"

Gaven studied a posted sign. He tapped the brief map with his finger. "St. Oran's. Just over there." He pointed toward an expanse of flattened stones littering the graveyard.

We crossed to the cemetery outside the famous abbey. Named the Graveyard of Kings, there was little regal about the space unless you counted the tranquil environment and pristine grounds. The headstones were worn by time, little of their markings visible.

"Great," I said. "A mishmash of royalty."

Gaven looked around, waiting until a trio of silver-haired women left the site. "Well, you are our resident hedgerider. Time to put those skills to work, eh?"

I sighed, addressing the stones. Gaven was right. There was nothing to do but get my hands dirty.

An hour later and I'd felt up nearly every rock in the place. I'd never reached out for so many men in my life, only to feel the cold stones of my current reality. Not that the graves were empty. The quiet shift of energy mingled with the ancient earth. What I felt was long gone, drifted elsewhere, leaving little besides bones and dust.

"We could try a metal detector?"

I sighed, rocking back on my heels. I'd spent too much time on my aching knees. With help from Gaven, I stood and brushed off the front of my pants. They were water-stained and cold from the ground. "Don't have one on me. Guessing that would look suspicious, too."

"You're right," Gaven said, eyeing the grounds. "Even I have the sense to avoid such trespasses. Can you at least tell who is down there?"

"Well, no, not really." I admitted the limits of my abilities. "Might be because I'm not versed in this history...or it is a bag of bones at this point. Coffins disintegrate, as do remains. There's little left for me to find. Do you see that man?" I asked, staring over his shoulder.

"Where?"

"By that first little house, the one with the yellow door."

Gaven tented a hand over his eyes as though to scan for the incoming ferry. He turned toward the town. The shrouded figure, smoking a cigarette against the corner of a house, was in his view. "I see him. Doesn't look familiar."

"Saw him when he got off the boat. Kind of odd to stare at the comings and goings of tourists."

Gaven regarded the stones at our feet, the tourists streaming out of the abbey in search of their next stop. He inhaled through his nostrils and nodded slowly. One crow cawed from atop the cross. "In this country," he said, "when a situation appears hopeless, and more than a little odd, and you've already sought your peace at a church, there's only one thing left to do."

"What's that?"

"Go to a pub."

∼

In the dark room, its stone walls peppered with yellowing newspaper articles about residents who made it off the island and the scores of a favorite football team, we each sat with a pint in front of them, faces glum. I stared at the walls, my mind lost and forlorn.

"We tried," Gaven said. "It was a good hunch. Maybe

Hollis made a guess, that's all. I mean, if he knew where the crown was, why wouldn't he have taken it for himself?"

Indeed.

I sat up. "I didn't check the walls!"

"The walls?" Gaven sipped from the glass, a rim of foam lining his mouth.

"There could be a chink, a place where the crown was tucked inside." I couldn't explain the backstory of my hunch, not yet. "I should go back, feel the stones. If one is loose, the crown could be behind it. Hollis wouldn't have been able to dig up the place any more than we would have. If he hid the crown, he'd have to have it somewhere accessible."

I downed the rest of my beer. With a raised eyebrow, Gaven did the same. When we left the pub, headed back to the abbey, a familiar figure sat hunched over his own glass, face hidden by a hat pulled low over his profile.

Back at the abbey, a tingle ran through my nerves. Had the man been watching us? In a place this small, with so few strangers, it was possible there was little to do but keep tabs on tourists. But that explanation didn't sit with me.

"How is it?"

Gaven had stood back while I ran my hands along the walls, lichen and moss padding my touch, unbothered by the sightings of the cloaked man. He waited while I ran my hands over almost every stone twice, heartache filling the spaces where hope had been.

"Nothing. This has to be it, though. The quote spoke of Macbeth's ambition, the very thing that got him crowned."

"It was a good effort, EJ. Let's go back, report. Maybe the others will have some ideas. It'll be dark soon enough, and we've got to get back."

Dark. "Wait. Where are the Macduffs buried?"

"Fife," Gaven said. "Why?"

Nineteen

In the old ruins, my hands fluttered over the crumbling rock as though called by an ancient song. I'd all but run up the pathway toward the ruins on the hill, brickwork jutting out at odd angles, archways on the brink of collapse. Now, I tuned in to my growing association with the otherworld, seeking insight into what was hidden here. I'd made the amateur mistake on Iona, seeking remnants of an ancient king when I should have searched for those of my uncle. He would have heralded the man who took out the mad king. Some stories had long faded, others were fresh, still open wounds.

Gaven remained as the lookout below. When I'd told him where we needed to go, he didn't argue but smiled. "For someone new to all of this, you're sure ready for the next adventure, aren't you?"

Here we were, scrambling over the abandoned Macduff estate, twilight promising us little time in which to seek our outcomes, when I felt it. High on a precipice, my feet wedged in unintended footholds, belly scraping against stone, rain pouring down the collar of my jacket, I felt the tug of a familiar line. The ink along my skin glowed as I pawed at a pile of rock, a shimmer pressing back at my hand.

"I think it's warded," I called to Gaven.

"Fair to assume. You're a witch. It'll be no problem for you, right?"

Gaven had more confidence than I felt. I reached for the rubble once more, stretching my fingers wide over the ripple of energy. "Please, Hollis, it's me."

One crow cawed, and beneath my hand, the rocks shifted. I brushed some away and dropped others to the ground, praying Gaven was far enough away to avoid the downfall. I probed into a small nook, the press of metal finding purchase against my palm.

"Oona's stars," I whispered. "We did it!"

∽

Six pairs of eyes stared at the crown resting on a bar towel. It sparkled in the dim room, its emeralds capturing the street light and rocketing it around the room like sunlight through a forest.

"It's...stunning."

Iris had been the first person we'd found, not trusting ourselves to call anyone. The Apothecary was closed, Uzma long gone home to her apartment with Blythe, and Christopher slept when Gaven and I returned. We'd crept from the weir room, out the back door of my shop, and through the atrium to Morgan's. Behind us, the giant tree loomed, its branches casting creepy shapes on the walls. Iris, cleaning up after closing, ushered us into the darkened bar. The pin ball machines were off. Only the lamp at the bar was lit in the big room. Even the kitchen lights were dark, the machinery quiet for the night. Iris took one look at the wrapped bundle in my arms and darted for the stairs. Ansel called Joaquin, who'd invited Lotte. When all had assembled, I'd unwrapped our find and laid it on the clean cloth.

"Dunno," Joaquin said, cocking his head in that rakish way. "Looks like what they use in beauty pageants. So sparkly it looks fake, you know?"

Iris made a face at Joaquin. "How many beauty pageants have you entered?"

Joaquin crossed his arms. "I'll have you know I won Mr. Tiny Tot Tucson when I was a boy. That damn suit was a polyester nightmare. I can still feel the dig of that itchy collar into my neck." He ran a finger around his neckline, shrugging away from the fabric in response.

"Cute," Lotte said, smiling. When everyone looked at her, she blushed.

"When EJ pulled it from the castle wall, the thing was covered in dust." Gaven bent lower to observe the piece without touching it. As the one fae in our midst, I assumed he'd have been the most comfortable with the crown. Instead, he'd balked at holding it, let alone carrying it back on our journey. Instead, he stared at it like a repulsive insect. "Cleaned up, I think it's rather pretty."

"Let's put it on something dead," Joaquin said, ever practical. "See what happens."

Iris snapped. "Are you volunteering?"

Joaquin rolled his head back in mock irritation.

Ansel, who'd remained silent since he set eyes on the crown, its jeweled surface reflecting in his pupils, shifted his jaw from one side to the other. "I thought it would be...different. Imposing. This one is...brief."

"Brief?"

"Underwhelming."

"Most people wouldn't call a hunk of gold and jewels light," I said, bristling. Gaven and I had traveled across an ocean to find this treasure, and Ansel, without having touched it himself, was all but ready to dismiss it.

Iris interrupted our bickering. "Is it or is it not one of the Four Crowns?"

Gaven sucked in a deep breath. "Should be easy enough for me to test. Don't know why we didn't do it there."

"Maybe the growing dark and the cloaked man following us?"

Gaven poked out his lower lip. "Could be. Anyway, here we go." He held his hands over the crown, murmuring a few words in a language that would never fit my tongue. In the dark bar, the circle of gold glowed, its green gems sparkling as thought stars generating their own light. "It's legit," Gaven said. "Don't know which it is, but this is one of them."

"Easy now," Iris said, rushing to the windows to draw the shades past the sill. "That thing could be a demi-god beacon."

"Those don't exist," Lotte said, matter-of-fact. "They answer only to themselves. It's their downfall."

"Right," Iris said. "Still, it doesn't pay to advertise."

"We need to confirm which crown we have. Gaven, any chance you can feel that out?"

Gaven nodded. "I can get more specific with my questions. Look for images."

"Good."

"How will we store it until we can get the thing to Sharon?" Joaquin was all business, talking to Ansel.

"Been considering that," Ansel said. "Iron box—the Armory?"

"Makes sense to have weapons nearby."

I scoffed. "Wait a minute, what makes you the best keeper?" My protest was a weak one. It wasn't as though I had a better spot. My crown was a vulnerability, and I knew it.

"Because nothing gets past me," Ansel said.

A sultry voice joined the discussion. "Except me." Ophelia

appeared behind the bar. She wore a dark satin cape, the outside a deep navy, the color of the night sky. The inside was lined in black. It draped over her, covering every inch of her skin in the darkness. She reached across the bar and plucked up the crown. "Thanks," she said, and raced for the door.

Joaquin dove over the bar, missing the woman and crashing into the racks of glasses, sending them cascading to the floor.

Gaven flung his hand outward, slamming the back door shut as Ophelia opened it. She backed away and raced for the kitchen. Iris vaulted off a barstool and landed on Ophelia, clawing up her back to grab the crown. Ophelia flipped over, like a lion tossing a hyena, and ran for the front door. She grabbed a napkin holder as she ran, throwing the plastic brick at the glass. It didn't break, no doubt warded against infiltration. Ansel yelled for Gaven. "Guard the office."

Ophelia braced herself against the front door, her back to the glass. A neon sign spelling *Shut* glowed at her shoulder. "I should thank you, EJ," she said. "For making this easier. Never thought I'd be saying that." The woman's chest heaved as she considered the ring of people closing in on her precarious position.

"What are you going to do with it?" I asked. "Put it on and pretend you rule the world?"

Ophelia plastered on a smile and shook her head. "Much too dangerous. That would bring attention even I don't want."

Two shadows appeared on the other side of the door.

"That's Yanric and Grace," Joaquin said, "and I'm willing to bet they'll choose our side of this little entanglement."

"Then I shan't stay to be introduced." With a cheeky grin and a quick movement of her lips, Ophelia disappeared.

The table to my right shook, then toppled. There were stamping sounds atop the bar, then the back door flew open once more. Before Gaven could close it again, a woman's deep throated laughter rang through the atrium.

We bolted for the back door, tumbling down the stairs. The door to the Apothecary burst open, and Christopher stuck his head out. He balked at the sight of the six of us staring his way.

"What is going on?"

I didn't mince words. "I found the crown, but Ophelia stole it."

"What? How?"

"She was here," Joaquin said, neatly ignoring the fact that Christopher somehow knew about our plight. Those details could wait. "Then—poof—she was gone."

"Godsdamnit." I rehashed the last few minutes, seeking when we'd erred in our control over the situation. I smacked my hand to my forehead. "The ring!"

Iris pushed her way to me. "What ring?"

"Of course," Lotte said. "The ring. It makes the bearer invisible."

"The one she offered me that day Joaquin booted her from the shop."

Joaquin kicked at the ground. "Godsdamnit. We should have kept it for compensation."

"She offered it to me when she was desperate," I told Iris. "As a tithe. That's when she started hating my guts."

Ansel tore at his hair. "It was right here and now it's gone."

Iris looked at me. "Why was she so desperate? What would the crown have to do with any of it?"

"Oh," Lotte said, softly. "The poor, poor woman."

Twenty

We circled the bar, a bottle of single malt scotch between us. Iris had done the honors, pouring for everyone, Christopher included. He'd thrown on a gray hoodie and joined us.

Ansel glared at him, then me, in alternate forms of silent threat. Either he was saving questions when he'd reached his peak of irritation or he still debated how much I'd told my roommate.

Never one to linger in the sticky details, Christopher brushed off the death stare and savored his drink. "This is gorgeous," he said.

"Of course it is, it's an eighteen-year," Ansel said. He turned to address Lotte. "You will tell me why you, of all of us"—he raked his eyes among those gathered, then continued—"pity that thieving, conniving she-beast."

I raised an eyebrow at Christopher, who mirrored my expression. These conversations smacked of the most epic brawls we'd seen in the hundreds of weddings we'd worked. Someone, often after a little too much to drink, would speak a truth they'd longed to utter. The intended recipient, often deep in their own cups, would reel on the accuser, flinging accusations of their own, and it was off. Our boss told us to stay out of fights at all costs. The company's reputation relied on our professionalism and discretion—but that never meant we didn't like to watch.

"Ophelia is a descendent of the Bandorai," Lotte said, leveling a steady gaze at Ansel. She hadn't touched the liquid lubricant in the glass at her wrist. Instead, she turned in her seat to face the rest of us, her shoulder a cold signal to Ansel. "From an old family. She bears the Ring of Eluned, a treasure gifted from a knight to Angelica, a princess, when he proposed to her. He died, struck down in a battle he did not start, leaving his lover brokenhearted and alone. Angelica's tears became a lake of sorrows in which she drowned herself, desiring to give up her life rather than live with the grief. From EJ's description and what we just saw, Ophelia bears this very ring. When placed under the tongue, it makes the wearer invisible, as Angelica felt in her time of grieving."

I wanted to continue my grip of coldhearted disdain for Ophelia, but I felt the binds slipping, ever so slightly. "She was ready to give me something that powerful for the chance to sneak into the Otherworld—but why?"

Lotte swirled her glass, watching the liquid turn against the crystal. "For love," she said, and tossed back the contents.

Joaquin choked on something, gasping for air. Iris reached over to whack him on the back. His eyes watered as he regained his breath, but he wouldn't take his gaze off Lotte.

"How romantic," Christopher commented. "But I still don't follow." When the eyes of all the extranormals turned his way, he raised his hand. "Human, here. I need a lot of hand-holding."

Lotte gave him a kind smile. She reached out a manicured hand to give him a squeeze. "Young Ophelia fell hard for a refugee from Mali who loved heavy metal music. She met him in a bar along the Seine one night, and they were smitten. A week later, he'd moved in. Two months later, he was killed in the attack at the Bataclan."

"I remember that from the news," Iris said.

"Tragic," Ansel said. I shot him a look, but he focused on Lotte. "But why here, why now, and why *my* crown?"

I set my glass down, the sinking feeling in my gut spelling out the answer. My eyes met Lotte's. "She wants to see him again."

"Oh fuck," Joaquin said. He closed his eyes, then opened them again. "I'm such an ass." He turned to me, pointing two fingers at my chest. "You, too, newbie."

I held up my hands. "How was I supposed to know? She was some pushy woman ordering me around like a servant."

Ansel slammed his hand on the bar as his voice thundered through the room. "What are you talking about?"

I took a deep breath. This wasn't my fault, I knew that, but I had a new understanding of what had really been at play. Ophelia had been desperate, falling apart in grief. She'd brought me her most valuable asset, a symbol of her own pain, for a chance at hope. Out of fear, I'd thrown her out. Sure, she'd been a tyrant—but a brokenhearted one. A knot of guilt formed inside my heart as I told the story. "She must have thought I had the weir to Nether, not you. She wanted to go to him."

"After all this time," Lotte said, her eyes wistful.

Joaquin followed our thoughts. "So, somehow she found out about the crown—and will try that next?"

"Possible," Gaven said. "But even I don't know which crown she's got. What will she do if it's one of the others?"

I drained my glass and stood. "The same thing we will. Keep looking."

∼

To say the next day was tense was akin to describing a wedding for five hundred as a simple gathering of friends and family.

The night before, Ansel made us each swear to spend every waking minute on its recovery and sourcing another. Gaven had left after our meeting, disappearing into the weir to search. Joaquin insisted on escorting Lotte across the park, Iris tagging along toward her own apartment. Christopher and I, drooping with exhaustion, headed off to bed. He'd left the bedroom door open—in case.

The following morning, each of us were quieter than usual, tiptoeing around the shop. When I bumped into Christopher, knocking a tray of labeled mini bubble wands across the floor, I called us out.

"Say she was in here. It's not like we could stop her if she's invisible, right?"

Christopher grabbed fistfuls of the tiny tubes with his hands, shoving them back in their box. "Except that a tithe is not a choice, right?"

"True," I said, sitting back on my heels, bubble wands filling my hands. "It is possible to *make* a weir, though," I said.

Christopher's eyes went wide. "Does she know this?"

"Guessing not," I said, blinking. "It takes a special type of blade—or so I'm told. One made from the bones of the fae. Joaquin says such weapons are super rare and cursed." I thought of Little White, tucked upstairs alongside the crown. For a moment, a full confession lingered on my tongue. I swallowed it back down. "Anyway, without a blade, she's stuck with what exists, and that means we remain on alert."

It was now a game of cat and mouse with Ophelia. Her shop had gone dark, a *For Rent* sign in the window.

To their credit, Uzma and Blythe agreed to re-ward Ansel's and my block without explanation. Uzma probed when the request was first made, but after a steadying look from Blythe, she'd let it drop.

"So, no one can come in," Christopher said, watching Blythe through the window. The empathic witch ran her fingertips in trail along the building as she walked, murmuring words too quiet to hear. "How is this going to work again?"

"If we know them, we let them in. Those warded out will have targets on their backs."

"Right. This is the first time I'm thankful for your tight circle."

∽

At the first blast of pre-summer sunshine, my shop roasted. Heat from within the Apothecary, coupled with the rising temperature outside, made for an uncomfortable afternoon.

We'd closed up early after three hours passed without any sign of a customer. Even the square was quiet, folks retreating indoors to shade and air conditioning. Christopher poured himself a second gin and tonic, heavy on the ice, and retreated to the shadier part of the shop, out of sight of the clearstory windows.

"I'm getting caffeine." The effects of an iced mocha would last only so long, but they would help. "Want anything?"

"I'm good," Christopher said. "I'm headed over to Lotte's in a tick to order the candles. Rowdy's giving her all the beeswax she can handle, but I've got to think through a centerpiece count. I tell you what, that place will smell like honeyed heaven, if nothing else." We'd spent more than one night trying to picture what a hundred Fallen would do at such an event. Christopher and I agreed—and it was my job to tell Rowdy—that the minute any elixir came out, we were out of there, no refunds. "But when you get back, we need to go over the linens. You, my dearest, are losing your edge."

In the chaos of the second crown, I'd neglected my party planning duties. On top of missing the order, I was out of two of my flagship teas, a wildflower blend and a barrel-aged black that was a popular coffee replacement for some of my regular customers. If I was going to manage not one, but two successful businesses, I would have to fit hunting down mythical objects between managing my more tangible responsibilities.

Christopher was right. I'd built a career on anticipating chaos, carving order into the most unexpected of situations. When an ex-boyfriend showed up, threatening to take the microphone for a toast, I cut the power cord until the groomsmen could usher him out. The time a well-meaning future mother-in-law swapped sugar for salt in her patented cake recipe, I dashed to the nearest grocery store and sweet-talked the bakery into stacking readymade kid's birthday cakes into an impressive tower—the guests hardly noticed the rainbows of character icing between the layers. And when the bank of high-class portable toilets clogged at a ranch wedding thirty miles from the nearest town, I helped hitch up a hay wagon to cart people to a neighbor's house. If anyone could handle disappearing ancient treasures, creatures with unknown powers, and a business, it would be me. But Christopher was right, I was falling apart.

It was Ansel. I wanted to direct all my anger his way. I resented every rebuff, the judgment, and all the times he'd dismissed me as incompetent and dangerous, a loose cannon. But then I remembered he was once again chained to his own hell, all because of me. While this didn't excuse him treating me, a grown-ass woman with feelings and a backbone, like a complete idiot, it explained why he didn't believe the world would save him. Because it hadn't. Not yet, and possibly not ever.

To distract myself from the newest wave of guilt, I ran through my to-do list as I set off down Montezuma. In the square, a woman walked a half dozen dogs, their leashes threaded between her fingers. A couple flirted, the girl balancing as she walked along the top of a low wall, the boy beneath her, looking up into her smiling face. A dozen people gathered in front of a towering oak, practicing Qigong, their instructor guiding the group through their poses.

Second Shot had a new barista, a young woman who was all too happy to leave a note for her boss on my behalf. Grace must be on the hunt, I assumed, and figured I should hurry back to my own duties. Drink in hand, I pushed back into the sunshine.

At the light, I stopped, waiting for the crosswalk sign. When red changed to green, I followed the crowd to the other side. Midway across, a body sidled up behind me, a sharp blade pricking the skin of my back.

I yelped, and a harsh voice hissed, "Don't say a word."

Ophelia.

We kept walking, continuing my trek back to the Apothecary. Ophelia skirted the door to Morgan's, the wards pushing at her. At the Apothecary, there was a click in her mouth. She bared her teeth to reveal the ring.

"I know your boy toy will be back in moments, but this won't take long. Give me permission to enter or I'll make this painful, and no one will be the wiser as to how you ended up a slashed and bloody pile on the sidewalk."

I squeezed my eyes shut, but could summon no immediate means to circumvent her threat and stay alive. Under my breath I whispered the words Blythe taught me to allow entrance past the wards. There was a bitterness on my tongue, an ache in my gut.

The wards dropped, Ophelia ushered me inside and away from the windows. I kept quiet, both for personal safety and as I searched for an escape route. She shoved me down onto a stool, then dragged the blade along my side, pausing when she faced me, its point aimed at my chest.

"I have something you want," she said, a wicked grin on her lips.

"Correction," I said. "You have something Ansel wants. And he's not happy you took it."

Ophelia's smile faltered at the corners for a moment before she propped it back up. "No matter. Perhaps he'll trade." She glanced around the shop. "Too bad this place is light on anything of worth. Would have thought Hollis would be more of a collector."

"He was more into plants than money," I said. "Comes from being a green witch and all." This was my meager attempt to remind her I was related to the man, with powers of my own. Which, if any of them, would help me in this moment, I had yet to decide, but a threat couldn't hurt—however empty.

"Hmm," she said, eyeing my smaller shelf. "What's this?" She pointed to the dried mass of the resurrection plant that sat on my shelf. I would pull it out when kids came into the shop, loving their cheers when they saw its assumed magic.

I made an attempt at nonchalant. "An old thing. Haven't had the heart to throw it out."

Her eyebrow shot up. "Ah, let me help you with that." She aimed a finger at the plant, and it lit with a flame. Dry as it was, the whole thing was ashes in moments. A tiny gold dragon stood along the remains.

"My son gave that to me!"

"Oops," she said, widening her eyes in mock surprise. "Silly me, always using more oomph than is necessary. Funny how it feels when we lose the things we love. The people we love. Things we cherish can go up in smoke, just like that."

Ophelia snapped, and I flinched. I needed a new tactic. "Look. Lotte told us what happened to you, and I'm sorry. That's horrible and I can't imagine how you feel, but I had nothing to do with—"

"You're *sorry?*" Ophelia turned the knife in place. The fabric of my shirt twisted around the blade. Under my shirt, a trickle of blood snaked down my chest. "You've only begun to know the meaning of that word, Ember James, but I'll make sure it's one you say to me every day for the rest of your miserable, insignificant life."

And with a sick sneer, she lifted the blade, wiped it on my jeans, and left. I sat shaking on the stool, unwilling to move. Moments later, Christopher bustled in, his arms full of candles. When he saw my face, he hurried over. "Gods, what happened to you?"

His question gutted me. Tears spilled down my cheeks, and I released a huge sob that blew snot on my already bloodstained shirt. I looked down at the mess, at my once capable hands I counted on to fix any situation, and I fell apart.

Twenty-One

"I can't compete with this madness. Let Ansel deal with her." The minute I said the words, I knew they would never happen. "Or I guess that would have to be Joaquin, because I fucked that up, too." I buried my face in my hands, my sense of ability slipping by the minute. My breath quickened, and I swayed in place, the damning voices in my head pressing down on me, outlining every mistake I'd ever made in an endless chant. I squeezed my eyes shut, willing the world to stop spinning so I could step off for just a moment and get myself together. Instead, the weight of my failures pressed on my chest as a familiar panic pounded from within. "I can't do this, Topher. I'm supposed to fix things, not smash everything to pieces, ruining lives."

Christopher pulled me in, not giving a damn what I smeared on his designer tee. I clutched my filthy tissues in my hand as I curled into his embrace.

"I know that, Emma Jane. I've seen you kick absolute ass time and again. The real you is the most competent woman I've ever met. You are a firestorm of efficacy in a crisis, and no one manages them better than you. Hell, when that kid poured fondue chocolate in the coq au vin, you rebranded it as molé. Grossest stuff ever, but the guests called it exotic, and the kid's mom paid for the catering. And who corded off the area when the maintenance guy plowed into one of the swans? You called the local bird society and turned the whole thing into a rescue mission, complete with a newspaper photo op. The bride loved the attention—remember that fat tip?"

Memories. Nostalgia wrapped up in the stories we tell ourselves, the way we rewatch the movie of our lives. Reminders that life wasn't always such a complete dumpster fire of drama. You pick up, move on, and put the past behind you. "I gave all the money to the swan's owner. That poor bird."

"She's fine," Christopher said. "Probably chowing down on all the bugs—"

"Don't they eat plants?"

"Sure. All the plants she can eat. Popping out swan-lets or whatever they are."

"Cygnets."

"Yes, those. The point is, you make this happen. You think faster than anyone I know. When everything goes wrong, you are the first person to go after a solution. You come up with Band-Aids no one else ever could. No one flips a script faster than EJ Rookwood."

My chest lifted as I inhaled all the air I could fit into my butterflied lungs. "Thank you."

"You are right, though. About one thing, anyway."

I lifted my head. "What's that?"

"Letting Ansel and those guys go after her. That woman is unhinged, EJ, and she's playing on a whole new level. I don't want to see you try to match like that." He shrugged his arms for emphasis. "You're figuring things out. Starting behind all of them in what it means to have a whole other set of responsibilities on top of a normal, messy life. And selfishly, I need our business to work or I'm cooked, too. Fully admitting it. You need help on this one, darling."

I let my eyes roam over the shop. I remembered that first day when I opened the door into an inner jungle, vines everywhere, potting soil paving the floor. My uncle's pride and joy, neglected as he drove himself mad, searching for the relics that could balance the realms, make his home, his business, and everywhere around safe again. Prevent power hungry people like Ophelia from rolling into town and terrorizing people because of her own tragic luck. I'd spent the weeks since tidying up the place, chalking the neglect up to an old man with more chores than he had energy to do them. In fact, he'd spent all he had on an attempt to protect me and everyone else from destruction. That was too big a burden to bear alone. I had Christopher, Gaven, Lotte and Iris, Grace, Joaquin, and even Ansel, in a way. Hollis had been alone, overwhelmed, and a target.

Ophelia had a mission. I had to assume that the destruction of my life, from my business to my sense of safety, was its crux. It didn't matter that I hadn't known what happened to her lover. She didn't care that I hadn't meant to dismantle her plan to turn back the hands of time and find her love again. Never mind the fact that she had the wrong weir and that she wasn't fae, she would have given me her most valuable possession in order to walk.

And could I blame her? The answer, a quiet resounding no, popped up from within my chest. People die. Shitty things happen. But very human vulnerability sounded in everyone's heart. That, I could understand.

I nodded, then sniffed. "She'll never forgive me, and I get it. I'll call Joaquin."

Twenty-Two

Joaquin was easy. He'd breezed in, pigeon feathers dusting his hair.

"On the roof," he explained, as though we'd understand without question.

I glanced at Christopher. He perched on the stool next to me, ankles crossed in the casual stance of *You've got this.* I laid out my request.

"I'm on it," Joaquin said, a simple response, then left as fast as he'd arrived.

"That man is efficient," Christopher said. "And so, so good-looking. Did you see those pants? Painted on. Too bad he's not your type. The two of you would be unstoppable. Your babies would be president of everything."

I laughed, relief filling my belly. There was solace in having a request for help granted. "One down, one to go."

Unwilling to hedge my bets on the crew at Morgan's, I'd decided to consult Lotte, too. Unlike Joaquin, she arrived with enough provisions to camp out.

"I stopped at the market on my way," she said, handing one paper sack to Christopher and carrying the other to the counter. "Figured a little sustenance wouldn't hurt anyone." From within the bag, she withdrew a bottle of bubbles, a pink version I'd loved from our night at the winery. Next came a demi baguette, a couple of jars, and a container of dried apricots.

"I can smell all of Italy in this bag," Christopher said, his nose deep in the paper confines. "What magic have you brought us?"

"Some olives, prosciutto, a container of romesco. There's manchego and a soft cheese the woman talked me into. When I get strategic, I get hungry."

"A woman after my heart," Christopher said, and popped up from the stool, bag in hand. "Let me help."

"How about you get cleaned up," Lotte said, with a quick glance at my shirt. "We'll be waiting when you're done."

While my two friends went to work on a makeshift charcuterie plate, I headed for the spiral staircase near the back of the shop, one of my favorite architectural pieces in the whole place. The wrought iron steps twisted upward, broad at their base and narrowing as they approached the loft. At the top, I found my futon, duvet rumpled atop it in a heap. The pull to collapse into the comforting pile was real. Instead, I trudged into the tight bathroom.

I flipped on the light switch and grimaced at the face that greeted mine. Mascara streaks, smeared concealer, and a line of dried snot topped off with limp hair that clung to my tear-stained cheeks. The front of my shirt was a mess, a salmon-colored stain spreading outward from a ragged hole in the center. I stripped off the shirt and dropped it in the trash. Some damage isn't worth the effort to repair. My sandstone bra was no worse for the wear, so I moved on to my face.

With a squirt of cleanser and a gentle scrub, I removed the worst of the mess from my skin. I blotted the wound dry, taking care not to press too hard, and assessed the damage.

There was a small hole in my skin, slit-shaped and fresh. We'd covered puncture wounds with the kids in Patrick's scout troop, but stabbing hadn't been the focus. I followed the basic care with a swipe from a cotton ball dipped in alcohol. The liquid stung and I hissed. In the medicine cabinet, I fished out a bandage, a relic from Patrick's younger years. The outer wrapping revealed a camouflage colored strip printed with Brave Solider over the padded part. I daubed some antibiotic ointment on the wound, filling the pink gap. The bandage stuck, its message backward in the mirror.

"That would count as a nightclub outfit in Boys Town." Christopher popped up behind me, appraising my efforts. "Some rolled up denim and combat boots and there'd be no stopping you."

I pulled my hair into a ponytail with my hands. "Just the look I was going for, nineties punk."

He reached over to give my arm a squeeze. "Lotte and I are carrying the picnic out back. See you in a sec."

Out back meant the atrium. Steps from Ansel, the man who, by now, knew how weak I felt, how ready I was to give in. All I could do was wait for his answer. I dug out a button up blouse from the plastic tub that had served as a makeshift closet since my arrival and slipped my arms into the sleeves. Buttoning as I descended the stairs, I checked that the front door was locked, the Closed sign in place, and headed for the back door.

Christopher had dragged two of my still-unpacked moving boxes into the sunshine. The bottle and three flutes waited on one box. On the other waited an incredible spread. Above them, the magnificent tree held silent vigil, its handful of flower buds remaining chaste. My ever-present murder waited in the branches as though they, too, had received an invitation.

"Voila," Christopher said, gesturing to the plated food. "It was all Lotte. Well, I sliced the bread."

"And found the knives," Lotte added.

"Figured you wouldn't mind if we borrowed a little honey, too. Especially since you seem to have a thing going with the bee man."

"I do not have a thing with the 'bee man' as you call him. But thank you, this is magical."

They'd draped a baking sheet with tea towels and arranged a rainbow of goodness across the surface. Prosciutto swirls and cheese triangles kept the olives from rolling away and a trio of jam and mustard jars each held a knife for spreading. There was even a pile of sugar and spice-crusted pecans next to the bread, sliced on the bias.

Christopher patted the seat between him and Lotte. He spread a soft cheese on a slice of bread, drizzled honey on top, and added a sprinkle of my favorite garnish, Maldon salt. The first salty-sweet bite was divine, the crusty bread a perfect flavor vehicle.

Lotte poured the champagne and handed me a glass. Bubbles burst against my tongue. My world may hinge on the moment, but this was far from a bad way to occupy my time.

"You had a few droopy *Spathiphyllum wallisii*," Lotte said. "Gave them a bit of a drink."

I swallowed my bite. "Thank you," I said, taking another sip. "For the watering and all of this."

Lotte smiled. "Christopher said you needed a bit of a pick-me-up. It was my pleasure."

"He is rarely wrong, especially about me and what I need."

Christopher saluted me from his seat and reached for another snack.

"Want to talk about it?" Lotte popped a piece of cheese in her mouth, picked up her own glass, and tucked her feet up on the bench so her whole body was angled my way.

This was one thing I loved most about Lotte. She was an odd friend, disappearing for days and weeks on end, quiet when everyone else was loud, and mysterious about her own abilities, but what she said, what she did, and how she felt, were never anything short of genuine and focused. Maybe one day I'd know what kept her at a distance, mitigating risk, but for now I was just happy to have her here.

"It's this thing with Ophelia. More than the knife, which was a whole new level for me. It's that she's made no secret of surveilling me, waiting for a moment of weakness. I'm afraid to leave the shop, even in broad daylight. While she's out there"—I pointed toward the city at large—"I'm not safe anywhere. She's made it crystal clear that until she gets what she wants, my safety and sanity are the least of her concerns."

Lotte listened, her eyes on me. She accepted a stack of prosciutto and mustard from Christopher before responding. "What would make you feel safer?"

"Besides her being gone-gone?" I couldn't say dead. That wasn't something I was ready to do, no matter how much the idea played in the back of my mind. "If I felt in any way able to stop her. If I knew that the next time I came up against her, I would win."

Lotte chewed, thoughtful. "I'm told there are few weirs left, though there are more beyond these. There were rumors that the fae queen had sealed them all, but we know this to be false. How would the queen travel if all were closed? Still, there are far fewer. If Ophelia wants to get to Nether, Morgan's might be her only hope."

"Except she seems to think it's through the Apothecary," I said. "No clue why."

Christopher polished off a sophisticated finger sandwich of manchego, honey, and romesco sauce. He brushed the crumbs off his lap and reached for his glass. "Here I was, existing in my tiny townhouse life, and all the while, this madness is taking place all around. More chaos than a hundred weddings."

"We've got a little more than the average town, I think," Lotte said, selecting another olive.

"I've heard about all the vortices and whatnot. The healing water and the red rocks. But isn't that east of here?"

"A ruse," Lotte said. "Or a smart PR move—however you want to look at it. If we tell tourists where to look for the paranormal, they don't look here. Not that most know what they're looking at when it's right in front of their faces. Truly, it's a win-win situation."

Christopher kicked his heels up on the low retaining wall. He leaned back, glass to his lips. "Checking Sedona off my list..."

Lotte laughed. "It's still worth going, but I'd be surprised if anyone has some sort of metaphysical experience while there. I mean, I suppose it's possible. But I think it's important to remember why things can feel like chaos. So many think existence is this ordered place, but..." She trailed off, growing quiet. "I think what I'm trying to say is that this is a collective experience. We need everyone here. Each playing a part for a better good. Even you," she said, turning to me. "Especially you. We can't afford to lose anyone who wants to help."

"She's right," Christopher said. "You made your life smaller, again and again, so others could have their big days. I watched you give and give, which is noble and all, but when does EJ get to take center stage?"

"Is this a coded message to tell me you want me to get married again?"

Christopher frowned. "While I would look amazing as your Maid of Honor, that is beside the point. When are you going to fight back for your piece of all this? If you give up and give in, then we're all stuck in here with him, waiting for future freedom that may never come."

"If Ophelia keeps the crown, if she places it on her head, she becomes a ruler. Of what, we don't know," Lotte said.

"Dangerous," Christopher quipped.

"If she loses it, or if it's stolen, you could be stuck in this cycle all over again, hunting down an opponent before they get to you."

"Double dangerous." Christopher handed me a slice of bread. A viscous aubergine jam spread thickly across the pillowy softness. "If ever I was to learn the meaning of being between a rock and a hard place, this is it."

The back door of Morgan's swung open, startling the three of us. I dropped the slice on the stones at our feet. One crow hopped down from the branch, snatched the bread, and flew to a higher branch with its snack. Joaquin strolled our way, an imperceptible expression on his face.

"Boss says no," Joaquin said when within earshot, and my face fell. Before I could beg him to ask Ansel to reconsider, somehow upping my offer without completely groveling, he continued. "Says he'll do it for free. The Apothecary may not be under his control, but Ansel's not about to let anyone threaten Whiskey Row. Not even an ex."

Lotte looked at me, her eyes round. "What did you offer him?"

I didn't answer. Her question was background static to the word he'd said which now reverberated between my eardrums.

Twenty-Three

"The weir."

"But you can't!" Lotte turned her heat to Joaquin. Her voice lowered. "How could you even take him that offer?"

"She called me!" Joaquin protested. "It's my literal job to act as a go-between for that man. This isn't a secret. I didn't force her or anything!"

Lotte stood to square off with Joaquin. A head shorter than the mercenary, she stared at him with a ferocity palpable to all of us. "Did you even try to talk her out of it?"

"Ex?" The word slipped out as a question, as though I was without definition.

Joaquin looked from me to Lotte and back, as though deciding which question could have a more imminent effect on his personal safety. He held up both hands in surrender, like a captain on a sinking ship in want of a white flag. "I'm just the messenger," he said, in a nod to both inquiries. "People don't hire me to analyze decisions, past, present, or future. They hire me to deliver."

Christopher held up his glass to Joaquin in acknowledgement. "Amen. That's how I felt at the Deluca nuptials when the bride wanted to get married at a bowling alley. No one could hear the ceremony, and she lost her ring in the ball return. I warned her, then let it go."

"Did they find the ring?" Lotte asked.

"They had to take apart the machine. Paid the place a hefty fee to have it done," Christopher said. He turned to Joaquin. "So, what *is* he going to do about Ophelia?"

"Unclear," Joaquin said. "My first job is to confirm she still has the crown, then to see if I can find out what she wants with it—or for it."

Lotte flopped back on the bench with a sigh. After a moment, she leaned forward to make another stack of goodies atop a bread slice and handed this to Joaquin.

Joaquin's face lit up. "For me?"

"For doing your job. But if EJ gives you any more harebrained offers for giving her life away to that man, they should all go through me first. Got it?"

Joaquin dipped his chin in agreement, then Lotte looked at me. I nodded, too, however reluctant to give up on my single biggest bargaining chip.

"Then we're agreed," Lotte said, the expert negotiator.

"Ansel and I are putting all we have into finding her and the crown. All you have to do is sit tight and stay out of the spotlight. His name goes far in our world."

Joaquin said *our* world. Had he meant the world with me in it, joined up with all of them, or their world where I was constantly treated as a liability and an outsider?

"Good," Christopher said, putting both hands on his knees. "You've got some protection on deck."

"Cheer up, EJ," Joaquin added. "I've yet to let that man down, and I don't intend to start."

"But what about the event?" I asked. I'd wanted to ask about Ophelia and Ansel, to get details on Joaquin's admission that they'd once been a couple, but couldn't spit out the question.

"What event?"

Christopher grimaced, then reached for the bottle to refill his glass. "Oh, you know. Over a hundred people on Rowdy's farm with food, booze, and a live band. Did we mention the guest list is mostly the Fallen?"

Joaquin's jaw dropped, and he closed his eyes to exhale a controlled breath. "Guess I'm now busy that night. Better be a damn good party."

⁓

The next few weeks proved a whirlwind of party planning. Christopher and I spent every waking minute working. If we weren't working in the shop, we talked about our upcoming events. Worry about Ophelia took a back seat, yet my fear continued to undermine my thoughts, cropping up at random moments to shake me from any sense of accomplishment to remind me I was, in fact, a prisoner in my own life.

Christopher and Lotte did their best to distract me with the tiniest details: size of favor, the quantity of tiers on a cake, and the time allotted for speeches at a bar mitzvah. With Ophelia missing in action, our client list grew in a slow and steady march that painted the months ahead with possibility and a hint of hope. Still, the party occupied the bulk of our time.

"She's wearing white," Christopher said. He handed me another spool of golden grosgrain ribbon.

Lotte crossed her arms, resting slim fingers on her bare skin. She wore a buff-colored jumpsuit and gold gladiator-style sandals that wrapped to her knee. "And what is wrong with that?"

"Not a single thing," Christopher insisted, handing her

some ribbon and a handful of lavender stems. "Painting the picture for you as she wants her bridesmaids to wear rainbow sheaths."

Lotte cocked her chin. "Striped?"

Christopher sketched a fast silhouette on his notebook. "As in, one will wear red, one orange, one yellow…"

"Oh gods," Lotte said, making a face. "How many are there?"

"Three on each side. The groomsmen are continuing the color war."

"Tell her the best part," I said, enjoying their casual banter as my hands wove the ribbon between the folded-over stems, encasing the flower buds within. We planned to use the lavender wands at each place-setting, an elegant nod to the setting and the season. Rowdy requested a gilded event but let us select the secondary colors. We would highlight purples and natural greens so as not to veer on the side of Versailles-level decor, yet stick to the requested theme.

Christopher leaned closer to the both of us, his upper lip curling back. "He's wearing brown."

"What?" Lotte scrunched up her face in horror. "You're kidding."

"Truth," Christopher said, holding up several fingers in a scout's salute. "Teddy bear brown."

"This can't be allowed! Just think of the pictures."

I laughed. "That's what I said. Christopher is meeting with the groom on Monday. I told him to suggest a dove gray suit and pray for the best."

"That's two hundred," Christopher said as I added my last wand to the stack. "Finished four days early."

"Are we really ahead?" Our whiteboard to-do list leaned against the counter, too many items filling in the space. We'd crossed out some big ones, including sourcing a kitchen, the last of the decorations, solidifying the menu, and creating a schedule. Rowdy didn't want staff, instead insisting that his own workers would take care of everything. All we had to do was delivery and setup. While a part of me wanted to stay and watch whatever would enfold, my sense of survival told me to count my blessings.

Christopher carried the basket of wands toward the workroom. "Positive thinking, darling."

"Candles will be ready tomorrow," Lotte said.

"See?" Christopher returned from the back and picked up the marker. "Crossing off candles."

∽

Sunday arrived sunny and hot, a bright and promising May Eve. As we packed up our rented van with the decorations, catering trays, and linens, I continued to glance over my shoulder. Ophelia had remained unseen, despite Joaquin's best efforts. Neither he nor any of his crew found a trace of her. While we knew she hadn't entered the weirs, she could be in any infinite number of other places, hiding out until her next opportunity to wield the power she'd stolen. Wherever she was, I couldn't let go of the sensation that she had me in her sights.

I'd avoided Morgan's, too ashamed to face Ansel after my rejected offer, aware of my position as once again in his debt. When Iris popped by to bring me my to-go order of fries, I shrugged off her check-in, chalking up my distance to the impending event.

Gaven remained missing in action. After our jaunt through the weir and the subsequent blowback of having the crown stolen, he'd vowed to hunt down the remaining leads on the crowns, not resting until he made a discovery. There'd been no word—yet.

Uzma continued to pop into the store. Her presence was a

balm I didn't know I needed. We paid her, of course, but what she offered couldn't be backed with some minimum wage salary. She got to learn about plants from me and Lotte—well, mostly Lotte—and I had a competent witch renewing wards, teaching me about the coven, and screening the Gentry who came to use the weir.

That afternoon, she carried an unusual tithe back to me. With little ceremony, she plunked the item into my hand.

"A...bean?" I peered at the item in my hand. The length of a tube of lip balm, the pasty pod rocked in my hand like a canoe on land.

Uzma shrugged. "The guy said you'd know what to do with it. Want me to put it with the others?"

I held the bean up to the sunlight. Within the shell, the shadows of several oblong shapes rested. I slid it into my pocket. "I'll show it to Lotte. She's a walking plant encyclopedia. If anyone will know what it is, it's her."

"Got everything?" Uzma stood with her hands in the back pockets of her pants.

"Think so," I said, and shut the back doors of the van. "You good to watch the shop?"

"Blythe is coming over to hang out," Uzma said. "She's obsessed with this British drama in which there's a murder by the sea and everyone's a suspect. We're going to binge watch a couple of episodes until I can't take any more of their gray skies."

I held the door for her as we entered the Apothecary. The sunbeams scattered across the shop, the very leaves reaching for the windows. The air verged on uncomfortable, the temperature ratcheting up with the seasonal changes.

Christopher stood in the center of the shop. He held the whiteboard anchored to his midsection. He scanned our list once more.

"We've gone over this a dozen times. Everything is ready.

All we have to do is drop it off. We are hours away from relative freedom."

"What is it about these kinds of events? I count down the minutes until they are over as I'm too stressed to think, but then the minute I'm free, I miss the comfort of the whole thing."

"Might need to get that checked out," Uzma said.

"Ha ha," Christopher replied with a wink.

In the weeks of relying on Uzma, her sharp exterior had softened somewhat. She made it clear her alliance was first with Blythe, then the coven, and therefore June, but she'd become a comforting presence. "Do your thing. Tell me everything when you get back."

~

With the afternoon fading into the start of a beautiful sunset, we took to the winding highway, Christopher behind the wheel. Joaquin followed on his bike. Rowdy gave us a specific time slot to arrive, set up, and leave prior to the start of the party—and we intended to deliver. We debated what details from this party would go in our client book. Christopher and I agreed that the money alone made the adventure worth the risk. Rowdy paid us well, and we intended to earn it.

At the gate, one of the Fallen greeted our van. Joaquin peeled off before the entry, planning to seek a vantage point from somewhere on the periphery, tucking his bike somewhere it wouldn't be discovered while he kept an eye on the two of us. Christopher had yet to see Joaquin's other form, but I'd told him about the shifter's transformation, and my best friend was more than willing to trust me that Joaquin could follow our scent.

We wound our way past the first fields and back toward

the barracks. Our guide signaled for Christopher to park near the back.

The space was transformed, evidence of countless hours of preparation clear in the scene before us. The lounge area outside one of the barracks was clear of recreation equipment, the couches swapped for bar-height tables and one corner rigged with instruments, microphones and amplifiers, a sign of musical entertainment yet to arrive. Beyond the covered area were round dinner tables ringed with chairs

The other barn had its large doors open. Our guide waved us inside, not stopping to wait for us to follow.

Christopher leaned in close to whisper. "You weren't kidding about this place. Or them."

I gave a quick nod. I'd debriefed him on my visit, of course, but also of what we knew of the Fallen. Former members of the Order, the royal courts of Elysium, they'd been ejected from their home, cast out into the human realm to survive or perish on their own accord. Most tried to escape to Otherworld, an asylum in which they could live forever, however diminished, yet few made it. Travel required access to a weir, something those like me and Ansel fought hard to prevent. The Fallen forced to remain among the humans relied on the fae elixir to sustain their lives and to forget the loss of their past. The problem with the substance was that its sole source was from the fae, and most weren't willing to give of themselves to their forsaken brethren. I'd warned Christopher that if we saw any dealing in elixir, also known as the Angel's Share, we were out of there.

But I doubted anything would happen, at least not from Rowdy's crew. While the Fallen I'd encountered in town were brutes, drugging humans, attacking me and my friends, and desperate to do anything to get themselves through a weir, Rowdy's workers were calm, docile, and almost mechanical in their movement and communication. Unlike the day I'd visited, there were no workers in the fields. Lights on in the barracks signaled occupation within.

Our guide introduced himself as Jake but said little else other than to point out our work area and the sign preventing those without permission from entering the back half of the facility. Inside, the cavernous building was cordoned off, the front half providing an ample kitchen and work space for setting up. Industrial kitchen equipment gleamed in the overhead lights.

"Seven o'clock," he said to us, before leaving Christopher and me to our work.

At half-past six, we had set the drink station, assembled bouquets of flowers for every table, and set the food out on its designated platters. At several central tables, we'd assembled hibachi-style grills with everything from vegetables to meats and several sauces. I'd crafted two signature cocktails for the bar area and posted printed directions for the bartenders who'd yet to make themselves known. One was a tropical-style drink, rum-based and complete with a flaming sugar cube in a lime wedge boat. This drink was a solid yellow, its color stemming from a healthy portion of pineapple juice. The other was a smokey old-fashioned, its base a rich honeyed bourbon, giving the drink a more umber shade of gold. The bartenders would use miniature blow torches and wood chips to create the desired effect. We'd also included several jugs of an iced tea I'd brewed for the event, chamomile and calendula with a hint of turmeric, and lemonade. Rowdy wanted a golden-themed and fire-based gathering—Christopher and I did our best to deliver.

"Not sure why we have all of this if they don't eat," Christopher said, wiping the edge of a silver tray with a bar towel.

"Shh," I hissed. "We don't want to insult our hosts."

Christopher moved on to the next tray. "I'm just saying, if I didn't eat food, I wouldn't bother putting it out."

"They eat," I said, second-guessing the words the moment they left my mouth. "I think they do. I've definitely seen them drink." I flashed back to Plush, Bryce's bar that had welcomed the Fallen and anyone foolish enough to seek their company while they were high on elixir. He'd pedaled the elixir, keeping the Fallen indebted to him at their own expense, not to mention the other casualties of his business.

"It's Rowdy's money," Christopher quipped. "Let's set these out, do a last check, and then get out of here. My guy is coming back into town this weekend, and I want to surprise him with a little...you know."

I lifted both brows. "Sounds like it's getting serious between you two." Christopher had remained uncharacteristically quiet about his man friend. I'd been curious but respectful, not wanting to ruin a good thing with too much analysis.

Christopher gave a little shrug. "He does this thing where...well, it's like he knows me from the inside out already. Like he can read my mind."

I smiled at my friend. He'd dated plenty in our years together, but this was the first time I'd seen him crushing hard, and it was adorable. "Then I'm sure he'll love the surprise. Let's get someone to verify we've done what we came to do and get out of here."

We hefted the last of the food trays and carried them out to the event space. The party lights, extended via poles out over the dining tables, glowed. Near the closest field, there was a circular clearing. Within a circle of stones stood a massive ram, its shape formed from many sticks woven together. It faced west, as though to watch the dipping of the brilliant ball of bar below the horizon.

"There," I said, pleased with the display. I'd snapped a few pictures, too, when the lighting was great. Who knows if we'd need them, but I didn't want to miss the chance. "Now, where can we find the man in charge?"

Six o'clock, and there was no sign of Jake. My conscience said to leave, to call Rowdy on our exit and let him know we'd fulfilled our end of the contract and to be in touch. Another part of me wanted confirmation the job was done.

"Shit, we forgot the banner," Christopher said, eyeing the small bandstand. The sign remained rolled into the depths of the van.

As though operating on alert, Rowdy's workers streamed out of the barracks, moving toward our set up. In an unusual display, all wore black from head to toe, save a golden face mask. They surrounded the tables, buzzing over what they saw. A pair of the Fallen manned the bar, and a queue formed in front. Several others stepped onto the stage and tuned their instruments.

"We need to get going," I said, fear fighting for control over my voice.

"I'll get it. Just a sec."

Christopher hurried off to the van. I ducked into the staging area to check for anything we'd missed and make one last attempt to find Jake.

The room was empty. I stuffed our reusable grocery sacks under one arm, tossed a chunk of raw potato in the trash, and moved toward the exit. I was almost out the door when the voices from the other side of the wall stopped me in my tracks.

"I've come with an offer you're unlikely to see again in your lifetime, no matter how long that may be. I've got exactly what you've been looking for."

Ophelia's voice, cold and clear, shook at the end, as though failing to convince herself of her resolve.

Fuck.

"Oh, I doubt that," Rowdy said. "That you, a *bandorai*, could tempt me is laughable at best."

This wasn't the Rowdy I knew, his words and very being a honeyed existence meant to sooth and sweeten. He spoke with dismissive authority, someone uninterested in the inconvenience brought before him. I didn't want to meet this Rowdy. With a glance back, I tiptoed toward the doorway, ready to sprint for the van. Banner be damned, we could take that hit on the invoice.

Ophelia changed her strategy. "I know who's coming. Your *special* guest. Perhaps I'll offer it to him, instead."

I was almost outside, the fresh air of a late spring evening dusting my cheeks, when I collided with a tall man on his way in.

"Whoa there," he said, catching my shoulders in his hands.

"Excuse me...er...um. I was just leaving, so sorry." I glanced up at the man, painting the most apologetic expression I could muster on my face. His irises were a pale gray, his eyes probing my face as his fingers squeezed the sides of my arms.

"No need to go." He slid an arm around my shoulder. "I've traveled a long way to get here, and you smell divine," he said, his nose to my hair. "Stay a while. My brother won't mind."

I forced back a shudder at the sensation of his nose in my hair. *Brother?* "I couldn't, really. We're just the caterers and we—"

"Neil?" Christopher stood at the edge of the tables, his eyes on the man with his arm around me. Behind Christopher, a dark shape darted through the tall grasses, low and sleek.

The man—Neil—blinked once, then again, before responding. "Chris. What a surprise."

"What..." Christopher struggled, his lower lip quivering. "What are you doing here?"

The man called Neil, whose name was probably anything but, plastered on a grin. "Why, I'm the guest of honor. And as such, I think you and your colleague here"—

he wrapped the arm around my neck a little tighter—"should stay."

There was movement behind us. "Brother." Rowdy's voice was dark and foreboding. Neil turned in place, forcing me to follow his lead. "So glad you could join us. Had you alerted me to your arrival, I would have afforded you a proper welcome."

"I much prefer surprises, as you know. It's why you set all this up, is it not?" Behind Rowdy, Ophelia fought the hold of Jake and another one of the Fallen, each with their hands gripped on her arms. She was gagged. Her eyes were wild as she appeared to mutter incoherently to herself. "Who is this?"

"No one of consequence." Rowdy's flippant tone was a mismatch to the warning look he gave me. "I'll send the staff on their way so we can begin the festivities."

"Thank you," I said, ducking out from under Neil's arm. "Enjoy the party." I grabbed Christopher's arm, dragging him toward the van. He continued to stare, mute, at Neil, who waggled a few fingers in Christopher's direction.

A great cry went up. Circling the ram, its shape stark against the growing twilight, several of the Fallen held lit torches to the magnificent beast. The wicker sculpture burst into flame as though it were a forest made of matches. Within moments, it was engulfed in fire. At the van, I blinked at the blaze, lost in the burning light, before shoving Christopher inside and sliding the door shut.

At that moment, Ophelia spat out her gag. "I've got the crown," she shouted, heaving. I froze, the driver's side door open, not wanting to miss a word. "I'll tell you where it is if you—"

There was a wet smack as Jake slapped a hand over her mouth. But it was too late. Neil turned from the fire, his own pupils reflecting the blaze. "What did you say?"

"Mmmumph," Ophelia mumbled over Jake's fingers.

Neil flicked his wrist toward Jake as though swatting a fly. His target crumpled to the ground.

Ophelia, freed, ran for Neil. "All I ask in return is—"

"Stop!" Rowdy faced Neil, his skin bright like glowing embers. "This woman is mine, as is her property."

"Bullshit," Ophelia countered. Her proximity to Neil amplified her bravery. "I'll give the thing to whichever one of you will get me what I want." She spotted me, frozen by the scene, and broke out into a smile. "There's a bonus if you'll take care of a little problem on the side."

But Rowdy didn't spare her a glance. He faced his brother with an unwavering display of strength. Behind him, Fallen, tired of their burning effigy, returned their interest to the party at hand. Several made their way to the growing conflict, curious. "You have no rule here, Tethra. This is my domain."

"Really now." Neil/Tethra flapped his hand at Rowdy. "There you go, ever the brutish one. Here we could have celebrated this *find*"—he grabbed hold of Ophelia. To him, she was a rag doll, a plaything for powerful beings—"together. But oh, no. You wanted to keep it to yourself. After all we've been through." Tethra tutted at Rowdy. "Perhaps it is indeed time for a *rebalancing*."

"The only thing that needs rebalancing, *brother*, is your tenuous grip on how things work in this realm." The tips of Rowdy's fingers sparked, as though he embodied the sun itself. Heat radiated off him, his clothes burning off in blackened rags.

"Ever the show off," Tethra said. "I see some things never change. But perhaps you're right." Tethra clutched Ophelia tight to his side, his words icicles in the night air. "I should strengthen that hold."

Rowdy started forward, a golden heat in his wake. Several Fallen attempted to rush Tethra from the side, but it was too late. He opened his mouth, and a wall of water flooded the night.

Twenty-Four

I hit the gas. The van skidded outward as my shorter body slid forward in the seat. With a tsunami headed our way, I hadn't stopped to adjust the seat from my taller best friend's reach.

For his part, Christopher clung to one of the handles in the back, his eyes outside. The thunk of his head against the window was audible. "Ow," he yelped, when I took a bend in the road faster than his reflexes could match.

"Hang on," I said, fingers gripping the steering wheel. My hands shook, but my determination drove me forward. I backed down the gravel road, rocks flying out from beneath the tires. Shadows danced through the field at my side, a dangerous distraction. I kept my eyes forward, gritting my teeth.

At the gate, one of the Fallen lounged, his lot to guard the perimeter while the others partied. When my headlights striped his reclined pose, he was up like a shot. He dove in front of the gate, waving his arms.

"Stop!" Christopher cried. "You'll hit him!!"

But I didn't stop. In another world, a different EJ would

have slowed. Maybe she would have acted as though nothing was wrong, pulled over to request he open the gate, ignoring the paranormal display of power happening across the fields and opting for the innocent approach. This EJ barreled toward the gate.

At the last second, our bouncer dove for the bushes. The van popped the gate on its hinge; metal falling flat in the dust. The van rumbled over the former barrier and my teeth clattered in my head. As I spun onto the road, a motorcycle buzzed along my side, the familiar shape of a black-clad rider astride the bike. I followed him, the taillights blurring as I fought back tears long enough to put serious distance between us and whatever we'd left behind. There was a roaring in my ears, and my head pounded, adrenaline flooding my body.

Minutes later, I squealed into a parking spot along Goodwin, heart thumping in my chest. Joaquin roared past us and up the alley. Christopher and I followed on foot. He ditched the bike in the atrium and held open the door to Morgan's.

"What about Uzma?" I glanced at the back door to the Apothecary.

"Blythe is there," Iris said, ushering us inside. "They picked up food an hour ago. I'll call them, tell them to sit tight, then you all need to explain this incoming train wreck. Boss!" Iris hollered up the stairs.

"I tried calling him," Joaquin said. He crossed behind the bar. "He didn't answer." From the shelving below, he withdrew something with a long barrel, the steel glinting in the bar light. He reached below once more to extract two daggers. He kept one and handed the other to Iris.

I scanned the bar—empty. On a Saturday night, the place should be bursting.

Iris followed my gaze. "Told them we had a downed refrigeration system," she said. She stuck the blade in the band of her cutoffs and headed for the stairs. "Ansel went down to the storage room. I'll get him."

Christopher had collapsed in a booth, his long legs hanging out over the vinyl bench seat.

"You okay?" I hadn't said anything since we left, though I'd been dying to ask him about Neil.

"Okay?" Christopher sat up. "No, I am everything short of okay. The man I've been dating is some kind of water demigod freak. I let him—" Christopher put a hand over his open mouth and shuddered.

"Hey," I said, sliding into the booth and wrapping my arms around his shoulders. "You didn't know. How could you?"

"But don't you see?" He turned his teary face my way. "Neil—or Tethra, or whoever he is—could have used me to get to you. Or the weir. Or anything else. I'm just a human. A plain-ass gay man from South Bend. I can't tell when someone is some kind of evil. I'm a walking, talking liability to you all."

"Stop it right now. I will not let you count yourself as anything other than my amazing best friend."

"Make up later," Joaquin said. "Yanric said company is on the—"

The back door to Morgan's burst open, a wave of water rushing up to our ankles. Ophelia stumbled through the door, catching herself on the stair railing, her top and jeans soaked through. Her hair hung in damp ringlets, dripping. Neil pushed in behind her. "Get it, and be quite quick."

Shaking, Ophelia sloshed across the bar, headed our way. She avoided my gaze as she stooped to reach under the billiard tables. With both hands, she wrenched something out from under the table. Its black wrapping slipped, revealing a cluster of emeralds. She'd hidden the crown in the most obvious and among the safest of places—somewhere no one thought to look.

"Ah, the *staff*," Tethra said, looking at me, a smile spreading across his face. "My brother is forever hiding his toys from me. And my Christopher," he said, voice dripping with a saccharine sweetness. "I will miss our afternoons together."

"Fuck that," Iris said. She'd descended the stairs, splashing down into the pooling water. With a stamp of her boot, the liquid froze outward in a great sheet of ice. Tethra spun to address the sprite of a woman, ice cracking around his feet. Iris paled in a flash of reverence, then squared off with him, hands twitching at her sides.

The man from the party, a cocky guest who got far too handsy and destroyed my month's worth of work and possibly Rowdy's entire farm with a single yawn, had transformed. He was dry, as though his skin were a repellant, but bigger, too. His features, too, had altered. The stretch of his earlobe connected to his neck, the space between his fingers webbed together, and there was a growing protrusion that parted the hair on the back of his head.

"Ooh, someone new," Tethra said. "And she's got her own talents. No wonder my brother built up his little kingdom here. There are so many of the gifted from which to choose."

Ansel pushed his way into the bar through the kitchen doors. He stomped onto the ice, bringing up a swirl of flakes in his wake. "This has never been Rowdy's kingdom."

"As I live and breathe, if it isn't one of the guardians. Then I must be close." Tethra shook his feet free from the chunks of ice clinging to his ankles and approached Ansel.

Iris aimed the bar hose at Tethra's approach, flicking off shards of ice from the stream. They shot out like throwing knives, aimed for Tethra's side.

With one hand, Tethra blocked the onslaught. With a flick of his wrist, the water in the stream exploded in a burst, ripping through the hosing and knocking Iris into the wooden bar with a sickening thud. She collapsed against the surface, sliding to the floor.

"Tell me, big boy," Tethra continued as he stalked toward Ansel, stepping over Iris. "Did Sharon promise you, too, some kind of release one day?"

Ansel didn't answer. He remained an immovable mountain, his eyes never straying from the focal point. Ansel was a big man, yet he stared down someone even bigger.

Ophelia crouched at the corner of the billiards table, clutching at its carved leg. Her head bowed, the crown on her lap, she was murmuring something under her breath. Christopher bunched himself up against the back of the booth. When he met my eyes, he gave an imperceptible shake of his head, as though to warn me away from doing anything stupid. He knew that very decision was on my brain. But I had to do something.

The inside of Morgan's was devoid of plant life. The bird ferns sat outside on the railing, dripping from their weekly watering. Joaquin had forced a few into Ansel's office, telling his brutish boss they'd bring in oxygen to the stifling room, but those were upstairs and out of sight, along with Ansel's cache of weapons. I was a witch with no tools at my disposal and little in the way of natural ability. My tattoos remained dark and shiny, damp with the excess of water in the room.

Ansel said nothing in response to Tethra's taunts. Instead, he reached behind his back and withdrew Blazewing. He held the blade in front of him, its metal bouncing light back from the ice at their feet.

"And I see she kitted you out," Tethra said, eyeing the weapon. He gave a half smile. "I'll have to get inventory under control with that one. Can't have one's new employees giving out treasures like candy."

"She gave me nothing," Ansel said. "I took this. From *Bres*." He drew out the name, giving it meaning intended to influence Tethra. "It wasn't like he would need it anytime soon, according to Sharon."

Tethra smirked. "Fine. Then let's see what you can do with it, *halfborn*." Tethra held out both hands and beckoned to Ansel.

There was a twitch at the corner of Ansel's eye, a spark of recognition. Without further hesitation, he swung the sword in a graceful, angled arc designed to kill.

Tethra evaded the blow, whirling out of the way. "Not bad," he said. "But you brought a knife to a water fight." Tethra opened his mouth, and a torrent rushed forward, a wave that crashed against Ansel, knocking into his knees and drenching him from the waist down.

"You'll have to give me more than a splash from a kiddie pool," Ansel said, shaking water from his hair. "Or have the years weakened you?"

I looked at Christopher, who again shook his head. He hadn't known. Ophelia watched the door, her lips moving, ignoring us. She clutched the crown in her hands, her knuckles turning white.

"Adorable halfborn," Tethra said. "You know, I have more than one trick up my sleeve."

Ansel's nostrils flared, Blazewing at the ready. "You talk too much. Must have been lonely, all these years with no kingdom of your own."

Tethra sneered. He held his hands up to his mouth as though to form a tunnel, when two dogs burst in from the back door: one black and shaggy, sharp teeth bared and white, the other long and brown, his growl echoing in the room. One was Falinis, Ansel's extranormal hound leant to Uzma and Blythe for protection. The other was a shifter I knew on sight.

Each animal leapt for Tethra, aiming for his neck. Tethra turned from Ansel, releasing a torrent of water that slammed into the dogs, knocking them back. With his hands, he used the floodwaters to carry the stunned animals out the door, tossing their bodies as though swept up in the winds of a hurricane.

In their place, Uzma and Blythe ran in, eyes blazing.

Uzma reached back through the door's opening. Ropes of vines slipped in and around her, snaking their way to Tethra.

Ansel seized the distraction as an opportunity to dive for Tethra, attempting a tackle. He collided with Tethra's middle, sacking the man against a booth. Blazewing flew across the remainders of the ice sheet, clinking against a pinball machine. The men wrestled, chairs flying. I crawled into the booth with Christopher, the two of us covering our heads. Ansel was quick, but Tethra was faster. He slipped from Ansel's hold, taking advantage of the booth as leverage, and kicked Ansel in the jaw. Ansel scrambled to take hold of Tethra's foot, wrenching hard to send him to the ground. Tethra shot water at the wall next to Ansel's face, both temporarily blinding his opponent and giving him a boost to escape. Ansel patted at the surrounding surfaces. He tried to stand and fell. He pawed at his face.

Tethra laughed at the sight. "Aren't much without them, are you? A lumbering brute with no direction." He blasted off Uzma's vines with a stream of spray then grabbed the next round she launched and cracked them like a whip. The vines caught Uzma in their tendrils, knocking her to the ground. He rushed her, wrapping her in her own vines until she gasped for air. Tethra blasted her with water, shoving her against the wall with a sickening smack. She choked on the spray, unable to free herself from the stream.

"Stop!" Blythe's cry split the room, the ache in her voice palpable.

Tethra closed his mouth to regard the woman, studying her from head to toe. I jumped over the back of the booth and raced to Uzma's side. A nasty gash streaked her face and blood seeped into her hair. She was wet from head to toe and shook. I clutched her to me.

"I know who you are," Blythe said, her voice wavering in pitch. "More importantly, I know *what* you are." Her chin lifted in defiance.

Tethra's eyes shone when he took in Blythe. "Yet another, and this one so pretty."

"You are weak," Blythe said. She cocked her chin to the side, regarding him. "And even you know this. No one is afraid of you, and this eats at your soul."

Tethra's eyes went wide as his jaw hardened. What was Blythe doing? She was an empath, but did this translate into foolish sacrifice? Tethra grinned at Blythe's bravado.

Blythe glanced at me. I mouthed, "She's okay." I dug my hands under Uzma's shoulders and hauled her backward, hiding her slumped form behind a toppled booth.

"Such a mouth on this one," he said, reaching for Blythe. He grabbed her chin in his hand and squeezed hard. Blythe gasped. Tethra dragged her closer as she stared defiantly into his face. "Who taught you to address one of the ancients this way?"

"Maybe you were something, once," Blythe said, her periwinkle eyes shifting to navy, a whimper in her voice as Tethra squeezed harder. "But you're nothing now. A washed up has been with no realm to call his own. And worst of all," she said, and gave him a pitiful look, tears at the corner of her eyes, the skin under his hand purpling from the pressure, "a part of you knows it."

Tethra raged at this, his head flying back. He fixed his eyes on Blythe's and opened his mouth, locking his against hers in a sickening kiss. Tethra flooded Blythe's body with water, clutching her tiny body to his own in a lover's embrace. Blythe choked and gagged, struggling to be free of his grasp. There was a sob, and her torso slackened against him. A moment later, Tethra let her body drop to the floor. Water poured from Blythe's mouth, her eyes glassy and empty. She was gone.

"Don't cry," Tethra said to me, spotting my hunched form, horrified. I crouched to block his view of Uzma. "Witches were a mistake, a poor attempt to cover up the abject failure of a queen to oversee her own realms. It doesn't have to hurt, you know," he said, approaching me in a slow, deliberate way. "I can give you incredible pleasure before I turn out the light. That choice is yours," he said, then cast a glance back at the limp form of Blythe. "But escaping me is not."

"As if anything about you is pleasurable." Behind Tethra, Ansel shook his head, then blinked several times. He pushed himself up to standing. I shifted my attention back to the true enemy in the room. *"Neil."*

"That's not what your boyfriend said the other night," he threw at me, smirking. He hadn't noticed Ansel's return to consciousness.

I rolled my eyes. Yet another person who insisted that people of the opposite sex who hung out together had to be banging. "Not my boyfriend. Or yours anymore, either." Christopher ducked his head back down into the booth. "Besides, Rowdy will find you. This isn't some secret lair. You're in the most popular building on the most visited street in the city."

Tethra smirked. "Someone's behind on her lessons," he said. "Let me help. Rowdy can't hurt me. Our destiny is linked. Neither can some weak-willed witch stuck in a tourist trap. The Fomori are a force of nature, not a crime family to be taken out one by one. Our end lies only in our beginning."

Falinis slunk in, his ragged shape saturated. The dog slumped against the back door, panting. I wanted to hug the beloved hunter, Ansel's closest companion, but I stood frozen, like Ansel, unable to risk a moment of weakness.

"Don't look so sad, puppet," Tethra said to me, noting the

wretched despair across my face. "Imperfect beings like yourself and this pathetic hound are disposable. It's not your fault."

In my periphery, I watched Ansel reach for a knife in his belt. He stepped toward Tethra's back, preparing to leap. If what Tethra said was true, he and his brother couldn't be killed. Dread crossed my brow. Ansel risked a wound from which Tethra would rise again. It might buy time, though.

"Now," Tethra said, turning to scan the room, "where did that baby druid go with my crown? It's high time I claim what is mine and make plans."

Ansel leapt. He lodged the blade into Tethra's shoulder, the handle jutting out at an odd angle. Tethra shrieked. He reached for the handle and yanked the blade out. Water seeped from the wound.

"Ah, I see you're up, halfborn," Tethra said, a nefarious grin stretching his face as he strode over to Ansel. "I won't make the mistake of assuming you're gone again. I've got too much to do to play, and you're getting in my way."

Before Ansel could block him, Tethra locked his mouth against Ansel's. Only this time, instead of flooding the bridge he'd made, Tethra swallowed, again and again. In Tethra's grip, Ansel's body went lank, skin shriveling against his flesh and bone. When Ansel's eyes rolled back into his head, Tethra turned to spit out a stream of water that included what looked like blood and other material I didn't want to identify. When he'd drained Ansel, Tethra tossed his body into a booth where it sagged, emaciated. His once muscular figure was skeletal and jagged.

I screamed, frozen in horror. Falinis howled, a sound that pierced the night.

Tethra laughed, maniacal. "Now," he said, clapping his hands together. "Where's that crown?"

Twenty-Five

Tethra crowed, strutting through the bar in surveillance of his win. "Now that the formalities are out of the way," he said, "where did that divine druidess go? Come out, come out wherever you are. My, my, so many bodies. Someone's going to have to clean this up. Not me, of course." Tethra's feet crunched on shards of glass and ice. "I could take a page out of my dear brother's book. Hire some of his rejects—if any survived—to do my bidding. Build an army. With followers, I'd be unstoppable."

So that's why Rowdy hadn't come. Tethra had destroyed the farm.

Uzma was battered, but stable. I'd managed to drape her over a pair of chairs. Her shallow breaths came, however weak. I couldn't get to Iris, and I'd yet to bring myself to look at Ansel. I needed to find out what happened to Joaquin.

Where had Ophelia gone? Then I remembered the ring. Whether she was there or not, none of us would know unless she slipped. I couldn't wait for her to distract Tethra—I had to do something.

The front door was cracked. It had popped open when Tethra and Ansel had crashed against its bulk.

While Tethra continued to survey his new domicile, I waved my hand at Christopher. He'd been crouched in the booth where Ansel lay, hands over his ears, tears streaming down his face. When he met my eyes, the fear within his was raw and unmatched. My self-confident gadabout of a best friend was terrified, and had every right to be.

I pointed to my chest, then toward the front door, and gave a quick nod. Christopher turned his head toward the sound of Tethra's conquest and shook his head, eyes round with panic. I nodded, a slow and steady movement to show it was happening. Christopher pressed his lips together, his expression panicked, but echoed my nod.

Tethra's boots thudded against the stairs. He kept up the sing-song voice, treating his hunt for Ophelia like a game of cat and mouse. "Don't make me hunt you down, princess. Give me that pretty crown and I promise to take good care of you. I'll even let you live in my court. You can feed me grapes while I deliberate what to do with the souls who desire entrance into my kingdom. You and Sharon can be friends. She loves strong women..."

Tethra would find Ansel's office locked. Even if he kicked in the first door, the halls beyond were heavily armed. He would be frustrated and back down the stairs in minutes. I had to go—now.

With one last look at Christopher, I made a beeline for the door. Its bulk creaked open at my touch.

On the sidewalk, the Saturday evening crowd milled about. With Morgan's closed, neighboring bars burst with patrons, people spilling out under the awnings. Some smoked, others stared like zombies at their phones. All were clueless as to the force of nature loose within the walls next door.

Like a madwoman, I paused at the street corner. There

were no lights on in Lotte's shop across the square. Her apartment was blocks away, but I didn't know if she was home. Second Shot was never open at night, so there was little chance Grace would be around. If I risked either and was wrong, I would sacrifice precious time that could make the difference between utter destruction and any chance of salvation.

Instead of heading away from Morgan's, I bolted for the Apothecary. The green *Open* sign bid me through the front door, and I stepped over the threshold. The sisters had left the door unlocked in their rush. Moths flitted about, their rest disturbed. I ran through the shop. A half-eaten bowl of popcorn sat on the counter, a couple of beers nearby. A laptop played a Ryan Reynolds romance, the one where he ends up with his overbearing boss. One glance showed the weir room door closed and undisturbed. Ophelia hadn't made it through —at least not yet. I raced for the stairs, taking them two at a time, praying my plan would work.

∽

Christopher was the first person I saw when I slipped back into Morgan's. His eyes were saucers. I should have forced him to follow me out. But I'd left him to the mercy of this madness and he'd remained, frozen in fear. He jerked his head toward the kitchen where a clash of metal signaled a rampage.

I dashed to Ansel, or what was left of him, and untied the velvet pouch I held. The covering fell away, revealing the crown. I lifted it from the bag; the metal searing against my skin as the circle of gold sparkled, its diamonds stunning in their mounts. My hand shook as I placed the crown atop Ansel's head, or what was left of it, his skull pressing against the thin paper skin. I stepped back.

Nothing.

The kitchen door burst open. A hulking version of the

demigod I'd left moments ago was now spitting mad, his head swinging in a wild fury. "Where. Is. That. Crown? I smell you here. I don't know what trick this is, but the longer you make me wait, the more you'll suffer my wrath, *kitten.*"

Tethra turned once more to the bar and saw me, obvious and upright, a deer in headlights. *"You."* His words were venomous, barbed and lethal. "What do you think you are doing?"

"N-n-nothing," I lied. Christopher gulped.

"Did *you* hide it?" Tethra, his skin now a grayish blue, dry and scaling, prowled my way. Water dribbled from the sides of his mouth, trickling down to join the growing river that flooded the bar. Ice chunks heaved and swayed on the tides created by Tethra's movements.

I opened my eyes wide in a display of innocence. "Hide what?"

Tethra tutted at me, his movements slow and deliberate. "Don't play stupid. The crown. You know," he said, hands rising to the top of his head where he mimed the placement of a royal circlet. "Fancy hat, made of precious metal and jewels?"

"I don't have it," I said, which was true on a technicality.

Tethra shook his head, his lip curling. "I know you don't, *witch*. What I want to know is who *does*?" He took another step closer, his pale eyes haunting in the low light. "If you can't be useful, I'll have to get rid of you. Probably will anyway."

He was two feet away from me. His breath smelled of seaweed, the docks, and the tang of sulfur. I met his gaze with my own. I gulped.

Tethra leaned in closer. His lips, bluing by the minute, were inches from my own. With one of his webbed hands, he finger-walked up my arm until he booped me on the nose, forming each of his words with deliberate emphasis. "Find me the crown—or die."

A glass smashed near our heads, the shattered bits exploding outward. Several bit into my skin, the pain sharp and raw. A second glass flew at the wall, and we both ducked, seeking the source. On the bar top, pint glasses lined up along the edge. As we watched, another one left its mooring and flew in our direction.

When the last glass shattered behind us, Tethra stomped toward the bar.

Iris wobbled to her feet, a lump on the side of her head. She reached into the thin air above her. There was a gasp as she lunged for something and then jumped back. A thump on the floor signaled the landing of someone—or something—at the end of the bar.

Tethra traced the movement and grabbed at the space where the sound had been. The back door opened, and a cackle disappeared into the night. Tethra stood in the pooled water, blinking at the open door.

"Get the fuck out of my bar."

Tethra whirled around, impossibility taking shape in his mind as the floodwaters sloshed around his feet.

Ansel stood, shaky but whole. His skin lay slack in some places but was filling out by the minute. If anything, he looked bigger than ever, as though compensating for the depleted form. His eyes stormed, his mouth set in a grim line. The air snapped around him, cut by electricity. Atop his head was the crown, glittering in its immortal glory.

"Out of the water!" Ansel yelled. Iris jumped on top of the bar, and I scrambled onto the pinball machine.

"Boss!" Iris yelled. Both Tethra and Ansel looked her way. "Catch!"

Without taking his eyes off Tethra, Ansel snatched an object out of the air. He jammed it into Tethra, not stopping to plan his attack. He held tight to the object as a black cloud formed over his head and the crack of thunder snapped through the air. A bolt of lightning broke free from the cloud, making contact with Ansel's hand and the fork he'd jammed in Tethra's flesh. The electrical charge shot through them, branching down into the water at their feet and outward in the bar. Tethra opened his mouth, stunned, releasing a puff of black smoke.

Electricity spread across the pond that was the bar. There was a surge of power, in which every light in the place brightened then dimmed again. Black zigzags ran up the vintage paneled walls. A moment later, the bar was dim and quiet again. Ansel had his arms wrapped around the semi-conscious Tethra.

"Iris, get the irons."

"On it," Iris said. She swung out from around the bar, something tucked close against her side. She limped her way to the stairs and clambered upward.

"EJ, can you move?"

I scanned the floor, my brain refusing to ignore the crackling water from moments before. I gulped. "Maybe."

Ansel spoke to me as though a firefighter calling a kitten down from a tree. "Could you climb down—careful, one foot at a time—and get Blazewing for me? It landed over there somewhere." He gestured with his chin, not daring to remove his hands from around the incapacitated Tethra.

I nodded, then followed his directive. The sword was in the corner of the bar, wedged under a booth. I wrenched it out and ran back to Ansel. He leaned against the bar a little, the remaining wear on his body evident in the pale hue of his skin.

"You're alive," I said, in what will go down as the dumbest statement I've ever made.

"I am," he said. "Thanks to you."

Iris rushed in, heavy chains draped on her arms. "Do you want the ones with spikes or just the regular type?"

"I'll take them all," Ansel said, and winced. "Wrap me up

with him if you have to. I'm not taking any chances. EJ will stand guard." He nodded at Blazewing in my hands.

I lifted the weapon and regarded its hilt. Tiny carvings like swirling clouds covered the metal. The blade was so sharp it sang in my hands. Blazewing was stunning, and incredibly lethal.

When Iris had secured Tethra, Ansel gave his next requests. "Iris, get Yanric and Grace. Gaven if you can. We need to find Joaquin, and we're going to need the Nurse."

Iris nodded, then darted from the room.

"EJ—Ember James." My name was a cautious utterance from Ansel's lips. "Any chance you'd be willing to tell me the story of this," he said, his eyes looking upward to the weight above his brows, "over a pint?"

Twenty-Six

Eyes closed, I inhaled, drawing in oxygen from within the plants in my shop, letting the air fill my lungs with clarity. Christopher half joked that we should sell oxygen hits and heat come winter. I cracked a smile.

"Focus," a sharp but quiet voice said in my ear.

June. With Blythe gone and Uzma recuperating from her injuries and her broken heart with her coven sisters, I was relegated, once again, to begging for help. Their leader took every opportunity to remind me of my every failure.

"Every misstep is a moment of weakness. Mess up, and someone will get through."

She was right. I exhaled through my nose, a slow re-centering. Concentrating on the walls of my shop, the heat below, and the sky above, I traced a line around the shop in my mind, careful to picture every bump and jut of the walls, each nook and cranny of the ceiling. As I drew, I pushed outward in my mind, blocking out Ophelia and anyone else who sought to do me or my loved ones harm. When I'd drawn the perimeter thrice over in my head, I opened my eyes.

"Did it work?"

June glanced around the shop, appraising my work. "There's only one way to test for certain, and I wouldn't recommend it. At least not by yourself."

I glanced at the loft, where I knew Christopher lay. He'd taken to watching reruns of *Supernatural* while he waited for a twisted ankle and bruised pride to heal.

"He doesn't count," June said, matter of fact. "Couldn't hurt a fly if you paid him."

"I heard that," Christopher called from above.

"Anyway," June said, reaching for the bike helmet she'd abandoned on the coat rack. "Wait until Gaven's back, then get Joaquin to lure one in. You'll know then, and you'll have others around to help clean up the mess."

I swallowed, sickened by the cavalier way June dismissed the life of a potential intruder as someone to be obliterated by me and my extranormal friends in a random test.

Iris pushed in through the back door after June's exit. "I admit," she said, shifting a pair of paper sacks from one arm to the other, "to waiting until I saw that old broad ride past. Like the Wicked Witch of the West, that one. Is his royal highness upstairs?"

"I'm here," Christopher said, a faux whimper in his voice.

Iris handed me a bag and smiled before mounting the stairs. "One double-decker burger, hand delivered, coming up."

I unrolled the top of my bag, inhaling the scent of greasy magic. "What flavor is it tonight? Smells amazing!" I'd started the tradition of ordering dirty fries when I'd first moved in. In the months that followed, Morgan's morphed my odd request into one of their most popular rotating specials.

Iris peered over the loft. "It's a vegan gyro. Made with seitan. Loaded that sucker up with olives, pepperoncini, tzatziki, all of it."

Humming to myself, I grabbed a fork from a drawer, then

reached into the bag to stab at the fries. They dripped with sauce and chunks of tomato. "Can you stay for a drink?" I shoved the magical meal in my mouth, savoring the bite.

"What have you got that I don't?" Iris rounded the landing. A grin striped her face.

I bit my lip, considering. "Rose water. Thyme. A gin from a tiny distillery in New Hampshire."

"Count me in," Iris said, mounting a stool as I assembled a few ingredients into a shaker. "Boss can handle things by himself for a bit. So, what did June want today? She railed on Ansel something fierce. Blamed him for Blythe's death and Uzma's catatonic state. And all this because that lovesick tart couldn't leave well enough dead."

I popped the glass into the shaker. With both hands, I shook the contraption, allowing the ice to do the bulk of the work. Finished, I knocked the heel of my palm against the side of the shaker and removed the glass. With a strainer firmly in place, I filled two coup glasses with the light pink liquid. Last, I dropped a pair of rose petals into the foam floating atop each drink. I knew Iris was speaking of Ophelia, though she hadn't mentioned her by name. "June came to help me learn to ward my shop. She said it's my own fault I didn't learn earlier."

"That woman goes down in history as the most sour of lemons," Iris said, taking a sip. "Ooh, this is good."

I beamed. "Thanks."

"We should do a collaboration. I could feature your recipes, make a menu..."

I smiled into my glass. "I doubt Ansel would go for that."

"I don't know," Iris said. "He hasn't cursed your name in a full day. Things might be a little different now, after you saved his life and all."

I didn't have a response for her. Instead, I let her words and the temporary truce with Ansel settle on my shoulders. "I feel bad for her, you know."

"For who?"

"Ophelia. Love can do that, make you so desperate you risk your life for the chance to be with someone."

"True love can. Or so I'm told," Iris said.

I stabbed again at the pile of fries in my to-go container. "Don't know that I'll ever love any man that much," I said. "Especially given my history."

"Speaking of lying assholes," Iris said. "Tethra has been delivered to Sharon."

"What will happen to him?"

"The same thing as Bryce. Boss doesn't share all the details, but he's somewhere in the depths of the Netherworld."

"Got it."

"And the crowns are locked up for safekeeping. Boss says no one goes near them until Gaven gets back to verify what we have. If the one is in fact the Crown of Immortality, then we have a mystery as to the other." Iris drained her glass. "One question before I go."

"Shoot."

"How did you know the crown would revive Ansel?"

"I didn't," I said, matter-of-fact. "But I...I wanted it to." I looked down at my palm, where the now tattooed imprint of the crown traced a ragged, regal edge against my palm.

∼

"They're here, and they're gorgeous!"

Four days, a gallon of almond lattes, cheesecake flown in from the Village, and the first print of our calendar full of hot, semi-naked people was all it took to get Christopher up and functional again. On Friday he'd shaved, dressed himself, and was out the door before I'd made it down the stairs.

Christopher had returned with pink cheeks, a paper-wrapped package under his arm, and a coffee cup in each hand. He handed me my mocha before plunking the package on the table.

"Just wait until you see them. They did a bang-up job." Christopher set his own cup on the counter and ripped at the paper, dropping bits on the floor of the shop. He withdrew one of the spiral-bound calendars from the stack and grimaced, handing one over to me. "I hope you like them..."

I'd given Christopher complete creative control over the layout. He'd trained in it, after all, and had made a career out of making the average look extraordinary. I was best at spreadsheets and recipes, books and stats. At weddings, Christopher was right there behind the photographer, ensuring they caught the curve of a curl against the bride's cheek, the soft smile of a great aunt, and the ring bearer smooshing cake into his hair. Christopher observed life and knew just what to immortalize. I'd fussed over him like a mother hen while he moped around the Apothecary, struck low by the betrayal of Neil/Tethra and the horrors he'd witnessed. When my best friend had moved west, none of this had been part of the plan. The first few days, I worried he'd pack up and head back east, but by Friday, he'd steeled himself, committed to this new reality.

Also, I'd been more than occupied. With my training and preparations for the party-turned-chaotic-nightmare at the farm, I'd been more than happy to have him take something off my plate.

He'd handed me the calendar upside down. On the back was a paragraph about the project, World Naked Gardening Day, and great houseplants with which to get started. He'd added the Apothecary logo to the bottom, along with our contact information and a heads up to look for the second installment next spring.

"So, we're already planning another one?" I said.

Christopher shrugged. "I think when you see how good it looks, you'll go for it."

I raised an eyebrow at him before flipping the calendar over. Instant warmth flooded my veins and flushed my cheeks. "Our cover model is Joaquin?"

Christopher stared pointedly at the cover. "Can you blame me?"

I couldn't. On the cover, Joaquin held a Thai constellation balanced against each hip, as though he'd just been to the nursery—in the nude—to pick them up. Their broad leaves served as a chastity belt in the foreground. He wore a come-hither smile that leapt off the page. "Wow."

"And you haven't even seen the monthly spreads."

"These might need a warning on them tomorrow," I said, fanning myself with one hand in mock shock. The corner of Christopher's mouth turned up as I turned to January. "This is fabulous—how completely cool of them!"

The first month was a picture of several coven members, scarves draped around their necks, working on bikes in the shop. Balanced on the pedals, seats, and the floor were plants of all sizes, artfully cloaking the women's bodies. I recognized the woman who'd been at the shop, as well as some I'd seen at the market. There was Uzma, and nearby, her sister Blythe. I swallowed back a lump of emotion. "I don't need to see the rest."

"Keep going. There's more."

February was the darling older couple who owned the bistro. He held a watering can while she carried a Hoya Kerii. She kissed him on the cheek. "It's perfect. Absolutely darling."

March, April, and May highlighted the mayor, the gardening club, and several cowboys who wore little other than their hats. June's photograph was Rowdy, decked out in all his golden boy glory. Wildflowers brushed his middle, a perfect smile on his face.

"They're all so good," I said, my eyes lingering on the shot from the field. I remembered that day, capturing the exquisite balance of sunshine in his eyes.

July was Joaquin again, his hands wrapped around the pot of a spiral cactus, head thrown back in laughter, the muscles along his arms and neck corded with lean strength. His black hair shone in the lighting, his skin luminous.

"That is one pretty man," Christopher said.

I took another look. "Indeed," I said, and turned the page. August was Grace, a cup of coffee in hand as she stooped to smell a rose. September was the owner of a local vineyard and a few of their braver staff. October was Christopher.

"Topher, you look great!"

Christopher stood behind a table of Gaven's orchids, a mister in hand. His Clark Kent glasses added a level of sophistication to his shot. His salt and pepper hair slicked back, his tattoo of a tree barely visible around the edge of his shoulder and the slightest curve of a toned butt cheek made an appearance. "Thanks," he said, sheepish. "Figured either I'm out there, or I'm *out* there. Press can't hurt."

I turned to November and my heart skipped a beat.

Ansel.

The burly man held a bonsai in front of his chest, the tiny tree surrounded by a bed of pebbles. In one hand, he wielded a vintage pair of miniature shears as he consulted the plant. His stormy eyes focused just in front of the camera and his hair fell in loose waves around his shoulders. There was something incredibly delicate and sensual about the image. I couldn't stop staring.

"Yeah," Christopher said, and didn't have to elaborate.

Reluctant, I flipped to December. Iris peaked out from behind a Christmas tree in a Santa hat. The pic was adorable.

I flipped back to Ansel, gazing at the photo for longer than I should have. "These will sell like crazy."

Christopher beamed. "Don't I know it. And this is just

one version. There's a second one, too, just wait until you see it."

My phone buzzed in my pocket. *Patrick.* I pressed the speaker to my ear. "Hello, son of mine. How is Paris in May?"

"Better than I deserve. The term's almost over. I'm not sure how I did on exams, but I have some good news."

I loved the infectious energy in Patrick's voice. From a continent away, he was all cheer and light. "What's that?"

"I landed the internship. The one at that place on the left bank? I'm not doing much and it's only a month, but my professor said if I do well there, it will only open more doors. Or, as the French say, je suis en pleine forme."

"Congratulations, honey. That is wonderful news." I ached to hug my adult son. He'd made me promise to visit as soon as I could swing it. With one disaster after another after I opened the shop, I'd had to delay that trip again and again. With the sale of the calendars, though, and a few more events, maybe I could make it to the City of Lights sooner rather than later. "I can't wait for you to show me all that you've created."

"Oh, and there's one more thing. I...uh... have been dating. A little bit. One girl. It's not too serious or anything, but we've decided not to date anyone else—for now."

Christopher leaned in, ever the eavesdropper. He raised both his eyebrows as I fought to maintain a steady voice. My son, ever the awkward kid who hid behind a sketchbook, had done little in the way of dating as a teenager. Perhaps the City of Love had worked its magic. "Really? She must be special then. Tell me about her."

"She's great, Mom. A Parisian. And she's a party planner, like you. Here, I'll send you a pic."

There was a ping on my phone, and I clicked on the icon to start the download.

"She's a little older, but not much. Totally gorgeous. We've only been dating a few weeks, and she's been out of town a lot for work. But when she's here—"

I didn't hear the rest of what Patrick said. My mind fixated on the image before me on the tiny screen. Next to my son, who stood in front of the Eiffel Tower, was a woman I knew all too well.

Ophelia.

Twenty-Seven
Joaquin

"So we're not going to talk about it?" Joaquin speared another bite of eggs. He squinted at the specks of green that speckled the morsels on his fork. "Did you put thyme in these?"

Ansel grunted. He tipped the hot sauce bottle over his own plate and gave it a shake. Bright orange-red dots peppered his scramble. He flipped the cap back over and slid the bottle to his employee and most loyal friend.

Joaquin accepted the offering and upended it over his own food. "She saved your life, you know."

Ansel swallowed his first bite. "You think I need to be told?"

"What I think is that you need to thank her," Joaquin said.

The halfborn brute set his fork down on his plate, wiped his face with a napkin, and laid the fabric square next to the plate. He pushed back from the bar and headed for his office.

"It's just my opinion. You don't have to get butt hurt about it!" Joaquin called out to Ansel's back, but the man had gone.

Joaquin shrugged, then readdressed his breakfast. He

reached for the honey jar and inserted a knife to swirl out a blob of the thick, golden fluid. It spread over his toast like a yellow wave, soaking into the bread. He took a bite, sinking his teeth through the sticky sweetness atop the chewy bread. The sweet-savory combo was magical in his mouth, and he moaned over the bite.

"Damn that Rowdy, this is good shit." He swung himself off the bar stool and rounded the side of the bar. At the coffee machine, he poured himself a mugful and, after brief deliberation, one for Ansel as well. Both mugs went on the bar.

Back on his stool, Joaquin stabbed another bite and shoved it into his mouth. He checked his phone. Nothing. Where was she?

Joaquin had only insisted Ansel say something—*do* something—regarding EJ saving his sorry ass because he, too, felt the burden of repayment over his head. Ever since Lotte had peeled him off that pavement and breathed life back into his sorry bag of bones, he'd wanted to give her the moon and stars. Yet she'd kept him at arm's length—or further—away.

How could he tell her he was mad for her, that she'd been all he'd thought about since they'd met, and that he wanted to prostrate himself before her in adoration if she was never around?

Another fruitless scroll through his messages proved depressing, so he flipped the phone upside down and smacked it on the bar.

Iris breezed in, a heavy basket stuffed full of produce over her arm. "Morning." She leaned over the bar. "I see he's outdone himself again. Any left?"

"Might be—in the kitchen."

Iris unloaded a few limes and lemons, an orange, and a sandwich from the basket. She nodded at the other plate. "Where did he go?"

Joaquin shifted his eyes to the staircase.

"Great," she said, her voice dipped in sarcasm. "So, he's feeling better, I take it."

"Loads. What was the count today?"

"At the market? Maybe a half dozen."

"Still no Rowdy?"

Iris shook her head. A clomping on the stairs signaled Ansel's return. "I don't want to be caught in those crosshairs. I'll catch you later." She hurried into the kitchen, letting the doors swing shut behind her.

The footsteps drew closer. Without looking up, Joaquin said, "Your eggs are getting cold."

Ansel set his hand down on the bar, then reclaimed his stool.

"What's that?"

Ansel lifted a hand to reveal a small jade ring. "She gave it to me," Ansel said, before picking up his fork.

"I remember that day." Joaquin thought of the tree, EJ's guilt over the reinstatement of Ansel's indentured servitude.

"The ring. The crown. My life. It's hard to hate someone who does all that."

"That it is."

They finished the meal in silence, the ticking clock above the bar the sole sound in the room. When his plate was clean, Joaquin pushed back and patted his stomach. "You've outdone yourself once more, my friend. I'm on dish duty." He reached for his and Ansel's plates.

"I've failed."

Joaquin froze. "What do you mean?"

"You're right. I should have done something. Said something, at least. But how do you repay someone for your life? Especially when you don't think it's worth saving in the first place."

Ansel's voice was all anguish. Joaquin recognized it as his own pain, mirrored in the mind of another. He'd asked himself this same question dozens of times, coming up short again and again. It didn't matter that they were on the brink of conflict with an ancient family of overlords. He couldn't stop thinking about how to give all of himself to a woman who wouldn't grant him a moment, let alone a lifetime. They were a pair of wayward souls with raw hearts.

"Not that she'd listen. That woman never listens."

"You mean, she never does what you say," Joaquin added, a wry smile on his face.

Ansel sighed. "Am I that bad?"

"Worse," Joaquin said. Ansel's face fell, and Joaquin felt a pang of guilt. This man was his best friend. If anyone could get him to do something about the sorry state of his heart, it was on Joaquin Torres. "Good news or bad news?"

"Bad news. It's all bad news."

"Fine," Joaquin said. "Bad news first. You've got a sexy woman with a temper to match your own living right next door who literally saved your miserable life, and you keep screwing up every chance you get to tell her that she makes you remember what love is. What it could be."

Ansel buried his face in his hands.

"But you finally have your hands on that damn crown. That's the good news. And a bonus crown to boot. All you need now is the ring. You're so close to your freedom. Hard to go soft and give up right when you're so close to everything you've always wanted."

Ansel reached for a bottle off a shelf and poured some of the amber liquid into his coffee. He took a deep drink, then set down the cup. "You're right. I need to focus. I shouldn't even be thinking about EJ. That's a waste of time."

Joaquin frowned. "I didn't mean that—"

"No, it's true. I've got everything within reach. I can't get tangled up in a woman."

"Wait, I don't think—"

Ansel clapped Joaquin on the back and stood. "Good pep talk. Now get on out there and find that ring..." The halfborn whistled as he carried their plates to the kitchen.

"Roger that," Joaquin said, knowing with incredible newfound clarity what he must do. If Ansel was free, then he'd be able to pull his head out of his ass and go after EJ.

Joaquin stepped out onto the sidewalk, the morning already too warm and promising more. Above him, four crows now perched in the branches outside the Apothecary. One bird preened, striping lines through its feathers with its black beak, as though brushing off a new coat. The other three watched Joaquin, their beady black eyes expectant.

"If you keep my secrets," Joaquin said to the growing murder, "I'll keep yours."

The biggest bird tipped forward on the branch and cawed twice.

~

THANK YOU!

Thanks so much for reading! If you enjoyed this book, please consider leaving me a review and I'll be so very grateful. Reviews help me find readers and I am thankful for you. ♡

If there was something that tugged at your mind as you read, I'd love to hear from you at erin@erinlark.com.

I'm already back at the keyboard, working on book three —*The Southern Diadem*!

A free novella

Sign up for my monthly newsletter and you'll be sent a free copy of the Four Crowns prequel novella, Fallen, in your preferred digital format.

Each month I send monthly writing and reading updates, some personal stories, recipes, freebies from my author friends, cat pics, and more! I promise to never sell your email and hope you'll hit reply once in a while and let me know how you are, too. :)

Read the Serial

L ove the Four Crowns crew? Read the companion serial, Weir Walker—for free on Ream, a great platform for readers.

Hope to see you there!

Afterword

Sophomores can be a tough lot. No longer freshman, forgiven for their every transgression as high school newbies, and not yet the forward-facing upperclassmen, respected for their almost-adult status. Sophomores are right in that tough spot of knowing they are on a path, yet fully aware that there is much to come.

Second books in a series are no different. Tiara Borealis is one player in set of four full novels, with a few novellas tucked around them for good measure. This book was designed to drive the characters closer to their ultimate fate but not all the way.

Still, there was growth to experience. Learning to do. Plans to set into motion. Fun to be had.

World Naked Gardening Day is a real thing that happens each year in May. If you are plant-minded, I encourage you to check out this celebration of people and their plants, and consider joining in for the good cheer.

Gaven takes EJ to a place loosely based on the island of

Iona, part of the Hebrides. Many a royal was laid to rest there, and it's a gorgeous place as is all of Scotland. If you go, keep your eyes open for a chink in the wall that doesn't look quite right...

Local farmers markets can be a wealth of goods and services that not only allow you to support your community, but let you learn about all that is happening where you live. The market in this book is an amalgamation of all those I've attended over the years. I hope you'll find out if there's one near you, and make an outing of it.

I found myself back on the actual Whiskey Row back in September for the wedding of two dear friends. Standing on Montezuma, I pictured my characters in their shops, living out their lives. If you're ever in Prescott, I hope you'll do the same, and send me a picture.

—Erin

Acknowledgments

This book would not be what it is without the feedback from my sister Stephanie about the characters, the plot, and all things connecting-the-dots in a grand plot scheme.

I'm also thankful to our Scottish tour guide, Keith Fraser, for his lessons on Iona and the history buried there. If you're ever on the islands, there's no better driver to have at the wheel.

Green hearts to Katherine who first tuned me in to World Naked Gardening Day. There's little cooler than this good energy flood of photos in appreciation of bodies and plants.

Much thanks to Paula Lester, my longtime head editor who never fails to point out her favorite phrases and delights in every "next" book.

Thank you to Ava and Bryan who tolerate having a writer in the house who sequesters herself away when it's drafting season. You two are the best!

Readers, you get all my adoration for this one. It's one thing to write one book, it's another to build a series because people fall in love with your characters and their world. I'm excited to bring you more of the Four Crowns crew you've come to love.

About the Author

Erin is a lover of fountain pens and the trail they leave behind. She is an award-winning author of the Four Crowns romantic contemporary fantasy series. Her work is highly praised for its heart and snark as well as her knack for breathing magic into the everyday. Erin also writes cozy mysteries for those who walk the gentler side of fiction.

A diehard gadabout and champagne fanatic, Erin is a firm believer in the tender and wild. A native Arizonan, when not behind a keyboard, you'll find her under the stars, howling at the moon.

Also by Erin Lark Maples

Four Crowns

Weir Walker
Fallen
A Circle of Stars
Tiara Borealis
The Southern Diadem (Coming in 2025)

The Declan Rosewood Mysteries

Bleeding Hearts

The Sheridan County Mysteries

The Sheriff's Wife
The New Teacher
The Sled Dog
The Dead Swede
The Master Mechanic
The Banjo Player

Milton Keynes UK
Ingram Content Group UK Ltd.
UKHW041948291124
451915UK00001B/32